"GET YOUR RIFLES!"
SERGEANT HANNAN SHOUTED.

The huge throng of jeering Blood warriors were a little more than a dozen yards away as the six red-coated Mounties lined up shoulder to shoulder behind the overturned wagon, their Winchester barrels leveled at the Indians.

"That is far enough!" Hannan shouted to the braves in their own tongue.

But a big lantern-jawed brave with red and blue zigzag marks that failed to hide the pocks on his face stepped forward.

"We have had enough of white man's law!" he shouted. He looked at the Mounties and shook his rifle at them. "Down with the redcoats!"

Then he lifted the rifle to his shoulder and tightened his finger against the trigger as the mass of Indians surged forward.

THE SCARLET RIDERS

#6 THE FLYING PATROL

IAN ANDERSON

ZEBRA BOOKS
KENSINGTON PUBLISHING CORP.

ZEBRA BOOKS

are published by

Kensington Publishing Corp.
475 Park Avenue South
New York, NY 10016

First printing: August, 1988

Printed in the United States of America

*Dedicated to Mary, my wife,
for taking "second place" to my books.*

Chapter 1

Easing himself in his creaking saddle, Johnny McNab looked anxiously up at the watery moon riding high in the night sky. Patches of cloud blotted out the stars, throwing black shadows across the rolling ground. Lowering his eyes, he gazed off to the west, where a sea of silvery peaks jutted upward like a giant ridge. Clouds were banking up over those mountains, and there was a nippy tang in the air. He hoped the weather wouldn't turn bad. He'd heard how raging blizzards could sweep down from across the mountains up in this part of western Canada, even as late as May. The cattle were restless, too. Maybe they sensed it.

He glanced over at the mass of black forms spread across the shadowed hills and dips on the undulating plain. They should have been lying down and resting, but too many were moving around, some grazing, a few chewing on their cuds. Now and then one or two bawled back and forth.

With luck they would reach Fort Macleod by noon day after tomorrow. It had been a long enough drive, from down Virginia City way, averaging fifteen miles a day. Johnny McNab looked forward to a good, cooked meal in a Fort Macleod restaurant and a night in a hotel bed, then the ride back down into Montana.

That thought comforted him, but he leaned forward over the horn of his saddle uneasily and looked around in all directions. Something wasn't quite right, yet he couldn't put his finger on it.

Farther off a large fire flickered in the blackness. Laughter and the sound of talking carried across the night air. The smell of coffee and tobacco wafted up from around the fire. Men lay propped against saddles or sat on a dead tree trunk as they ate and talked.

"Yep," said a young cowpuncher as he lowered a battered tin cup from his mouth, "it's been a long drive, herdin' these dogies up here to these Canadian ranchers."

"Long ride—hell!" exploded a grizzled cowboy. "This has been nothin'. Why, I remember the good ol' days back in the 'sixties when we used t' push herds along the Texas Trail. Back then we pushed steers—all horns an' tails—up along the Chisholm Trail, from Red River, Texas, all the way to Abilene, Kansas. Now, let me tell you, *that* was a cattle drive—fightin' off outlaws, Indians and Comancheros. Things have become plumb peaceful since them days. All the excitement has gone out of the drives. Back then the only law was a good old six-gun," and he patted the .45 holstered at his waist.

Vince Black, weather-beaten trail boss, snorted. "Fightin' Comancheros, my ass! The only fightin' you done, Sam, was in bar room brawls down in Kansas City and Wichita."

The other punchers, young men mostly, laughed. Said one, "I don't mind a piece of excitement, but I figger on livin' to a rip old age so's one day I can sit on a ranchhouse porch down in Wyoming an' tell my grandkids how things were in my day."

"Me," laughed another, "I'll take my excitement with the dance hall gals back in Virginia City."

"Any more coffee?"

"Yep, some still in the pot."

A cowboy leaned toward the fire and lifted a blackened pot off some hot rocks and poured the dark strong liquid

8

into an old tin cup. Another rolled a smoke. They all hung around close to the blazing fire. Like Johnny McNab, out riding herd as night guard, they too noticed the cool tang of the night air. Although it was getting on to late spring, since they had crossed the Canadian border they had seen pockets of deep snow in some of the coulees where the spring sun hadn't yet penetrated.

The trail boss pushed his sweat-stained hat back off his gray hair. "When we get to Fort Macleod, we'll turn this herd over to the Mounted Police. They're the quarantine authorities up here in Canadian territory. They keep 'em in quarantine for ninety days before the ranchers we drove these cattle up here for can collect 'em and drive 'em onto their own spreads."

"Wouldn't mind settlin' down on some of this grazing country up here in Canada. Looks good from what we've seen so far. Rich grass and plenty of it."

As the dozen or more cowboys lolled around smoking and drinking coffee, they could hear bawling from among the massed cattle grazing or resting out on the range.

"Them cattle sound a mite restless tonight. Hope there's not some bad weather comin' from over the mountains."

Several of the cowboys peered up at the sky, noting the clouds banking up over the mountains, visible even in the night.

"Yeah. We'll want good weather for the ride back home. Don't want to be hangin' around Fort Macleod too long. Not a bad little town, but them red-coated Mounted Police keep the lid pretty tight on it."

One of the cowboys ground out his cigarette on the heel of his boot, pushed his hat forward over his head and stood up. Reaching down, he grasped his saddle by its horn and lifted it up, slinging it over his shoulder.

"My turn to go out and ride herd for a while. Leave some coffee for the boys still out there."

"Old Ling will fix some more," said Vince Black, inclining his head toward the chuckwagon just beyond the fire. "As for you other boys, you'd better put a rope on the

9

chatter and hunker down into your bedrolls. We'll be pullin' out before sunup."

There was more bawling. The cowboys lolling around the fire peered into the darkness in the direction of the herd. "Them animals sure are restless."

"Yeah. Strange. Ain't been like this before. Maybe they sense they're near the end of the trail."

Johnny McNab, riding slowly around the fringes of the herd, listened to the bawling. There was more of it now. He looked around uneasily. Maybe there were wolves out there. He'd heard of the big gray buffalo wolves up on the northern plains. Or maybe there were Indians around. But this was Canadian territory. The Indians were said to be law-abiding.

Not far away, no more than an arrow's flight, shadowy figures sat their horses just below a long ridge and watched the herd. A tiny red glow showed momentarily in the darkness as one of the herd night guard drew on a cigarette. There was whispered murmuring among the shadowy figures as they leaned over their horses talking quietly among themselves. The silvery moon showed their buckskin clothing but little else. A rifle barrel glinted dully in the subdued light.

Minutes passed, then the shadowy horsemen legged their horses down from the ridge, spreading out as they went. The next instant rifle shots exploded in the night, followed by whoops and high-pitched shouts and the sound of pounding horse hoofs.

The startled night guards wheeled their horses around to face the unexpected disturbance. Dark shadows swept toward them from all directions. The cattle jerked their heads up and looked around in the darkness, suddenly frightened.

Back in the range camp the resting cowboys jumped to their feet, hands reaching for rifles and saddles.

"Hell! Sounds like a war's broken out."

10

"War be damned! That's Indians attackin' the herd! Come on, boys!"

Men ran for their horses, throwing on their saddles and swinging up onto them.

Shots, shouts and terrified bawling intensified from the direction of the herd. Pounding hoofs increased in tempo until they sounded like the roll of thunder. Minutes later horses galloped out of the camp and headed toward the herd.

The cowboys were too far away to see the flash of rifle fire but they covered the distance very fast.

The scattered night guards took the brunt of the attack. Those who got in their way were stamped into the ground or shot from their saddles. Cries of pain split the air. Horses whinnied and screamed as razor-sharp horns ripped into them. Suddenly balls of fire erupted as horsemen towed bundles of burning sagebrush across the grass toward the cattle. Terrified, the frenzied beasts lumbered around and around and stamped back along the shallow valley, back along the way they had come only hours before. The nightguards tried to stop them but they didn't have a chance.

Back toward the camp, the cowboys galloped their horses toward the sound of the commotion. Topping a rise they saw the burning sagebrush bundles half a mile away, saw the muzzle flashes of exploding rifles in the darkness.

"The herd's bein' run off, boys," shouted Vince Black, the trail boss. "We gotta stop 'em!"

The cowboys pressed spurs to horseflesh and rode pell-mell after the stampeding herd. But the cattle raid had been well planned, and as the pursuing cowboys attempted to close the gap they suddenly ran headlong into a wall of hot lead from unseen riflemen.

Shouted curses erupted from the cowboys as horses and riders tumbled headlong in death and destruction.

"Son of a bitch!" shouted Vince Black.

"We've run into an ambush!" shouted another.

"Pull out! Scatter!"

11

The cowboys not hit reined their horses to a stop, pulled rifles out of saddle scabbards and jumped down from their saddles. Throwing their rifles to their shoulders, they took aim at the flashes and returned the fire.

A cowboy's bullet found its mark and one of the buckskin-clad riflemen slumped to the ground. Two of his companions picked up his body and carried it a short distance to where another figure in buckskin held their horses. They slung his body over one of the horse's backs, mounted up and rode off.

The cowboys, seeing the fire against them had lessened, drew heart. "They're not firin' as heavy," shouted one. "I think we got a couple of the sons of bitches."

They renewed their fire until finally the shooting at them stopped. "We either got 'em all or they've pulled out," shouted one of the cowboys exultantly.

"Careful," shouted Vince Black. "It might be a trap."

"But the dogies—they're gettin' stampeded away."

The trail boss did not reply.

The stampeding herd pounded on southward, driven by a dozen or more fast-riding figures in buckskin who whooped and yelled, firing their rifles into the air. The stampede was in full swing, leaving behind it flattened grass, swirling dust, and the bodies of seven dead or injured blood-smeared cowboys and almost as many dead or dying horses.

Johnny McNab lay on his back in the trampled grass, blood seeping into the dust beside him as he lay dying on foreign soil. He coughed twice, pain wracking his chest. The last thing he saw was the pale moon riding high in the dark night sky.

Chapter 2

Hugh O'Reilly sat beside the window of the Canadian Pacific Railway carriage gazing at the rolling prairie passing by. He gazed, fascinated by the sparkling, snow-crowned mountain peaks some sixty miles off to the west. He had sailed around the continents of Africa, Europe and Asia but had never seen anything as spectacular as the Rocky Mountains.

Ahead, the locomotive belched smoke into the blue sky as it pulled its two carriages southward at the rocking speed of thirty-five miles an hour. Occasional sparks floated by O'Reilly's window, and he remembered hearing how these coalburning locomotives started prairie fires in the long grass as they rattled by.

O'Reilly was pleased. In the prime of life at twenty-three, he was a magnificently built man with deep chest, broad shoulders and lean waist emphasized by his form-fitting scarlet tunic, dark blue breeches with wide yellow cavalry stripes down the sides, and highly polished boots. His face, tanned by several years of exposure to sun and wind, gave the impression of strength and determination. His features were regular, with a straight nose, a firm mouth and square jaw. He sported a neatly trimmed military moustache, while his black hair, cut to regulation length, was worn brushed back from his forehead. On the seat beside him lay a blue pill-box forage cap with a yellow band around it, known within the service as a *one-ear* because it was worn at a jaunty angle on the head, slanting down over the right eyebrow and ear, and held in place by a narrow leather strap worn around the point of the chin.

Constable O'Reilly had been a member of the North-west Mounted Police for one year. He was on his way to Fort Macleod, Northwest Territories, to report for duty, on transfer from Depot Division at Regina, the territorial capital. He was keen to experience the adventures he expected would come his way in the service of Canada's elite Scarlet Riders, a force that in May 1893 was not quite twenty years old but had already earned world fame.

He was becoming impatient to arrive at Fort Macleod. It had seemed a long time on the train. He had boarded a Canadian Pacific at Regina two days earlier, traveled west to Calgary, then disembarked to board the day train to Fort Macleod, ninety miles to the south. It would have been more direct to have changed trains farther back east at Medicine Hat, caught the North-Western Coal and Navigation Company's narrow gauge to Lethbridge and then boarded a stagecoach for the final thirty miles to Fort Macleod, but the engineers and conductors of the North-Western Coal's railway were on strike, which had left south-bound passengers no other alternative but to travel the extra distance to Calgary.

One of the reasons for O'Reilly's pleasurable frame of mind was his posting. Fort Macleod was acknowledged as one of the best Mounted Police stations in the Northwest Territories. As well as possessing a generally equitable climate in a country known for its severe winters, the Fort Macleod district — the heart of western Canada's booming young cattle industry — contained some of the West's most spectacular scenery.

He was about to pull his pipe and tobacco from the white haversack that, together with his pill-box, occupied the seat beside him, when he felt a tap on his shoulder.

14

Looking up, he saw a squirrel-like face with thick gray hair underneath a black cap bearing in gold lettering the word *Conductor*.

"There's a bit of a problem on the carriage behind, Constable," the conductor said, jerking his thumb over his shoulder. "Couple of young dandies back there are bothering one of the passengers. I think they've had a bit too much to drink. I told 'em to behave themselves, but they told me to get the hell away or they'd shove the carriage right up my ass."

The conductor looked thoroughly miserable as he added, "If I was a bit younger I'd have given 'em something to think about, but I'm getting too long in the tooth for that sort of thing now."

O'Reilly stood up, all seventy-four inches of him. Picking up his pill-box forage cap from the seat, he put it on his head and adjusted the narrow leather strap around his chin, pulled on his white gauntlets and followed the conductor along the aisle between the seats toward the second carriage behind.

Heads turned as O'Reilly passed, his spurs jingling behind him. He was a sight to behold, his fine physique filling the famous uniform as he carried himself straight-backed and proud, as befitting a member of the North-west Mounted Police.

They stepped out of the first carriage, crossed the steel platform connecting the two carriages, and opened the door leading into the second carriage.

Halfway down the coach two young men in smart city suits and bowler hats stood in the aisle laughing and carrying on. Seated primly on the seat below them was an obviously embarrassed young woman, her face flushed red underneath a wide straw hat. She couldn't be any more than twenty, O'Reilly thought, and she was very pretty.

The two young men quickly became aware of the approach of the conductor, and of O'Reilly's blazing scarlet tunic following him. One of the young men nudged the other, who looked up from the young lady, saw the object of the first's attention and grinned.

"All right, boys," the conductor said, brave now with the presence of a Mountie behind him. "You'll have to behave yourselves and sit down."

"To hell with you, old man," one of the dandies said. He was a big fellow, about O'Reilly's age.

"You're talking big now that you've got that redcoat with you," said the other. "Not big enough to handle your own problems, eh."

O'Reilly stepped around in front of the conductor. He was about to handle his first police case, two liquored-up dandies on a Canadian Pacific train. Not what he had imagined when he left the training depot at Regina, not a case of riding alone in an armed Indian camp and laying down the Queen's law, or chasing a dangerous criminal through the north woods. But at least there was a pretty face involved.

O'Reilly looked down at the young lady. His white-gauntleted hand went up to his pill-box in an informal salute. "These two men bothering you, ma'am?"

The young woman looked up, large violet eyes complementing her lavender jacket and skirt. "Well, I . . . I . . ." She seemed totally flustered and O'Reilly felt sorry for her as she sat clutching a handbag on her lap.

"Why don't you mind your own business and get back on your horse where you belong, redcoat?" one of the dandies said.

The other laughed as he joined in. "Yeah — with all the other horses' asses." He broke out into a peal of raucous laughter.

There were several other male passengers in the coach, but none had been inclined to get up and say anything to the two robust young dandies. Dandies they might have been, city-slickers, but they were big and bold. No one to trifle with.

O'Reilly turned to the conductor. "Stop the train."

The conductor's eyes widened. "Stop the train . . . ?"

"Yes. These two are getting off. They're going to walk

16

the rest of the way."

The expressions on the two young dandies' faces changed as the conductor reached over to the communication cord and pulled it. A moment later the train started to slow down.

As the train ground to a stop, O'Reilly pointed to the rear door. "All right, get off. If you can't behave yourselves and not bother other passengers, you don't have any business being on this train."

The two dandies glared hard at O'Reilly. One thrust out his jaw belligerently. "You just try putting us off the train!"

O'Reillys' brown eyes flashed. A challenge had been tossed down and he wasn't inclined to ignore it. His scarlet arm shot out, his hand grabbed the dandy by the shoulder and twirled him around so that he was facing the back of the train. Then, with one hand on the dandy's shoulder and the other on the seat of his pants, O'Reilly ran him down the aisle to the back door. The dandy's bowler hat rolled down the aisle behind them. A passenger sitting beside the door got up and obligingly opened it. O'Reilly and the dandy passed through. Once outside on the platform, O'Reilly heaved the young man down the steps and off the train, where he landed in a heap on the prairie beside the rails.

O'Reilly turned around, stepped back into the carriage and strode back along the aisle toward the second dandy. He reached him in great bounding strides. But the second man, the bigger of the two, turned ugly.

"You red-coated son of a bitch!" He took a wild swing at O'Reilly's head. O'Reilly ducked. The dandy's fist sailed past his ear but struck the Mountie's pill-box, snapping the strap and knocking the cap off his head.

O'Reilly came back with a solid right that caught the dandy in the midriff, knocking the air out of him with a plainly audible whoosh. The dandy doubled up. O'Reilly reached out, grabbed him by the collar and dragged him along the aisle to the rear door. Out on the platform

17

O'Reilly pulled him to the edge and rolled him down the steel steps so that he landed in the prairie dust beside his friend.

Turning around, O'Reilly saw the conductor standing beside him, holding the two dandies' bags. Grinning, the conductor tossed the bags down onto the ground beside the pair.

The conductor then pulled the communications cord and a moment later the train chuffed off to resume its southward journey. Bewildered, the two dandies sat in the dust beside the shiny steel rails watching the train disappear into the distance.

O'Reilly walked back along the aisle until he reached the young woman. Picking up his cap, he put it back on his head, the broken strap dangling down the side of his face. He lifted his white-gauntleted hand to his cap in an informal salute again.

"Sorry those two men bothered you, ma'am. They won't be doing that again."

Standing in the rocking aisle of the day carriage as the train picked up speed, O'Reilly looked down at her. He noticed now the few freckles on her face, but far from detracting from her looks, they enhanced them. He revised his earlier opinion of her as being pretty. Attractive was a better way to describe her. She was the type of woman, O'Reilly guessed, who would not have caught the boys' attention while a school girl — she would have been something of an "ugly duckling" — but one who had blossomed out into a very attractive young woman. O'Reilly couldn't think of anything else to say, and he had no reason to remain, but he didn't want to go.

A shy smile pulled at the corners of her mouth as she looked at the dangling strap of his pill-box. "Your . . . your cap. It's broken . . . because of me. You've been so kind, er . . . ." Her eyes moved to the Austrian knot of gold Russian braid around the lower sleeve of his scarlet dress tunic. "Er . . . Sergeant. I'm so sorry."

O'Reilly reached up to the cap. "Oh . . . that's all

right." He took it off his head and examined it. It wouldn't look so good when he reported in to division headquarters at Fort Macleod. He would get reprimanded over it. Maybe he could borrow one from one of the other men before he was marched in and paraded before the commanding officer.

"If you'd like to sit down," the young woman said, moving over in her seat to leave the space beside her vacant, "I'd be pleased to see if I can mend it."

O'Reilly flashed her a gallant smile. "That's very nice of you, ma'am. But I wouldn't want to bother you."

"Oh, it's no bother, Sergeant. It's the least I can do. I have a sewing bag in my case." She pointed up to a case on the luggage rack above her seat. O'Reilly reached up and handed it down to her. Placing it on the seat opposite, she opened it and extracted a small bag. O'Reilly sat down on the seat beside her.

O'Reilly held his pill-box in front of him while she quickly threaded a needle, despite the rocking of the railway carriage. He handed her the cap. As she lowered her head and examined the break, O'Reilly inhaled the fragrance of her perfume. Her closeness intoxicated him.

"You're going to Fort Macleod, ma'am?" O'Reilly asked. The rail line ended at Fort Macleod, but she could have been taking a stagecoach to Lethbridge or some other place.

"Yes," she replied. "I'm going to visit my uncle."

Now he noticed her clipped Eastern accent. "Is this your first visit to the West?"

She nodded. "Yes. In fact, it's my first visit to your country. It's so exciting out here, all these wide open spaces, and those beautiful mountains over there." She nodded her head in the direction of the Rocky Mountains. "It's so different from anything I've ever seen before. I'm from New York."

"New York?" O'Reilly smiled again, his teeth showing white and even against the tan of his face. "We're practically neighbors. I'm from Halifax." When her face didn't

19

show anything, he quickly added, "That's in Nova Scotia."

She smiled back at him. "Yes, I've heard of Halifax."

"I've heard of New York, too."

They both laughed.

They didn't speak again for several minutes as she turned her attention to sewing the broken strap on his cap. He watched her expertly repair the break. He ended the silence by saying "You're pretty good with a needle."

"That's what a woman is for."

"I'm not a bad hand with a needle myself, although I'm no expert by any means, and I certainly wouldn't be doing anywhere near as good a job with that strap."

"You don't have a wife to sew for you, Sergeant?" she asked, her eyes riveted to her task.

O'Reilly liked the sound of her addressing him as *Sergeant*. It sounded good, although he felt he should tell her that he wasn't a sergeant at all, just a lowly constable. Yet, for some reason that he couldn't explain and didn't bother to analyze just then, he felt some need to impress her. Besides, he told himself, it couldn't do any harm for her to think of him as a sergeant. "No," he said, answering her question. "The Mounted Police doesn't take married men. The Force likes to keep most if its men single because they can be transferred all around the Territories at a moment's notice, whenever there's an outbreak of trouble anywhere."

"It must be exciting being in the Mounted Police. I suppose you've had lots of adventures."

"Well . . ."

Before he could answer, she suddenly turned to face him directly. Her eyes shone with an enthusiasm he hadn't seen in them until just that instant. "Have you ever chased a murderer across the plains? Or put down an Indian war?"

"Well, I haven't exactly put down an Indian war," O'Reilly answered, trying to sound modest. "At least, not alone. Myself and a couple of other men. That was up in the Saskatchewan country, where the halfbreeds and Indians rebelled, back in '85. You probably read about it."

"No . . . I can't say that I have. I was only about twelve then."

His face as straight as a poker, O'Reilly looked into her eyes. "It was a bit before my time, too."

A serious expression on her face, she looked into O'Reilly's brown eyes for a long moment before she saw the sparkle in them. Then her face colored and she laughed self-consciously. "Oh, you're teasing me."

She just as quickly turned back to the sewing and said no more for several minutes as the train chuffed southward across the rolling prairie. When she finished she looked at O'Reilly again and smilingly handed him the round blue and yellow pill-box.

"There you are, Sergeant. It's as good as new . . . well, almost."

O'Reilly took it and turned it over, smiling admiringly. "Thank you. You've saved my life."

She blushed. "Oh, come, now. They can't be all *that* strict in the Mounted Police."

O'Reilly's face went stern. "Oh, they're strict, all right. Discipline in the Mounted Police is as strict as it is in the British Army. Several of our officers saw service in some of the most famous regiments in the British Empire. The Commissioner himself, although a Canadian, served in a British regiment. He decreed that the Northwest Mounted Police would be the hardest force in the world to join and the easiest to leave. A man has to watch himself. If he steps out of line or breaks the disciplinary code, he's likely to do a spell in the guardroom and then find himself booted right out of the Force. That's the British influence. They make the best soldiers in the world."

The young lady tilted her chin in polite disagreement. "You don't seem to have heard of the United States Army. Particularly the cavalry. They're very dashing."

"Yes, but they haven't fought in the wars the British have. Look at India, Africa, Egypt, the Sudan, Afghanistan, the Northwest Frontier . . . just to mention a few."

"What about the Indian wars in the American West? The Little Big Horn, for instance?" A lightly indignant tone entered her voice. "What about General Custer and the famous Seventh United States Cavalry? There's even a former officer who served under the gallant General Custer in the Seventh Cavalry in your own—"

Whatever else she was about to say was interrupted by the conductor entering the carriage and calling, "Fort Macleod coming up, ladies and gentlemen. End of the line. We'll be arriving in a few minutes."

Immediately there was activity with the carriage as some of the passengers started gathering their luggage in preparation for disembarking, while others craned their necks at the windows, peering out in search of the signs of habitation.

O'Reilly's attractive young lady acquaintance looked out the window. She smiled happily. "Oh, I'm so glad. It's been a long train ride, all the way from New York and Montreal. I feel as though I've been on a train most of my life."

The train slowed as it crossed a wooden bridge that spanned the sparkling green water of a river. A short distance beyond, the train passed a few scattered buildings here and there, then the frame buildings of a one street town. Just then the conductor returned, carrying O'Reilly's white haversack.

"It's not very big," the young lady said of the town, still staring out the window.

"Two hundred people, miss, give or take one or two," the conductor said in answer to her remark as he handed the haversack to O'Reilly. "That is, in the town of Macleod itself. But there's lots of folks in the surrounding district. Heart of western Canada's cattle range country. Macleod started out nigh on twenty years ago as a Northwest Mounted Police fort. Nothin' out here then but Mounted Police and Indians. Named the place after Colonel James Macleod, the Forces' second Commissioner. He's Judge Macleod now, of the Supreme Court of the

22

Northwest Territories. The town became incorporated last year and they dropped the name *Fort,* at least officially. Didn't seem appropriate to call it a fort anymore, but most folks still do. Old habits die hard."

The train ground to a stop in front of the railway station. Excusing himself, the conductor left to walk along the aisle calling, "Fort Macleod. End of the line. Everybody disembark here."

The young lady stood up and reached for her bag, but O'Reilly was quicker. "I'll help you, ma'am."

"Thank you, Sergeant," she replied, smiling.

"If . . . if you're going to be around, ma'am," O'Reilly stammered, suddenly flustered, "perhaps I'll bump into you again. I mean . . . I don't even know your name."

"I'm Miss Ruth Baker. I'll be staying with my uncle, just out of town."

O'Reilly recovered himself. "Pleased to make your acquaintance, Miss Baker. My name is O'Reilly, Hugh O'Reilly."

"I'm happy to meet you, Sergeant O'Reilly."

They walked along the aisle and out onto the platform. O'Reilly stepped down onto the station platform, then turned to help Miss Ruth Baker down the steel steps.

They were no sooner on the platform when Ruth Baker's eyes lighted up and she started waving frantically to someone on the platform. "There's Uncle Jack," she exclaimed excitedly.

O'Reilly turned his head in the direction where she was waving. Instantly he froze! Striding toward them was a tall, military-like man wearing the blue tunic and Glengarry cap of a commissioned officer of the Northwest Mounted Police.

O'Reilly snapped to attention and saluted. The officer, the star of an inspector on his collars, looked briefly at O'Reilly and returned the salute, then reached out his arms for Ruth Baker.

"Uncle Jack!" she said, her eyes shining with excitement.

"Hello, Ruth," he replied. "So good to see you. My, you've grown more beautiful in the last two years. A real young lady in full bloom."

While O'Reilly stood at rigid attention, they embraced. At last Ruth turned to smile at O'Reilly. "Sergeant O'Reilly. This is my uncle."

The inspector studied O'Reilly through steel-blue eyes. *"Sergeant,"* he said, his eyes taking in the bare space on the upper right arm of O'Reilly's scarlet tunic, where a crown and three gold chevrons would have been if O'Reilly really was a sergeant. "I'm Inspector Cavannagh."

O'Reilly swallowed. *Inspector Cavannagh!* Christ! He had heard all about Inspector Cavannagh. Who in the Mounted Police hadn't? The instructors at the training depot at Regina had often spoken Cavannagh's name. The West Point graduate and former Seventh Cavalry officer who had come up to Canada in 1875, less than two years after the Force had been formed, and joined up. Cavannagh, who had backed down victory-flushed Sioux warriors after they crossed into Canada fresh from their victory over Custer back in '76. Cavannagh . . . a name to be mentioned in the same hushed tones as other Mounted Police immortals of those early years . . . *Macleod* . . . *Walsh* . . . *Steele* . . .

Cavannagh was an American, O'Reilly remembered. And Ruth Baker was, of course, American. That's what she had been trying to say when they were talking about British and American soldiers. The American cavalry . . . her uncle a former officer of Custer's immortal Seventh U.S. Cavalry. O'Reilly recalled her words . . . *"there's even a former officer who served under the gallant General Custer in the Seventh Cavalry in your own—"*

O'Reilly fervently wished he had admitted to her that he was only a constable, not a sergeant. His face colored to the same shade as his scarlet tunic.

"You're here on transfer, I take it, O'Reilly?" Inspector Cavannagh said.

"Er . . . yes, sir."

Inspector Cavannagh smiled. "Good. We can always use an extra man. In fact, we can use all the extra men Depot Division sends us. We've very busy out here. I have a democrat. I can give you a lift to the barracks."

"That . . . that's very kind of you, sir."

Inspector Cavannagh took his niece by the arm and led her to a spring wagon, where a red-coated constable sat waiting, holding the traces in gauntleted hands. O'Reilly followed.

"Climb aboard, O'Reilly," Inspector Cavannagh said after helping his niece up onto one of the leather seats behind the driver. "The barracks are just on the western end of the town. I'll send a man back to pick up the rest of your things. It'll take ten or fifteen minutes before the baggage car is unloaded, and I'm afraid I have to hurry back to headquarters to attend a conference the commanding officer has called. We've just had a bad outbreak of cattle rustling and several cowboys were killed."

O'Reilly wasn't sure whether Inspector Cavannagh was speaking to him or his niece. He presumed his niece; officers weren't in the habit of discussing official matters with constables, except to issue orders. Anyway, Ruth answered by saying how sorry she was that those poor cowboys had lost their lives, and expressing her hope that her arrival wasn't inconveniencing him. While Inspector Cavannagh assured her that it wasn't, and that in any event it wasn't every day that his niece arrived all the way from New York to visit him, O'Reilly climbed up onto the front seat beside the driver.

"What sort of journey did you have, Ruth?" Inspector Cavannagh asked. "You must be tired."

"Yes, I am a little, but it was very interesting. And for the last few miles I had the pleasure of Sergeant O'Reilly's company. He has been very charming, entertaining me by telling me all about life in the Mounted Police."

Sitting up on the front seat, O'Reilly winced, especially at the mention of *"Sergeant O'Reilly."* He felt his neck redden as he imagined Inspector Cavannagh's steel-blue eyes boring into him from behind. The red-coated driver cast a sideways glance at him. O'Reilly didn't like the mocking expression on the constable's face, and he knew he would be the subject of discussion in the barracks that night before the trumpeter sounded *lights out*.

They drove along the town's dusty main street, loose stones flying under the wagon's wheels as it rolled along between the string of false-fronted frame buildings. There was a hotel, several stores, a bank, lawyer's office, doctor's surgery, livery stables, restaurant, billiard parlors, blacksmith's shop and the trappings of a frontier cow town. Cattlemen and business men, a few Indians and a stagecoach characterized the main street.

Ahead O'Reilly could see the Union Jack flying from a tall white flagpole and beneath it the outline of the Northwest Mounted Police barracks rising neat and orderly against the rolling green and brown hills in the distance. Farther off, the snow-topped mountains thrust their irregular peaks against the blue sky some fifty or so miles away. To the south there was nothing but rolling prairie, blue sky and distance, to the north the same, while off to the northwest loomed the deep green bulk of a range of treed hills.

"Do you know," O'Reilly heard Inspector Cavannagh saying to his niece, "that you were still in school the last time I saw you? That young ladies' finishing school just out of New York."

O'Reilly heard Ruth Baker laugh. Then Inspector Cavannagh asked, "You're not engaged to be married yet, or anything like that?"

O'Reilly strained his ears to hear her reply over the noise of the clip-clopping of the horses' hoofs. Again she laughed. "No, Uncle Jack. I'm not engaged or anything like that."

There was a short pause in the conversation as Ruth looked all around, then she said, "I can't get over how far you can see in every direction out here in the West."

Inspector Cavannagh smiled as he glanced around.

"Yes, and the wind blows forever. But tell me, Ruth, how is your mother? And your father?"

The remainder of the short journey was occupied with talk of family events. Inspector Cavannagh seemed starved of family information and he utilized the time to hear everything his niece could tell him.

The wagon rattled into the barracks, light gray frame buildings with shingle roofs of a darker shade, formed in the shape of a square, with a large parade ground in the center and the flagpole, the Union Jack stretched full and flapping noisily in the brisk prairie wind. A pair of nine-pounder field guns stood within the square. Well-tended lawns and gardens graced the area around the buildings, with young pine and spruce trees growing alongside. The place reminded O'Reilly of the Regina depot.

The driver reined the team to a stop in front of one of a row of identical houses on the west side of the square. Officers' houses, O'Reilly guessed. Inspector Cavannagh stepped down from the wagon and helped Ruth Baker down. Ruth looked smilingly up at O'Reilly.

"Goodbye, Sergeant O'Reilly. It's been so nice enjoying your company. I hope we'll meet again. I'm going to be here a little while."

O'Reilly raised his hand to his cap as he looked down at her. "My pleasure, Miss Baker. Yes, I hope we see each other again."

Inspector Cavannagh said to the driver, "Take O'Reilly to the sergeant major, Constable. He's reporting here on transfer."

"Very good, sir," the driver said.

Inspector Cavannagh took Ruth's arm and led her up the board walk to his house. A golden haired woman, smiling radiantly, appeared at the front door. Inspector Cavannagh's wife, O'Reilly reasoned. He felt a pang of regret seeing Ruth disappear in through the front door. O'Reilly and the driver exchanged glances before the driver flicked the reins and the wagon moved off.

"I'll take you over to the sergeant major's office, *Ser-*

geant," the driver said with a sly grin. O'Reilly glared at him but didn't say a word. He knew he would have a long time to wear that one down.

Chapter 3

Major Sam Steele stood ramrod-straight beside his desk. He was a big, blustery man of forty-two, displaying a wide military moustache and the ribbon of the Northwest Medal on his blue tunic. The most famous officer still serving in the Northwest Mounted Police, he commanded the Fort Macleod district. Sitting on chairs in front of his desk were the four officers of his command— a superintendent and three inspectors. On the wall behind his desk hung a large map of the Northwest Territories, including the northern portions of Montana and Dakota. Outside his window stretched the parade square and its two field guns.

"I'm more than concerned about this most recent incident of cattle rustling, gentlemen," Major Steele said as he stood, hands clasped behind his back, looking at the officers in front of him. "Five American cowboys lost their lives as a result of it, two being killed outright by gunfire, two more were trampled to death, and a fifth subsequently died from gunshot wounds. Additionally, three more were injured, two by bullet wounds and a third by being trampled. On top of that, almost the entire herd was run off."

"Did they get any description of the rustlers, sir?" asked Inspector Cavannagh.

Major Steele stepped around his desk and stood behind his chair, his hands grasping its back as he looked at Inspector Cavannagh. Like Major Steele, Inspector Cavannagh also wore the ribbon of the Northwest Medal, awarded to members of the Mounted Police for service under fire during the Northwest Rebellion of 1885. At forty-three, Inspector Cavannagh was a year older than Major Steele, and was almost as much a legend in the Force.

"Only that they wore buckskin and no hats," Major Steele replied. "It was a dark night. There was a moon but there was a lot of cloud. There was also a lot of high-pitched yelling and whooping. The cowboys thought they were Indians."

"Certainly sounds like Indians," said the superintendent, a crusty, beetle-browed man.

"Our flying patrols have combed the Blood and Peigan reserves, but haven't sighted a glimpse of stolen cattle," Major Steele replied. "Besides, it's unlike Indians to rustle cattle. They'll kill an occasional rancher's cow or steer for meat, but they've never gone in for large-scale cattle rustling. If it were horses, I'd be inclined to suspect them. After all, that's what they did for generations, back in the old days when a brave was judged by the number of scalps he lifted and the number of horses he ran off. It was all an accepted part of warfare, but we've stamped out that sort of activity."

"What about a war party of American Indians?" the superintendent suggested.

Major Steele nodded. "That is a possibility, but I doubt they'd pull off anything like that so close to a reservation containing a large concentration of our Indians, especially a tribe such as the Bloods." He took his hands off the back of his chair, stepped out around his desk and paced backward and forward in front of his officers, his face stern. "No, gentlemen, I believe there's a common thread linking all the instances of rustling we've had over the past

30

two years. Every case that's been reported to us has borne similar characteristics. Each one has been well planned, well executed, each one has taken place when our patrols were occupied with other law enforcement activities, and in each case the stolen stock vanished without a trace. Whoever is responsible has a thorough knowledge of the country. They would need it to avoid our network of detachments and patrols."

"All of which points to Indians in my opinion," said the crusty superintendent. "They know the country better than anyone else by far. They have the communications and the riding ability. We should also remember that we've had reports from ranchers who have found tracks of unshod ponies where cattle were rustled from, and they've sighted Indians skulking around their herds."

Frowning, Major Steele stopped pacing. "If Indians are responsible, it's going to have an unsettling effect on the population of the district as a whole. Not only of the Fort Macleod district for that matter, but throughout the Territories in general. It will have a particularly bad effect on the rest of the Indians. If they see their own tribesmen getting away with this sort of thing, the young bucks especially are going to get the idea they can defy us and get away with it. This whole thing could indicate a growing restlessness on the part of the Indians, a mounting dissatisfaction with the transition that has seen them pass from proud, buffalo-hunting warriors answerable to no law other than their own and that of the Great Spirit, to reservation Indians dependent upon us and the government for their daily existence. A restlessness and dissatisfaction that might be foreshadowed by a growing tendency to defy the law. A restlessness that might express itself in one last, desperate attempt to throw off the white man's yoke by taking the warpath."

Major Steele paused to let the import of his words sink in. After a moment he went on. "Ominously, this most recent incident involved the loss of life for the first time.

31

Clearly, they're prepared to shoot it out whenever they're challenged. Gentlemen, if we don't bring the perpetrators of these criminal offenses to justice, we're going to face widespread increases in crime and lawlessness in general, to say the least. And perhaps much worse."

"The obvious answer," the superintendent said, "would be to more closely watch the activities of the Bloods and Peigans on the reserves and to increase the size and frequency of the flying patrols."

Major Steele nodded. "Yes, I agree." He looked at Inspector Cavannagh and an inspector sitting beside him. "Inspector Cavannagh, Inspector Ainsworth, you will visit the flying patrols in your respective divisions and personally instruct the NCOs in charge to increase the hours they and their men spend in the saddle. Examine all patrol routes to make sure every inch of the country is thoroughly covered as frequently as possible. Pay particular attention to geographical features that could be used as escape routes or hiding places. Mark them on the patrol maps. The prevention of rustling and the apprehension of those responsible is to be given number one priority. Put that in writing for the information of every NCO and constable on detached duty."

Inspector Cavannagh's face, weathered by years of exposure to sun and prairie wind, tightened. "An increase in patrol time could impair the health and stamina of the horses, sir. And the men as well, who already spend most of their waking hours in their saddles."

Major Steele's moustache bristled. "Duty makes demands upon us all, Inspector. I want every effort made to wipe out these infernal outbreaks of cattle rustling — and all other forms of lawlessness — and to bring the perpetrators to justice. And, by George, we *are* going to accomplish that."

For the second time that day, Constable O'Reilly stood

at attention in front of the sergeant major's desk. On the first occasion, the sergeant major told him to come back later as all the officers were in conference in Major Steele's office. Now O'Reilly, having returned as ordered, found he had a further wait.

"I'm Sergeant Major MacGregor," the big soldierly NCO sitting at the small desk said in an unmistakable Scottish accent. O'Reilly recognized the ribbon of the Northwest Medal on his tunic. It was sewn beside another ribbon, which O'Reilly did not recognize, but which he guessed represented some British campaign in some remote part of Queen Victoria's far-flung Empire.

Sergeant Major MacGregor looked O'Reilly up and down, critical gray eyes taking in the appearance of his scarlet dress tunic, the shine on his brass buttons, noting that each button was straightly arrayed with the Force badge and the crown uppermost, and his belt buckle perfectly aligned with the buttons. Apparently satisfied, Sergeant Major MacGregor continued speaking.

"You're t' report t' Inspector Cavannagh, but someone's in t' see him at the moment. As soon as he's free, I'll march y' in. Wait ootside in the hallway. And dinna y' lounge around. Just because you're oot of the Depot Division, dinna y' think discipline's any the less here, because it is not."

Anticipating that the sergeant major had finished addressing him, O'Reilly was on the verge of stepping out into the hallway when Sergeant Major MacGregor's voice stopped him. "Have y' unpacked your gear?"

"No, sir."

"Well then, dinna y' bother. You're nae going t' be around here verra long."

With that, Sergeant Major MacGregor nodded a curt dismissal. O'Reilly executed a snappy about-turn and marched out into the hallway, where he stood at ease, but remained ready to spring to attention and salute should an officer suddenly appear from one of the several doorways

33

leading off from the hallway. Besides being an effective, hard-riding law enforcement body, the Northwest Mounted Police was also a spit-and-polish military corps; discipline and the parade ground were ever-present aspects of the Force.

As he waited, O'Reilly heard muffled voices coming from the room next to the sergeant major's office. The door bore the name *Insp. J. T. Cavannagh*. It sounded like a heated conversation going on in there.

Having nothing better to do, O'Reilly strained his ears to hear what was being said. He heard a loud, rasping voice saying ". . . sick and tired of this God damn rustling. That's why we're paying taxes, so's you pretty soldier boys will do something to stop it."

Then another voice said something, but O'Reilly couldn't hear it. After that the raspy voice spoke again, and again he heard the word *"rustling."*

Suddenly O'Reilly heard yet another voice, this one much closer—booming in his ear. "What do y' think you're doing, mon?"

O'Reilly stiffened to attention. "Nothing, sir."

Sergeant Major MacGregor looked hard at O'Reilly for a moment. Although in his mid-fifties, the sergeant major was a solid six-footer with no flab bulging his close-fitting tunic. He was, O'Reilly had heard, one of the few still serving *originals*, men who had joined the Force when it was formed in 1873 and took part in the epic march west from Fort Garry in Manitoba to the foothills of the Rockies, where they had chopped down cottonwoods on the banks of the Old Man's River and built the original Fort Macleod. O'Reilly expected a withering blast, but the senior noncom's rugged face relaxed, as though there was something about the younger man that drew his approval. He nodded at Inspector Cavannagh's closed door.

"Inspector Cavannagh, he's listening t' 'Iron-Fist' Taggart mouthing off aboot all the stock he's lost t' cattle rustlers. The inspector's sympathetic t' him and all the ranchers, but the others dinna carry on like Iron-Fist Taggart. Aye, and it sounds like Iron-Fist's having it all his way, because y' dinna hear Mister Cavannagh raising his voice. But the inspector has a temper himself when he needs it. Generally, though, he's too much a gentleman to let it get oot of control. But I'll tell y', O'Reilly, Iron-Fist Taggart is nae going t' get much sympathy from him by carrying on like tha'. It's just nae the way with Inspector Cavannagh."

Just then the raspy voice exploded from the other side of the door, and the next instant the door was thrown open and a big, burly man stood framed in the doorway, his back to the hall. "If you redcoats can't do something about those God damn Indians who're doing all this rustling, I will!"

"What makes you think it's Indians, Mister Taggart?" Inspector Cavannagh asked quietly from behind his desk.

"Of course it's Indians!" Iron-Fist Taggart rasped. "They're always hanging around the herds. Who else knows the country so well that they can whisk large numbers of stock away so no one can find any trace of them. It's no wonder you redcoats can't catch them. You don't even know what the hell you're looking for. Maybe you should plant your arse in a saddle and ride around and see what your flying patrols are doing."

"That will do, Mister Taggart!" Inspector Cavannagh's voice was hard and sharp.

Without another word, Iron-Fist Taggart whirled around and stormed out of the office. His mahogany colored face flushed dark with apparent rage, he bumped into O'Reilly. At six feet two inches, O'Reilly weighed one hundred and ninety pounds, but Iron-Fist Taggart was taller and bigger, and the unexpected force of his body sent O'Reilly reeling. Taggart glared briefly at O'Reilly, but he didn't apologize. He merely grunted, the expression on his face seeming to say, *Get out of my God damn way!* and stomped on along the hallway.

35

"Ill-mannered bastard!" Sergeant Major MacGregor muttered, watching him go.

As soon as the headquarters building's front door slammed shut behind the irate rancher, Sergeant Major MacGregor stiffened his back and knocked on the door Taggart had just come out of.

"Come in," a voice called from inside.

Sergeant Major MacGregor stood in the doorway. "The new mon, Constable O'Reilly, sir, just posted here on transfer frae Depot Division. Reporting for duty, sir."

"March him in please, Sergeant Major."

At the sergeant major's command, Constable O'Reilly marched into the office and crashed to a spur-clashing halt in front of Inspector Cavannagh's desk. He swung his right arm up in a springlike movement, bringing his right hand palm-out, extended fingers touching his pill-box. It was a snappy, regimental salute, the way he had been taught at Depot, as laid down in *Regulations and Orders of the Northwest Mounted Police Force of Canada*, a book just one step away from the Holy Bible.

"Constable O'Reilly, *sirr!*" bellowed Sergeant Major MacGregor.

Inspector Cavannagh glanced at the sergeant major. "Thank you, Sergeant Major. That will be all. You may carry on."

"Sir!" Sergeant Major MacGregor saluted, turned about and marched out of the inspector's office, pulling the door shut behind him.

Inspector Cavannagh looked up at O'Reilly. "Stand at ease, Constable O'Reilly."

Inspector Cavannagh dropped his eyes to a manila file folder on the desk in front of him. The folder, containing O'Reilly's service file, bore his name and regimental number printed across the top in black India ink.

Opening the file, Inspector Cavannagh started reading from a sheet of paper. "You joined the Mounted Police in May 1882, O'Reilly, so you have a year's service."

36

"Yes, sir."

"And following completion of recruit training, you were assigned assistant riding instructor's duties."

"Yes, sir."

Still reading, Inspector Cavannagh continued. "You went to school in Halifax until you were thirteen, when you left because of the Depression and went to work in a grocery store to help support your widowed mother. You remained there until you were sixteen, then you went to sea. Since then you sailed most of the world's oceans and saw Europe, Africa, India, Asia, South America . . ." Inspector Cavannagh looked up at O'Reilly. "That's quite a background, O'Reilly. You must have seen some interesting sights and had some unique experiences."

"Some of it was, sir. Some of it was pretty monotonous, day after day of ocean."

"Why did you got to sea?"

"To see the sea, sir."

The inspector grinned. "Living in Halifax, growing up there, I would have thought you would have seen lots of it."

"I mean . . . I wanted to see the *seas*, sir—all seven of them."

"Hmmm," Inspector Cavannagh murmured, looking down at the file again. "The Depot Riding Master at Regina wrote on your file, '*first class horseman. Natural ability with horses. Recommended be assigned duties as rough-rider and assistant riding instructor.*'"

Inspector Cavannagh looked up from the file again. "Had you ridden before joining the Force, O'Reilly?"

O'Reilly shook his head. "No, sir."

Inspector Cavannagh looked down at the file once more. "You applied for a transfer out of Depot Division." He lifted his steel-blue eyes to study O'Reilly's face. "Why didn't you want to be a riding instructor, O'Reilly? That would have been an important job. We need good riding instructors. You would have earned corporal's stripes much sooner than you will out here on active service."

O'Reilly held the inspector's gaze. "Teaching recruits to ride horses wasn't what I had in mind when I joined the Mounted Police, sir."

"I see," Inspector Cavannagh replied, nodding slowly. "How are you with rifle and revolver?"

"Better than average, sir."

"Good. I've got just the job for you. I need a man who can ride and shoot well. You've heard of the flying patrols?"

A wave of excitement surging through him, O'Reilly nodded. "Yes, sir."

His eyes still studying O'Reilly, Inspector Cavannagh leaned back in his chair. "The Fort Macleod district is cattle country. It consists of rolling grasslands, foothills, coulees and buttes running all the way down to the Montana border, sixty miles away. We police it by means of a chain of detachment outposts fanning out from Fort Macleod. To supplement the coverage provided by the outposts, we have added flying patrols, which, as you will be aware, are small parties of mounted men, usually a sergeant and three or four constables, constantly on the move, day and night, fair weather or storm, crisscrossing the country regardless of trails, seldom touching the same place at the same time of day or night, unpredictable in their movements, always on the watch for crime or criminals, keeping restless young Indian bucks on their reservations where they belong, preventing whisky smuggling, stopping border desperadoes or Indian war parties from crossing the international boundary, questioning all strangers to find out their business, fighting prairie fires, and generally attending to anything they come across. For the last while we've been plagued by an outbreak of cattle rustling, and to date we've had no success in combatting it. The raids have been well planned and carried out at widely separated times, following no pattern and so far they've been quite unpredictable. Indians are suspected, but we have no proof and therefore we don't know who's responsible. Unfortunately, in the most recent incident the rustlers resorted to gunplay and several American cowboys were killed or injured. As with the other instances of rustling, the cattle disappeared without a trace. With literally hundreds of ravines and coulees between here and Montana, the country lends itself to rustling."

Inspector Cavannagh brought himself forward over his desk again. He closed the cover of O'Reilly's service file. "I'm transferring you to the flying patrol at Standoff. We have a sergeant and three men there. It's sixteen miles south of Fort Macleod, on the west side of the Belly River. The Blood Indian reservation is on the other side of the river. You will report to Sergeant Hannan, the NCO in charge. You'll leave tomorrow morning. Sergeant Major MacGregor will arrange transportation." Inspector Cavannagh nodded in dismissal. "That will be all, O'Reilly. Carry on."

O'Reilly snapped to attention and saluted. "Sir." He made an about-turn and marched out of the office.

The next morning O'Reilly stood at the edge of the parade ground in front of the headquarters building, his dunnage bag, bedroll and rifle beside him. He stood looking toward the center of the parade ground, watching the red, white and blue of the Union Jack throwing a patch of color against the azure sky as it snapped noisily in the prairie wind. He didn't hear the sound of light footsteps approaching from behind.

"Good morning, Sergeant O'Reilly."

He whirled around. Standing behind him, looking breathlessly lovely, was Ruth Baker. She wore a purple dress and carried a straw basket. O'Reilly's hand went up to his pill-box in an informal salute. "Good morning, Miss Baker."

"Are you enjoying the sunshine?" she asked.

He grinned. "I'm waiting for a ride. I'm being shipped out to one of the outposts."

She nodded. "Yes, I know. Uncle Jack told me, to a place called . . . Stand-back?"

"Standoff," he corrected.

She smiled. "Oh, yes . . . Standoff. Uncle Jack told me it used to be a whisky trader's fort back in the old days before the Mounted Police arrived in the West. He told me the story of how it got its name. Some whisky runners came up from Montana to trade whisky to the Indians in exchange for buffalo skins. They were wanted by a United States marshal who crossed the border after them. The border wasn't marked in those days and no one paid much attention to it anyway. When the marshal caught up with them and tried to take them back, they stood him off with their guns and he had to go back empty-handed. So they called the place where it happened Standoff. Uncle Jack said they even built a log fort, but it's fallen apart now."

"That's an interesting story."

"You must be going there in charge."

O'Reilly looked at her. "Hasn't your uncle told you? I'm not a sergeant, I'm only a constable."

Her eyes widened in obvious surprise. "No, he didn't. I . . . I just thought you were a sergeant, with all that gold on your tunic. I thought you had to be a sergeant, at least." She was quiet for a moment, then asked, "What should I call you . . . Constable O'Reilly? Or would you prefer Mister O'Reilly?"

Some women would have described O'Reilly as handsome. Although his dark, tanned face bore three small scars—reminders of bar room brawls he'd been in in different ports around the world, for O'Reilly liked a fight—they did not detract from his looks. If anything, they added to them, giving him a rugged, manly handsomeness. O'Reilly carried himself with a military swagger, characteristic of the select one thousand officers and men given the privilege of wearing the already famous uniform of scarlet and gold. The very sight of Hugh O'Reilly striding along a street or marching around a barrack square was enough to drive women wild. But he was largely unaware of the attraction he had over women. Neither time nor circumstances had allowed him much experience with them. Although always ready to take on man or beast, he felt ill at ease and even shy with women, and it took him considerable courage to say to Ruth Baker, "You could call me Hugh, and I'd like to call you Ruth . . . if I may."

Ruth dropped her eyes. She said, slowly, "I would like that . . . Hugh. I would like you to call me Ruth."

A wagon approached around the square. O'Reilly had seen it coming from the direction of the transport shed over beyond the southeastern corner of the parade ground. He guessed it was his ride to Standoff. He had been impatient to be on his way before Ruth had appeared, but now he wanted to dally with this very attractive young woman and he wished the driver would turn around and go back.

"I'm sorry you're going away," she said, her eyes still downcast. "I had hoped I would see you again. I felt as though I had a friend here."

"Oh . . . I'm sure your uncle will see to it that you won't be lonely," O'Reilly said, feeling suddenly and strangely jealous. "All the single men will be hanging around your uncle's house."

She lifted her eyes to look up into his. "Perhaps his rank will scare them away. Besides, I'd be pleased to have just one friend here, someone whom I'd just begun to know."

At that moment the wagon pulled up alongside the boardwalk where they stood. "You the man going to Standoff?" the red-coated driver asked.

O'Reilly glanced up at him, a straw-haired constable a couple of years older than himself. "Yes. I'll be right with you." He turned back to Ruth. "Well, goodbye Miss . . .

41

Ruth."

"Will I see you again?" she asked.

He looked into her eyes. "I hope so. If I get back this way, I'd be honored to call on you. That is, if your uncle doesn't object."

"I'm sure he won't," Ruth replied, smiling. "He looks stern and business-like sometimes, but he's really very nice."

O'Reilly went to pick up his gear. Ruth reached into her basket and handed him a cloth-covered package. "I thought you might like this," she said. "My aunt prepared it yesterday. It's good home cooking."

"Thank you, Ruth," replied O'Reilly, touched at the realization that their meeting wasn't accidental, that she had especially come over to see him and that she had been thinking of him. "It's very thoughtful of you. I'm sure I'll enjoy it. I haven't had any home cooking for a long while."

O'Reilly placed the package on the back of the wagon, then lifted up his rifle, dunnage bag and bedroll and placed them on the back of the wagon. He adjusted the white haversack over his shoulder, then turned back to Ruth. He reached out his hand for hers and shook it politely.

"Goodbye, Ruth."

"Goodbye, Hugh."

He turned and stepped up onto the wagon and sat down beside the driver.

"Giddup," shouted the driver, kicking free the brake and flicking the reins. The horses pulled themselves into their harness and the democrat rolled away from the boardwalk and out along the driveway around the parade ground. O'Reilly sat looking back over his shoulder at a small, demure Ruth Baker standing in front of the headquarters building as she watched him go. She lifted her arm and waved. O'Reilly waved back, then turned his head around and looked to the front.

Following a travel-worn trail, the democrat wound its way down toward a river bottom. The sun shone brightly from a cloudless sky, warming passenger and driver through their tight-fitting scarlet tunics. It was midday when they rounded a bend and saw, on a cottonwood-treed flat beside the sparkling, snow-fed waters of the Belly River, a pair of gray frame buildings with dark gray shingle roofs surrounded by a neat picket fence to match the color of the buildings. Just inside the fence rose a white flagpole, the inevitable Union Jack flying from the top.

"That's Standoff," remarked the straw-haired constable as he guided the horses toward the buildings. "The big building is the barracks and office, the other one is the stables."

O'Reilly nodded approvingly. "Looks as good as Regina or Fort Macleod. I didn't think the outposts would be this modern."

The driver laughed. "A lot of them aren't. These have only been up two or three years. They tell me the old barracks were just a couple of old log cabins. All the chinking between the logs had fallen out and in winter a man would wake up to find his bed covered with three feet of snow that had blown in through the cracks during the night."

The sound of hoofbeats and the democrat's iron-bound wheels attracted attention within the building. Two men appeared in the doorway, stepped out and watched them drive up. They were dressed in dark blue breeches with wide yellow stripes down the sides, but instead of scarlet tunics they wore brown duck jackets with cutaway fronts and brass buttons. The older of the two had a shock of flaming red hair, while the other wore a wide-brimmed felt hat with a leather band and four dents in the crown.

43

The driver pulled the democrat to a stop in front of the gate and nodded to the red-headed man. "Good day, Sergeant Hannan."

Sergeant Michael Thomas Hannan nodded in return. "Good day," he growled. O'Reilly flashed him a quick look of appraisal, noting the short but compact build, hard-bitten freckled face and heavy jaw. Sergeant Hannan looked back at O'Reilly with the same appraising look.

O'Reilly jumped down from the democrat and stood at attention. "I'm Constable O'Reilly, Sergeant. I've been transferred here to the flying patrol."

Sergeant Hannan scowled as he looked O'Reilly up and down, noting the Depot smartness of his uniform and the shine on his boots and buttons. "You won't have time for all that spit-and-polish routine they drummed into you at Regina. Can you ride? And I don't mean sitting on your ass going through the motions of troop and squadron drill. I mean rough riding—hills, coulees, crossing rivers, pounding saddle leather for sixteen, sometimes twenty hours at a stretch."

O'Reilly's jaw tightened. "I can hold my own."

Sergeant Hannan's bright blue eyes took in the blue and yellow pill-box on O'Reilly's head. "And you can pack that *one-ear* away. They're useless for patrol. Wear a hat, like the one he's wearing." He inclined his head at the man beside him.

O'Reilly frowned. "The quartermaster didn't issue me with one."

"They're not issue—at least, not yet. Major Steele has been after Headquarters at Regina to supply felt hats instead of those ridiculous white helmets they make us wear for ceremonial parades. One day Ottawa will realize that what's good for the British Army isn't necessarily right for the Mounted Police. Until they do, Major Steele lets us wear felt hats provided we all wear the same kind. They come from the States. Feller by the name of Stetson makes 'em, John B. Stetson. They cost six bucks apiece, but they're worth it. They protect your eyes from the sun's glare, keep your head dry in wet weather, you can use them to fan the embers of a campfire or to water your horse when traveling across alkaline country." He jerked his thumb over his shoulder toward the river. "There's a trading post down there. You can buy one there."

Sergeant Hannan stood looking at O'Reilly for a moment longer, as though undecided whether he really wanted this new addition to his patrol. Finally he flicked his head at O'Reilly's dunnage bag, rifle and bedroll on the back of the democrat. "All right, get your kit unloaded. You'll find a spare bunk in the barracks."

Relieved that he'd passed muster, O'Reilly sprang to the back of the democrat and grabbed his dunnage bag and rifle. The man who had been standing beside Sergeant Hannan stepped over and grasped the bedroll. "I'll show you where the sleeping quarters are," he said.

He led O'Reilly into the building, to a large barrack room at the back where there were several bunks lined in a row. One was empty and O'Reilly dropped his dunnage bag onto it. The other man placed the bedroll beside it.

"I'm Roy Wise," the constable said, offering his hand. He was, O'Reilly guessed, about twenty-five. O'Reilly shook his hand.

"Hugh O'Reilly."

"Been around Fort Macleod long?"

"No. Arrived there yesterday."

"From Regina?"

Unstrapping his dunnage bag, O'Reilly nodded. "That's right."

"Just get through training?"

"No. Six months ago."

"What did they have you doing at Regina? Guard duties?"

"No. Assistant riding instructor."

"Riding instructor?" Roy Wise grinned. "Good thing you didn't tell Mike that when he asked you if you could

45

ride. He would've tried you out. He hasn't got too much time for the training depot or parades or drills or anything regimental."

O'Reilly started pulling uniforms and clothing from his dunnage bag. "I sort of got that impression."

Just then Sergeant Hannan walked into the barrack room. Two other men followed him. One was wearing yellow-striped blue breeches with a pair of suspenders holding them up over his shirt, but no jacket. The other wore fatigues. They were both in their late twenties, unlike Sergeant Hannan, whom O'Reilly guessed to be in his mid-forties.

"O'Reilly," Sergeant Hannan said. "Meet Bob Scott and Tom McCormack."

They all shook hands. After Sergeant Hannan left them, O'Reilly asked, "Are you fellows all on the flying patrol?"

"That's right," Scott and McCormack replied in unison.

"We're a little different from the regular detachment patrols," added Tom McCormack, the one wearing fatigues. "We don't follow any fixed routes or time schedules. Our motto is, 'We ride farther and get there faster.' We've been out on patrol for the last eight days. We just got back late yesterday afternoon. Now we're resting up."

Bob Scott, the senior constable in service, hooked his thumbs behind his suspenders. "Us resting? Hell! We're resting for only one reason—the horses need it. The men don't count. The Mounted Police doesn't care how hard it works its men, only its horses. If there's such a thing as reincarnation, I hope I come back to this earth as a Mounted Police horse."

They all laughed.

The laughter had just died down when the sound of drumming hoofs caught their attention. Bob Scott looked out the window. "Someone's in a mighty hurry."

A voice shouted from outside the building. "Hey! Some Bloods just run off twenty head o' my horses down by the

46

Double Bar X. Fired a couple of shots over my head. Damn near hit me!"

A rancher reined his galloping horse to a stop in front of the barracks. Sergeant Hannan met him at the door. They exchanged a few quick words, then the sergeant turned around and, his spurred boots beating a staccato on the floor boards, ran down the hallway to the men's barrack room.

"Flying patrol! Turn out! On the double! Sidearms and bandoliers. Hurry it up, now!"

The men went into a flurry of activity. Sergeant Hannan glanced at O'Reilly. "You too, O'Reilly. You got a stable jacket in that dunnage bag?"

O'Reilly nodded quickly. "Yes, Sergeant."

"Get it on, then. We don't wear red coats on patrol. They dirty up too easy and stand out too much on the prairie. The people we chase can see us coming from miles away. Come on, hurry it up, man! Now's the chance for you to show me how good you can ride."

47

Chapter 4

From Standoff they rode southwest, following the high banks of the Belly River. Sergeant Hannan and the rancher, whose name was Barrett, led, with Scott, McCormack, Wise and O'Reilly following. Each Mounted Policeman wore a .476 calibre Enfield service revolver holstered at his waist, and carried a .45-75 Winchester repeater slung across the pommel of his California stock saddle.

After a while they veered to the west and headed toward the distant mountains, the white peaks glistening under their snow-jeweled covering in the bright sunlight, rising like a jagged irregular line against the blue sky.

They rode over rolling hills and down into deep coulees. They forded the Kootenai, cold and swift from melting mountain snow. Then they legged their horses up the bank onto grassy upland.

Shortly they drew rein. The rancher pointed to a cutbank a hundred yards to their left. "That's where they took a couple of shots at me, Sergeant."

Sergeant Hannan eased himself in his saddle. "Those Indians, they could have come from either the Blood or Peigan reserves. You get a chance to identify any of them?"

The rancher shook his head. "One was riding a black and white pinto. The rest of them, about a dozen I reckon, just looked like any Indians."

Sergeant Hannan scanned the rolling hills ahead. "They'll push straight west, I reckon. Then they'll swing southwest. They won't go too far west because they might run into the Pincher Creek detachment. If they head straight south they'll fall foul of the detachment at Kootenai. So they'll stay west for a bit. All right, let's go."

They legged their horses on again, continuing west toward the mountains. O'Reilly thrilled to the excitement of the chase. This was his first patrol. This was what he had joined the Mounted Police for. This was far better than teaching recruits how to ride.

The trail continued west, what they could see of it. It was all range country, cattle grazing backward and forward. The patrol followed the lay of the land, riding along the tops of the coulees instead of taking the time to ride down into them and tiring the horses with the climb up out of them again. Sergeant Hannan reasoned the Indians would have done the same, especially at first because they would be intent on putting as much distance between themselves and the scene of the crime as they could, trying to outdistance the pursuit they knew would follow. But after a while the Indians would resort to guile and do the unpredicted.

They swung southwest with the contours of the land. Off in the distance to the south, the snow-crowned obelisk of Chief Mountain towered against the blue sky, a landmark just below the Montana side of the international boundary.

O'Reilly was amazed at the way the country rolled and changed with every mile. Around Regina the prairie stretched flat in all directions until the human eye ran out of distance, and even on the train ride to Calgary the country lay flat, although the elevation gradually rose as they got nearer to the Rockies farther west. But now the country was one rolling hill after another, each one rising successively high than the one before, and the snow-topped mountains were coming closer and closer. As they drew closer to the mountains, the air became cooler.

In the distance green pines fringed the lower slopes of the mountains. O'Reilly thrilled to the smooth rocking chair motion of the cantering horse beneath him, the easy relaxed way of riding that he could enjoy out on patrol but which the discipline-conscious riding instructors would not allow around the Regina depot. He exulted to the feel of the fresh, cool mountain air in his face, the thrill of the chase, the promise of imminent action.

They had been riding for more than three hours when, cresting the top of a hill, Sergeant Hannan signaled them to stop for a brief conference and to rest their horses.

They swung down from their saddles. "They're continuing southwest, into the foothills. The going is harder now. We can't make the same speed as before, but neither can they. A thing about Indians," Sergeant Hannan said, looking at O'Reilly as though his next words were for him because he was new and didn't know Indians. "They push their horses a hell of a lot harder than we do. They knock 'em around, whereas we look after ours. That's an advantage we have over them. But man for man we can't ride as good as them. They're born to the horse. On the other hand, I like to think we're a little smarter."

Leaning with an arm over his saddle, he gazed across his horse's back to the rising hills ahead and the mountains beyond. He pointed. "Those bucks are going to keep heading in that direction. I thought they'd probably swing off to the south before this. I figured they'd cut the Dry Fork, keep on going until they reached the North Fork, then run straight south along the Kootenai until they hit Montana. Maybe that's what they figured we'd think. But we're going to outsmart them. We're going to split up. Three of us will ride straight along the top of that ridge and cut off those bucks if they keep on running the way they've been going. Now, they might figure that's what we'll do, so they might get smart and double back on their tracks and come back down that coulee they're following.

"I'll take two men. Bob, you and Tom have the best

50

horses. You two come with me along the top of that ridge to head off those bucks." Sergeant Hannan looked at Constable Wise. "Roy, you and O'Reilly take Mister Barrett, if he wants to go, and follow along the coulee bottom. If those bucks turn around and double back, you fire off three fast shots with your Winchester, and we'll come a'running. Open fire and keep 'em boxed in."

Sergeant Hannan turned his eyes onto the rancher. "Mister Barrett, this is a job for a volunteer. I don't want to expose a civilian to gunfire. You can pull out and we'll think no less of you. You've done your bit just riding with us this far."

The rancher shook his head. "Hell, Sergeant! They're my horses. What sort of man would I be if I were to pull out now? No, I'll stick with you boys."

Sergeant Hannan's eyes shone with approval. "Good man." He swung back up into his saddle. "All right, let's move."

Sergeant Hannan and Constables Scott and McCormack put legs to their horses and cantered off along the ridge top further into the foothills. Roy Wise, O'Reilly and the rancher wheeled their horses around and rode down the grassed slope into the coulee after the Indians and the stolen horses.

It was gloomy in the coulee. The sky above was clouding in, with massing white and gray cloud, and O'Reilly shivered involuntarily, despite being warmed up from the exertion of the fast ride. As they rode, his spirits tingled with the expectation that any minute might bring action.

They rode for several miles. Pine trees appeared on the hills as they rode closer toward the mountains. Each time they rounded a bend, O'Reilly expected to ride into a herd of horses and a party of painted warriors.

It happened when O'Reilly was least expecting it. The succession of endless bends revealing the same as each preceding one had lulled him into a sense of unrealized anticipation. Then suddenly they rounded a bend as a bunch of galloping horses exploded toward them, fol-

51

lowed by high-pitched yells as Indians drove them back along the way they had come.

It was hard to know who was more surprised—the pursuing Mounties or the Indians. O'Reilly, Wise and the rancher pulled their horses away to avoid a head-on collision. At the same time the Indians, six of them—half the number Mister Barrett had said—scattered in all directions, jerking on their reins and legging their wiry ponies up the grassy sides of the coulee.

O'Reilly and Wise lost valuable seconds deciding what to do next, until reaction took over and each constable galloped after the closest of the scattering Indians.

Rancher Barrett had no such indecision. His instinctive reaction was to recover his horses and he wheeled around and galloped after them. The horses were just as startled as the police, and they scattered to go around them. The result was confusion all around, with horses and riders going everywhere, amid swirling dust.

O'Reilly spotted a well-built young warrior racing his black and white pinto up the slope toward timber higher up. He was naked except for a breech clout but, contrary to O'Reilly's expectation, he wore no warpaint.

O'Reilly legged his horse up the slope to intercept the brave. O'Reilly's charging momentum narrowed the gap between them. But the brave saw him coming and veered his pinto from the course it was taking, which would have brought him and the Mountie into a collision. O'Reilly's response was to push his horse to greater speed.

Up the slope they raced. O'Reilly was two horse lengths behind. A fringe of pines loomed ahead, a little farther up, about a hundred yards distant. O'Reilly knew he had to catch the young brave before he reached them, otherwise he might lose him in the trees.

O'Reilly pushed his horse harder. He felt the animal starting to blow. "Come on, boy . . . just a little more effort. We're gaining on him."

The horse gave a final burst of speed . . . its bobbing head caught up with the pinto's hindquarters. The trees were only yards away now.

O'Reilly stood in his stirrups, reached out with his left hand and slapped it on the brave's bare shoulder. Leaning out of his saddle he pulled back on the brave's shoulder in an effort to unhorse him. But he leaned too far and felt himself clearing saddle leather. He tried to kick himself clear of his saddle and pull the Indian off the pinto. But the young Indian flung up his elbow and knocked O'Reilly's arm away.

The next thing O'Reilly was sailing through the air as the pinto pulled away. Seconds later he landed on the steep grassy slope with a jarring thud. The wind whooshed out of him. Then he started rolling over and over backward down the slope. He rolled and rolled, everything going around and around like a kaleidoscope of trees and grass and horses and coulee and sky. Finally he came to a stop at the bottom of the coulee.

For a moment he lay there. Then he tried to get up. The pines above were a whirling, dizzy circle . . . pines, mountains, sky . . . everything going around and around. Then he lost his balance and fell backward, sitting heavily on his backside in the grass and swirling dust.

Up on the slope just below the pines, the young Indian brave sat his pinto staring down at the unhorsed Mountie. Through a dizzying whirl of giddiness, O'Reilly sat looking up at him. Even at that distance their eyes met. Suddenly the young Indian threw back his head and let out a great bellyrocking laugh. He laughed and laughed, looking down at O'Reilly, still sitting on his backside in the dust below.

Finally the young brave lifted his rifle and waved mockingly. Then his bare legs thumped the sides of his pinto and he galloped off into the pines.

Red-faced, O'Reilly pulled himself to his feet, flashing dark eyes locked onto the pines above.

"You red-skinned son of a bitch!"

Chapter 5

O'Reilly stood grooming his horse in the corral yard behind the Standoff barracks when he heard the sound of approaching hoofbeats. Looking up he saw the blue-uniformed figure of Inspector Cavannagh riding down the trail from Fort Macleod.

The officer sat straight-backed in his saddle, moving smoothly with the motion of his cantering horse. O'Reilly couldn't help but admire the officer's seat. There was a real horseman, he thought. Then, by association, his thoughts turned to Ruth Baker and he wished the inspector had driven a democrat and brought her along to show her the countryside.

"Good day, O'Reilly," Inspector Cavannagh called from his saddle. "I presume Sergeant Hannan is here."

His tortured muscles aching with the effort, O'Reilly straightened to attention. "Yes, sir. He's in the office."

As Inspector Cavannagh reined to, O'Reilly stepped through the corral fence and limped painfully forward. "I'll take your horse, sir."

"Thank you." Inspector Cavannagh swung down from his saddle. "That's quite a limp you have, O'Reilly."

O'Reilly nodded. "Yes, sir. Had a bit of a fall yesterday. Just a little stiff, that's all."

He took the officer's reins. Inspector Cavannagh said,

"By the way, O'Reilly, my niece sent her regards. She asked me to tell you that she's looking forward to having you call on her the next time you're in Fort Macleod."

O'Reilly's heart jumped. He took it from the inspector's tone that he would have no objection to him calling. "Thank you, sir. I'll look forward to that."

Leading the officer's horse into the corral, O'Reilly unsaddled the animal. He noted from the bedroll on the back of the saddle and the weight of the saddle wallets that this wasn't just a pleasant day's ride from Fort Macleod. The inspector was obviously going to do some traveling.

Inspector Cavannagh was in the office with Sergeant Hannan for an hour. When the hour had passed, Sergeant Hannan poked his head out the door and shouted. "O'Reilly! Saddle up the inspector's horse. He's leaving."

After Inspector Cavannagh had mounted, he looked down at Sergeant Hannan. "Oh, by the way, congratulations on recovering those stolen horses yesterday. Has that Indian prisoner Constable Wise arrested given the names of any of the others who were with him?"

"No, sir. He won't say a thing."

"Well, he might change his mind after he's been sitting in the guardroom at Fort Macleod for a while. At least we know they come from the Blood reserve. You'll be escorting him into Fort Macleod, I presume?"

"Yes, sir. I'm sending McCormack and Wise in with him today."

Inspector Cavannagh nodded his satisfaction. "He'll get a stiff sentence for having been an accomplice when shots were fired at a rancher. Hopefully it will serve as a deterrent to the other young bucks. Major Steele wants every effort made to stamp out all instances of lawlessness, with particular emphasis being placed on the suppression of rustling. It's going to mean longer hours in the saddle for all of us. I'm on my way down to the other outposts to tell them the same."

"Right, sir." Sergeant Hannan stepped back and saluted. Inspector Cavannagh returned the salute, reined his

55

horse around and rode away on the trail toward the next outpost, Big Bend, some thirty miles southwest up the Belly.

O'Reilly went back to the corral at the rear of the stables. As he rounded the corner of the building, he felt eyes on him. Turning his head he saw a pair of black eyes staring at him from the cell block window. It was the Indian whom Constable Wise had taken prisoner the day before, when O'Reilly had suffered his humiliating fall.

O'Reilly stopped and stood looking back at the Indian. The face looked sad, the eyes haunting. Suddenly O'Reilly felt sympathy for the owner of the copper-hued face, the face of a member of a once proud and defiant warrior race.

Absorbed in his thoughts, O'Reilly didn't hear the jingle of spurs as Sergeant Hannan came around the corner, and when the sergeant spoke, his voice startled him. "Looks harmless enough behind those bars, but that buck would have killed you twenty years ago if you'd tried to lock him up. Inspector Cavannagh knows damn well he isn't going to name the others who rode with him. They all belong to the same society, those bucks. They don't see anything wrong in running off someone else's horses. For generations they've been brought up to believe the more horses a brave runs off, the bigger warrior he is. How do we bring a race of warlike warriors to understand a law that's alien to everything they've been brought up to revere? They were born to ride and fight. I reckon half the time they get into trouble it's because they're bored. How the hell do we expect 'em to be content to raise stock and grow crops? That buck in there, he'll go to the penitentiary at Stony Mountain. That's bad medicine to an Indian. They go there expecting to die. More often than not, that's exactly what happens. They pick up tuberculosis or some damn thing like that in the white man's prison and die."

They stood together a moment longer, then Sergeant Hannan's voice changed its tone and he abruptly said, "Finish up what you've been doing, then get out of those fatigues and put on your uniform. Inspector Cavannagh wants us to ride over to Iron-Fist Taggart's ranch and get descriptions of cattle he says have been rustled."

Scarlet tunics ablaze against the rolling spring-green hills, Sergeant Hannan and Constable O'Reilly jogged stirrup-to-stirrup on their way to Iron-Fist Taggart's ranch. O'Reilly wore his new tan-colored Stetson hat, which he had bought at Sergeant Hannan's *suggestion*—it had sounded more like an order—from the Standoff trading post. Like the sergeant's hat and those of the other three men of the Standoff Flying Patrol, it had a wide leather band around it, with a buckle on the left side. O'Reilly had also followed the example of the sergeant and the others by pushing four identical dents—one each at the front and back and on both sides—just below the crown, so that it conformed to the pattern Major Steele allowed members of his command to wear.

The wide-brimmed Stetson shaded O'Reilly's eyes from the glare of the afternoon sun as he gazed around at the richly grassed rangeland.

"Is this all Taggart's land?" O'Reilly asked.

"He leases it from the government," Sergeant Hannan replied. "But for all practical purposes, he might just as well own it."

"He seems to be a pretty important man, from what I've heard."

"He's a son of a bitch!"

O'Reilly glanced sideways. Sergeant Hannan's freckled face bore a heavy scowl, and his tone of voice left no doubt as to how he felt about the rancher.

"He drifted up this way from down south of the border years ago," Sergeant Hannan said a moment later. "But he's not an American. I'm not sure where he hails from originally . . . England, Ireland, or maybe Australia. He had some military experience somewhere. When he arrived in the Fort Macleod district, he owned nothing more than a horse, saddle, rifle and the clothes he was wearing. Now he's an aspiring cattle king with one of the largest leases in the district. I've even heard he's planning to run for election as local member of Parliament."

A few miles later they rode through a gateway consisting of a high log-pole archway with the Circle T brand burned into the logs. They could see buildings a couple of miles farther on, sitting up high on a rise of land overlooking the rangeland in all directions, while off to the west the white peaks of the Rockies plainly were visible against the cloud-streaked blue sky.

"Those buildings are pretty exposed up there," O'Reilly remarked. "If they were mine, I'd have picked a spot into the side of the hill, sheltered from the wind."

Sergeant Hannan snorted. "Taggart likes to be able to look around and admire his kingdom. Makes him feel like a big man."

A large, pretentious frame house sprawled across the hilltop. It was big enough to accommodate a family of several people, although Taggart lived there alone. Below the ranch house were several outbuildings—stables, barn, bunkhouse, cookhouse, storage buildings, hayshed. The bunkhouse was large and ample. It looked capable of holding twice as many hands as should be required to handle even the largest ranches in the Fort Macleod district.

As they rode toward the ranch house, they saw several men dressed in cowpuncher garb sauntering out of the ranch house toward the bunkhouse.

"Hard-looking lot," O'Reilly commented.

Sergeant Hannan nodded. "Every time I ride up to this God damn place I see faces I haven't seen before. I don't know whether Taggart has one hell of a lot of hired hands or whether he just fires 'em as fast as he hires 'em and they don't stick around very long."

They were reining to in front of the ranch house veranda when Iron-Fist Taggart's immense bulk filled the front door. He was wearing high-heeled riding boots under a pair of blue denims, a sleeveless waistcoat, open-necked checkered shirt and a brown neckerchief. He wasn't wearing his hat and O'Reilly noticed his hair was light brown, parted in the center and graying at the sides. Despite his bulk he looked very fit. It was hard to tell his age. He had obviously spent most of his life out of doors, and perhaps part of it in hot climates, for his skin was burned a deep mahogany, and his face was prematurely lined. That and a toothbrush moustache gave his features a hard-driving look. It was an appearance that matches his temperament. He scowled at the sight of the two Mounties.

Sergeant Hannan didn't waste any time with preliminaries. He didn't bother dismounting, and Taggart didn't bother inviting him to.

"Inspector Cavannagh said you had some stock run off a couple of nights back. We're here to get the details."

Taggart sneered. "He didn't have the guts to come here and get the information himself, huh? He had to send you two."

"Even you should know better than that, Taggart," Sergeant Hannan said.

Taggart's eyes locked onto the sergeant. "You better watch the way you talk to me, Hannan. I could have your stripes."

Sergeant Hannan looked right back at him. "If the day ever comes when you have that sort of influence with the Mounted Police, I'll turn in my uniform."

Taggart continued to glare at Hannan. He said nothing further for a moment, until, "What sort of details do you want, for Christ's sake? They were all wearing my brand, the Circle T. Isn't that enough?"

"Shorthorns . . . white faces . . . Anguses? Brands can be changed."

"You ought to be put to better use out on patrol like you're supposed to be instead of riding around lookin' pretty in those red coats."

"It might have helped if you'd taken in the details of your stolen stock the time you were in Fort Macleod belly-aching."

"Cavannagh told you about that, huh? I bet he didn't tell you I chewed out his God damned arse."

"The day you chew out Inspector Cavannagh's ass, Taggart, I'll pull down my breeches and shit on the main street of Macleod."

"You got a real way with words, Hannan."

"Just give me a description of the cattle you say were stolen. I'm in a hurry to get away from here and breathe fresh air again."

Iron-Fist Taggart hadn't paid any attention to O'Reilly. O'Reilly reckoned the rancher didn't remember bumping into him outside Inspector Cavannagh's office that day.

With a final glare at Sergeant Hannan, Taggart turned around and disappeared inside the house. He was gone for more than half an hour, while Sergeant Hannan and O'Reilly dismounted to take the weight off their horses. They stood beside their horses and waited. O'Reilly's eyes were everywhere. This was the first ranch he had been on and he was curious to see whether it was what he would have imagined. The hard-looking hired hands had disappeared. None made an appearance while the two Mounties waited.

"I'm surprised Taggart pays 'em to hang around doing nothing," Sergeant Hannan said. "I'd reckon there should be work for them to do to earn their pay."

Taggart eventually reappeared and handed Sergeant Hannan a few sheets of paper. Sergeant Hannan glanced down at the heavy writing, then folded the papers and thrust them inside his tunic. He nodded to O'Reilly and they stepped up into their saddles. As they rode away, O'Reilly could feel hidden eyes watching them. He had expected the customary Western hospitality at the ranch, to have been invited in for a cup of coffee or a meal. But this place exuded a hostile atmosphere and he was glad to be riding away.

Chapter 6

The patrol rode out of Standoff, Sergeant Hannan and Constable McCormack riding side by side in front and Constable Wise and O'Reilly following. Constable Bob Scott stood in the yard outside the barracks watching them go. Sergeant Hannan had left him behind to "hold down the fort," as he had termed it.

They followed the Belly southwest for a few miles before fording the river and patrolling the western limit of the Blood Indian reserve. They rode south until they reached Lee's Creek, which they followed eastward to the Mormon settlement of Cardston. From there they walked and trotted their horses along the banks of the St. Mary's until they were so close to Chief Mountain that it seemed all they had to do was reach out and touch it.

Sergeant Hannan signaled them to rein to. As they sat their saddles, he thrust his chin at the rolling green foothills stretching off to the south. "That's Montana," he said, glancing at O'Reilly. "We're straddling an imaginary line, the Canada-United States boundary. This is where our jurisdiction ends. There are stone cairns marking the border every mile or two. But don't ever think for a minute that the Indians living on both sides of it don't know exactly where it is, with or without markers. Being so close to it doesn't make our job any easier. Indians and whites alike can commit an offense damn near under our noses, then make a run for the border, knowing full well that if they can get across it, we can't touch 'em."

"What about the Montana law enforcement authorities?" O'Reilly asked.

"There aren't enough of them," Sergeant Hannan replied. "The United States Cavalry help whenever they can, but they can only act where they have jurisdiction, which is restricted to Indians mostly."

For the next several days they patrolled backward and forward along the international boundary, from Chief Mountain in the west to the Sweetgrass Hills to the east and back again, then wheeling off to the northwest along the foothills of the Rockies before veering off to the northeast back toward the rolling prairie. They rode from sunup to sunset, camping wherever they happened to be, sleeping under the glittering stars, building a campfire if they found timber, or sometimes stopping off at a ranch and sharing bunkhouse quarters with the ranch hands. They ate their meals beside their campfire—patrol rations of beef, rice, bread, dried fruit and tea or coffee. They rode at random, traveling in one direction for an indeterminate number of miles, then suddenly swinging off in another direction, turning up unexpectedly anywhere anytime. Sometimes they camped at sundown, only to saddle up again at midnight and resume their patrol. They moved at a good clip, but frequently rested their horses. Day or night they rode down innumerable coulees and gullies, up across hills, along river banks, over rolling prairie.

By the fourth day of their patrol they were half a day's ride west of the Blood Indian reserve, having made a wide if irregular circle since leaving Standoff. Just before noon they spotted a thin spiral of smoke rising from the other side of a hill a few miles away.

"No ranch over there," Sergeant Hannan mused, squinting his eyes against the glare of the sun.

"Could be some cowpunchers' camp," Tom McCormack offered.

62

"Could be," Sergeant Hannan said slowly. "Let's ride over and take a look."

They had covered less than a quarter of the distance when they saw a flash of light up on a ridge in the distance. It was immediately followed by several more.

"What's that?" O'Reilly asked.

"It's a warning signal," Sergeant Hannan said, suddenly spurring his horse. "Come on," he shouted, waving his arm to the rest of the patrol to hurry.

They galloped their horses over the hills toward the smoke spiral. O'Reilly sat his saddle easily, leaning forward with the smooth, rocking-chair motion of the galloping horse.

As they topped the last hill they saw something down in a hollow below . . . a blackened circle in the grass. But there was no one there.

The four Mounties rode down in the hollow and reined to beside the smoldering ashes of a fire. They ranged their horses around it as they sat staring down. The coals had been hastily kicked apart in an effort to put out the fire and eliminate the smoke.

Sergeant Hannan glanced at O'Reilly, saying, "Those flashes we saw . . . it's an old Indian trick, flashing a mirror off the sun's reflection to warn their friends of the approach of Mounted Police."

Handing his reins to Tom McCormack, Sergeant Hannan swung down from his saddle and walked slowly around the smoldering ashes, staring down at the trampled grass. He dropped to a knee and examined the ground more closely. O'Reilly and the other two watched.

After a moment Sergeant Hannan picked up some coarse hairs and held them in front of his eyes as he studied them. Then his eyes returned to the ground as he searched for more signs.

"What is it, Sarge?" Tom McCormack asked.

Sergeant Hannan stood up and walked around, his eyes still glued to the trampled grass. "There's been cattle held down there." He pointed. "Look at that . . . and that."

63

O'Reilly and the other two followed the direction of his pointing finger. They saw small patches of black on the grass, where the grass had been burnt.

"That's where someone's rested a hot branding iron," Sergeant Hannan said. "There's been some branding done here, and I'll bet a month's pay that, whoever it was, they were branding over someone else's brand."

He walked around a little more, dropping to a knee again to examine impressions on the trampled grass twice more before returning to his horse.

They were much closer to the Blood reserve than they were to the Peigans farther north. Constable McCormack nodded his head to the east as he handed back the sergeant's reins.

"At least we know we're not looking for Peigans," McCormack said.

Sergeant Hannan stepped back up into his saddle. "I'm not so sure it's Indians we're looking for. Indians don't worry too much about branding. And they don't shoe their horses or wear high-heeled boots."

His bright blue eyes scanned the surrounding hills, then he looked at the distant ridge from where they had seen the flashes. "Come on," he said, legging his horse into a canter.

They rode up out of the hollow, then across the rolling hills toward the ridge. When they reached it, Sergeant Hannan didn't bother looking for whoever had flashed the warning signal. Whoever he was, he would have been long gone. Instead, the sergeant pulled a pair of field glasses from his saddle wallet and studied the rolling rangeland for miles in all directions.

The ridge offered a good vantage point. Behind them rose the snow-capped mountains. Ahead of them, to the east, the prairie rolled away all the miles to Fort Macleod and beyond. The same to the north and south, except that to the north they could see the green bulk of the Porcupine Hills. Even without the aid of field glasses, O'Reilly could see distant herds of cattle grazing.

Sergeant Hannan examined the herds for a while, replaced the glasses in his saddle wallet and led his patrol back down the grassed slopes, heading toward the grazing herds.

They reached the closest herd and walked their horses in among the cattle. Sergeant Hannan looked at the brand on each animal. Some were unbranded and a few cows had calves with them.

From there they rode to the next herd, two miles distant. This herd was tended by cowpunchers . . . hard-faced men carrying Winchester butts protruding from saddle scabbards.

Sergeant Hannan nodded. One of the men, wearing tight-fitting black leather gloves, nodded back. But there was no warmth in his unspoken greeting, noticeable in a country where hospitality and open friendliness were a way of life.

"You boys are a piece from home," Sergeant Hannan said.

The man wearing the tight black gloves replied. "This is government range, open for public grazin'."

Sergeant Hannan looked hard at him for a moment, then said, "We'll ride among your stock for a look-see."

"Help yourself."

Sergeant Hannan reined his horse in among the stock, looking at the brands. O'Reilly rode beside him.

"Those gloves, young O'Reilly," Sergeant Hannan said, "you notice anything about them?"

"They're new and shiny, and they looked too tight."

A smile spread across the sergeant's hard-bitten face. "That's right. They didn't look like they've seen any hard work. A cowpuncher likes his gloves loose, comfortable and worn. That feller's gloves look more suited to handling a firearm. He looks more like a gunfighter than a cowhand."

"Who is he, anyway?"

Sergeant Hannan pointed to the brand on the rump of one of the steers. "Circle T—Iron-Fist Taggart's outfit.

65

That's a poor job of branding. Look at at those blurred edges. I've always wondered about those men on Taggart's payroll. They don't look to me like he hired 'em because of their worth as stockmen. I'd like to take a ride down to Montana some day and have a look through the *wanted* posters in the sheriff's office at Fort Benton. I reckon I'd find some faces I've seen around Taggart's place."

With O'Reilly at his side, Sergeant Hannan pushed his horse in among the cattle, looking at the brands. Constables McCormack and Wise did the same, moving through the herd at different places. They had been on the flying patrol long enough to know what they were looking for. O'Reilly reasoned the best thing he could do was watch his sergeant and learn.

Sergeant Hannan pointed to more brands on the rumps of the cattle. "They're all the same . . . damn sloppy branding. A good branding job leaves the markings clean, without any blurring."

The herd, numbering a few hundred head, was far too big for the patrol to check them all, so they did the best they could, spot-checking. They found animals that weren't branded at all, but these were mostly yearlings and some that could have strayed and missed out in the last branding. None of the brands showed signs of having been recently worked over.

After checking about a quarter of the animals, Sergeant Hannan and the patrol pushed their horses out of the herd. The half-dozen of Taggart's riders sat their saddles and stared mockingly at the four Mounties.

Sergeant Hannan walked his horse toward them. His eyes scanned their outfits, noting the ropes hanging from their saddles. He saw no trace of what he was specifically looking for—a running iron.

"There's been a camp on the other side of those hills," he said to Taggart's riders, pointing his thumb over his shoulder. "Looked like someone had been doing a bit of branding. Looked like they'd suddenly decided to pull out, as though they hadn't wanted us to see them. The only reason I can see for someone acting like that is because they were altering brands."

The man wearing the tight black gloves leaned across the pommel of his saddle and stared at Sergeant Hannan. His eyes were shiny and black, like his gloves, and they did not blink. "Not us, Sergeant."

"You see anyone come riding from that direction?"

"Nope. Only ones we seen all day is you boys."

Sergeant Hannan looked him back. "Changing brands without proof of ownership is an offense."

The black-gloved man's eyes still did not blink. "Why tell us?"

"Just in case you needed telling."

The man said nothing in reply. Sergeant Hannan stared into his black eyes for a moment longer. They were dangerous looking eyes, and Hannan guessed they had seen a lot of violence and undoubtedly had taken part in it. Although their owner intended they should, they did not unnerve the red-headed sergeant one bit. However, there was no percentage in wasting time staring the man down, so Sergeant Hannan nodded curtly to him and reined his horse around. O'Reilly and the others joined him and together they trotted their mounts away.

That night they camped at the edge of a grove of cottonwoods beside a river. Taggart's cattle were still on Sergeant Hannan's mind.

"Those Circle T brands were the sloppiest branding jobs I've ever seen," he said, repeating what he had said earlier, as they sat around their campfire, the smell of woodsmoke and boiling coffee tantalizing O'Reilly's nose. "It keeps going through my mind that maybe those brands were made sloppy on purpose."

"Why would that be, Sergeant?" O'Reilly asked, eager to learn.

"Because if Taggart's men were changing brands, the doctored up ones wouldn't be all that unlike the legitimate ones. With a bit of doctoring, that Circle T brand could be made to look like a Circle L. That's Bart Lane's brand.

67

His spread is bigger than even Taggart's and he's lost a lot of head. If anyone were to ask my opinion, I'd say that was why Taggart chose a Circle T for his brand. I'd bet a year's pay that Iron-Fist Taggart has made himself rich on Bart Lane's cattle."

"Pretty strong words, Sarge," Tom McCormack said.

Sergeant Hannan looked across the fire's flames at the constable. "Why do you think he's got all those hard-looking hands on his payroll?"

Tom McCormack shrugged. "I heard he hired them to fight off the Indians he reckons have been rustling his stock. Hell, he's lost his share of stock to rustlers, too."

Sergeant Hannan scowled. "How do we really know he's lost all the stock he says?"

McCormack opened his mouth to say something, but Sergeant Hannan cut him short. "I know what you're about to say, Tom. Ranchers have reported Indians hanging around their herds when rustling was going on. I know the Indians can't seem to get it into their heads that cattle are cattle and buffalo were something else. But don't forget that for generations they were raised in the belief that all life revolved around the buffalo. When the buffalo suddenly disappeared, the Indians couldn't figure out where they disappeared to. Then the white man, who the Indians see as being responsible for the disappearance of their old way of life, turned up with 'the spotted buffalo'—beef cattle. The Indians got it into their heads that they have some sort of right to 'em, so occasionally they shoot one and butcher it for meat. The Indian agents are supposed to issue beef and flour rations out to the Indians when game is scarce or they're otherwise short of food. Personally, I suspect some of those agents hold out on the Indians. The Indians get hungry and ride around and shoot themselves a steer or a cow every now and then. Can't say I blame them. If I was hungry and had a family to feed, I'd probably do the same thing."

Tom McCormack grinned. "You're getting a bit soft, Sarge. Didn't used to hear you talk like that."

Sergeant Hannan raised a tin cup to his lips and drank. After a moment he lowered the cup and resumed talking. "I came out to the Territories back in '77, when I joined the Mounted Police. There weren't too many people out here then . . . just us, the Indians, and the whisky runners we used to chase. It was better back in those days, before too many people and the likes of Iron-Fist Taggart turned up to spoil things. The Blackfoot and Bloods were generally inclined to be peaceful, thanks to the fact that Colonel Macleod had hit it off with Crowfoot, the big chief of the Blackfoot Confederacy. Colonel Macleod was *the* government back then, the Great White Mother's right-hand man. When he made promises to Crowfoot or Red Crow, he made damn sure they were kept. That was before there were any Indian Department officials out here to screw things up. That's not to say the Indians didn't give us some pretty close calls from time to time. They liked to let us know they hadn't forgotten how to fight. We had our share of excitement."

Reaching across to the coffee pot, Sergeant Hannan held it aloft for a moment as he looked around at the faces of his men about the campfire. "There's lots of coffee. Anyone want any more?"

O'Reilly reached forward and held out his tin cup. Tom McCormack did the same, but Roy Wise shook his head.

"There's two things a plains Indian likes better than anything else," Sergeant Hannan said as he poured coffee into the cups, then put the pot back beside the fire. "Running off horses and tucking into a good feast. He'll run off horses as quick as look at them. He'll run 'em off another tribe before he'll run 'em off a white man because it's a little more dangerous and a lot more fun. If there's no other tribes around for him to raid and run off their horses, then he'll pick on some white rancher. And when he's hungry, he'll kill a rancher's steer. But I've not known a Blood or a Peigan to rustle cattle. Why should he? He's got no need for 'em. What's he going to do with 'em? Eat the whole damned herd in one sitting? He's got no way of selling 'em, not without getting caught." Sergeant Hannan shook his head. "No . . . it doesn't make sense to me to suspect Indians of rustling cattle."

Tom McCormack tossed another piece of wood onto the fire. "How about Indians getting paid by white men to rustle?" he asked as a shower of sparks hissed upward into the blackness.

Sergeant Hannan drained his cup. "If I knew the answer to that, I'd be wearing a star on my collars instead of three stripes on my sleeve."

He stood up and dusted off the seat of his breeches. "All right, fellers, better turn in. We mount up at first light. We'll ride over to Kootenai and see what's happening there. Then we'll head back to Standoff. We should be home by sundown tomorrow."

Chapter 7

A wide grin creased Sergeant Hannan's face as he sat behind the table he used for a desk. "I just got word that Gus Breen is making a whisky run from Montana two nights from now." It was plain the information pleased him. O'Reilly hadn't seen him smiling like that in the short time he had known him.

O'Reilly had seen the fox-faced man ride up to the outpost earlier and disappear into Sergeant Hannan's office. They had remained together for ten or fifteen minutes before the man left. He had looked like any cowhand and O'Reilly had assumed he was some cowboy reporting an offense. But somehow the man had learned of the planned whisky run and informed the Mounted Police, perhaps for an informant's fee.

Sergeant Hannan looked at the four constables standing in front of him. "Breen figures on selling to the Bloods somewhere close to the reserve, then moving north a piece so he can ply his trade with the cowhands of the ranching country, then swinging east toward Lethbridge to sell to the coal miners and the navvies widening the rail line between Lethbridge and Medicine Hat. Breen is an elusive son of a bitch. I've been after him a long time. He's been doing this for longer than the Mounted Police has been out here in the Territories and he knows the country like the back of his hand. I've arrested him more times than I can readily recollect, but each time he's come up with the fine money or someone's paid it for him. He's no sooner out of jail than he's back doing the same thing. We've confiscated his outfit every time, but he's always come up with another one. But he's smuggled contraband liquor into the Northwest Territories once too often. This time he's not going to have the option of paying a fine. This time he'll get a term in Stony Mountain Penitentiary."

Pushing back his chair, Sergeant Hannan stood up, his eyes still on his men, the grin still on his face. "When Breen crosses that border, we're going to be there to give him a right cordial welcome. We'll ride out of here tonight, after dark. I don't want anyone seeing us leave. Like I said, he's an elusive son of a bitch and he's got friends on this side of the border. We'll ride all night and reach the border before sunup."

He looked briefly at Constable McCormack. "I want someone to be around here to throw out false leads in case anyone comes nosing around, Tom, so you'll be staying put. The rest of you, get some rest. It'll be a hard, fast ride."

There was no moon when they rode out of Standoff, but the night was clear and cold, the blue-black velvet sky studded with brightly glittering stars. They rode hard all night and by dawn had reached within a few miles of Montana.

Finding a clump of poplar, they reined in and sat their saddles, studying the country to the south. Sergeant Hannan pointed through the trees.

"He'll come up along one of those coulees down there. The question is, which one? There's too many for us to watch them all. But whichever one he takes, he wants to move north halfway between Fort Macleod and Lethbridge and alongside the Blood reserve."

Lowering his pointing finger, he inclined his head at

72

Constable Wise. "Roy, you and O'Reilly watch from this clump of trees. Breen might cut this way to get around on the west side of the reserve. Bob and I will scout the coulees farther along the line. He's not supposed to come through until tomorrow night, but I don't want to chance missing him in case he decides to slip through earlier. You can take turns sleeping, but I want one of you alert and on watch all the time. If you see Breen's outfit, let him pass until we return. Then we'll all four overtake the wagons, arrest Breen and his men and confiscate the whisky. If we spot 'em in the meantime, we'll follow them until they get within reach of here, then we'll pick you two up and all four of us will take 'em. They're likely to be running a wagon or two and a couple of men riding as escort. We should be pretty evenly matched."

O'Reilly and Roy Wise nodded.

Sergeant Hannan gathered his reins and nodded to Constable Scott. "All right, Bob, let's head on down toward those coulees."

O'Reilly and Wise watched them ride off in the morning sun, then they unsaddled their horses and settled down, hidden among the poplars, to their vigil.

They watched and waited all day, taking turns sleeping.

The sun was well on its way toward the mountains to the west when O'Reilly, sitting on the ground with his back against a tree, heard something that instantly sharpened his senses. He stood up quickly and listened. At first he heard nothing further, but after several minutes he heard it again. As he listened it grew louder.

"Someone's coming," he said to Roy Wise, who was lying on the grass with his head propped against his saddle, his hat down over his eyes.

"What'd you hear?" Wise drawled lazily, not moving, his voice conveying a sense of complete disinterest.

"Horses," O'Reilly replied.

"Probably the sarge and Bob comin' back."

O'Reilly quickly shook his head. "No. It sounds like more than two."

73

"Well, it won't be Breen," Wise replied. "He wouldn't be coming across in daylight."

O'Reilly listened further. Maybe Wise was right, he thought. He couldn't hear any wagon wheels, just a steady drumming of hoofs. "Maybe we should saddle up, anyway."

Roy Wise made no move.

O'Reilly picked up his saddle and threw it on his horse's back. He had just got the cinches tightened and his bridle on when the afternoon air was split by the sound of savage whoops, and an instant later Indians galloped by, driving a herd of horses ahead of them. O'Reilly's stomach tightened when he saw one of them riding a black and white pinto.

"That's the same bunch we chased before!" O'Reilly exclaimed excitedly. "They're running off more horses! We passed a ranch a dozen miles back on the way here, the same direction they've come from!"

Without wasting another second, O'Reilly leaped up onto his saddle and legged his horse into action. "Come on!" he shouted over his shoulder. "Now's our chance to catch them!"

O'Reilly raced his horse out of the poplars and across the rolling grassland after the Indians. They were several hundred yards in front of him, the wind blowing their long braids behind them as they rode. O'Reilly counted five of them, and about fifteen horses.

It was several minutes before the Indians became aware they were being pursued. Sensing something, one glanced behind over his shoulder and saw the uniform of a Mountie chasing them. He stiffened, then shouted to the others. They looked around. More shouting broke out, carrying back to O'Reilly over the sound of pounding hoofs. The next instant they scattered.

Without breaking his horse's stride, O'Reilly set his sights on the brave riding the pinto and rode after him, ignoring the others, remembering the time when he was unhorsed because of that buck, determined to redeem himself. The brave veered toward the mountains. O'Reilly swung his horse after him.

They rode like the wind. Both riders leaned forward low over their horses' backs. Hoofs pounded over the grassed ground, kicking up clumps of grassed earth behind them as they passed over the steadily rising upland.

They rode hard for what seemed a long time, and before O'Reilly realized it the mountains were closer. There were just the two of them. There was no sign of the other Indians nor of the horses. O'Reilly hadn't seen Wise; he assumed his partner was somewhere behind rounding up one of the other Indians, and perhaps recovering some of the stolen horses.

The brave was trying to outdistance O'Reilly, hoping to gain the sanctuary of the wooded foothills, where he could elude the pursuing Mountie until sundown and then escape in the darkness. But O'Reilly's horse was fresher and gradually he overtook the brave.

They left the rolling grassland behind and splashed across a stream. They rode a little farther before thundering along the sandy shores of a quiet mountain lake. Another hundred yards and they were into spruce and pine trees. Above, great, snow-covered mountains hovered.

At last O'Reilly's horse closed the gap to a horse's length. The brave looked over his shoulder and snarled at the Mountie. He swung around on the pinto's back and waved his rifle threateningly at O'Reilly. But O'Reilly kept after him. The brave pointed the rifle at O'Reilly's chest, but O'Reilly was in no mood to be warned off.

O'Reilly's horse drew closer still, narrowing the gap to half a horse length. O'Reilly could almost lean out of his saddle and touch the pinto's flowing tail. The Indian pulled on his reins and veered the pinto away to gain some momentary advantage, but O'Reilly stayed with him. The brave purposely rode past overhanging trees, ducking his head at the last minute, hoping the Mountie would be unwary enough to be swept off his horse's back by a low branch. He rode as though he was part of the horse, but each time he glanced back over his shoulder, the Mountie was right behind him.

They broke out through the trees and galloped across a clearing. With a final burst of speed, O'Reilly's horse drew level with the pinto. Careful not to repeat the mistake he had made the last time, O'Reilly reached out and grabbed one of the Indian's flowing braids of hair. With a sharp pull he unhorsed the brave. The brave landed in a rolling heap on the grass, his rifle flying through the air.

Reining his horse down as quickly as he could, O'Reilly wheeled around and galloped the animal back toward the Indian. The brave recovered immediately, sprang up and raced across the grass for his rifle. O'Reilly rode his horse hard at him. The brave jumped back quickly to avoid being run down.

O'Reilly reined his horse around again and pulled his Winchester from its sling across the pommel of his saddle. But before he could point it at the brave, the young Indian leaped up at him, trying to pull him from his horse. O'Reilly tried to kick him away but the brave managed to clamber up partway onto the horse's back and got his arm around O'Reilly's neck. O'Reilly's horse reared. O'Reilly let go of his rifle as he grasped his reins to bring the animal under control. The brave released his arm from around O'Reilly's neck and dropped back onto the ground to scoop up the Winchester. O'Reilly leaned over in his saddle and swung his fist, catching the Indian across the side of his face. The Indian landed flat on his back in the grass.

Reaching into his pocket for a pair of handcuffs, O'Reilly jumped down from his saddle. But as he approached the prone form of the Indian, the young brave suddenly sprang up and kicked out with both feet, catching O'Reilly in the stomach and sending him reeling. Before O'Reilly realized it, the brave was upon him. O'Reilly grappled with him but the brave's ferocity sent him sprawling backward. They hit the ground together and wrestled on the grass. They rolled over and over, thrashing around wildly. One minute O'Reilly was on top, the next minute the brave was on top. Finally O'Reilly hit him full in the mouth, which sent him spinning sideways.

O'Reilly bounded to his feet and threw himself onto the Indian, jerking his arm up behind him. Holding the arm with one hand, he reached for his handcuffs with the other and tried to clap the steel manacle around the brave's wrist, but the young warrior twisted loose, swung around and got his arm about O'Reilly's neck. O'Reilly jabbed an elbow into his stomach. It was as hard as a rock. O'Reilly jabbed again but the brave again flexed his stomach muscles. The next instant he was able to wrench his arm free, and he spun around so that he was on the Mountie's back.

O'Reilly reached both hands behind him and grabbed the Indian by his head, one hand grasping a fistful of hair, the other hand the brave's right ear. O'Reilly squeezed the ear and pulled the hair. The brave strangled a howl of pain and the arm around O'Reilly's neck loosened. With a violent movement, O'Reilly dropped to one knee and threw the brave over his head. The brave went somersaulting and landed flat on his back with a jarring thud a few feet away. Before he could move, O'Reilly threw himself onto him, pinning him to the ground.

But the brave, wriggling and writhing like a threshing snake, twisted himself free and tensed himself to spring back onto his feet. O'Reilly flung out his arm and grabbed the brave's shoulder, holding him down. The brave rolled sideways and kicked hard at the Mountie. His moccasined foot caught O'Reilly in the groin. Hot waves of pain and nausea washed over O'Reilly, stars swirled in front of his eyes.

The brave leaped back onto his feet. O'Reilly struggled painfully to a standing position. Before he had quite made it, the brave aimed another kick. Fighting off nausea, O'Reilly clumsily but effectively blocked it. They were evenly matched in size, although O'Reilly stood an inch

77

taller and was deeper in the chest. But the young brave wore nothing more than breechclout and moccasins and had much greater agility than the Mountie, restricted by tight-fitting breeches and jacket and the gun belt strapped around his waist.

They stood face to face, sparring, gesturing threateningly at each other. Gradually O'Reilly's nausea lessened. Circling warily, O'Reilly threw a punch at the brave but he darted back beyond O'Reilly's reach. The next instant the brave retaliated, kicking out with his foot, aiming high for O'Reilly's head. O'Reilly saw it coming, grabbed the brave's ankle and, with a mighty heave, lifted him off his remaining foot and flung him through the air. The brave landed on his back on the grass a dozen feet away.

Amazingly, the brave recovered immediately and sprang back up. But as he was doing so, O'Reilly rushed at him. The Indian met O'Reilly's rush with lowered head, butting O'Reilly in the stomach above his belt buckle, wrapping his coppery arms around O'Reilly's waist. The brave tried to wrestle O'Reilly to the ground, but O'Reilly got his hands under the Indian's chest and lifted him off his feet, throwing him sideways. Stubbornly the brave hung on, pulling O'Reilly with him. O'Reilly lost his balance and they fell heavily to the grass, where they thrashed around and fought, punched and kicked as they rolled over and over. Finally O'Reilly got the heel of his hand under the brave's chin and forced his head upward and backward. The brave tried to claw O'Reilly's eyes out but O'Reilly exerted his mighty shoulders and almost broke the brave's neck. The brave grunted painfully, then suddenly tore himself loose.

Springing to his feet, the Indian broke into a sprint, making for his rifle lying in the grass a dozen yards away. He scooped up the rifle, but contrary to O'Reilly's expectations, did not whirl around and point it at him. Instead he kept on running, running toward his pinto standing a short distance away.

O'Reilly raced across the grass after him, moving with

the speed of a charging grizzly on a downhill slope. The Indian was about to leap up onto the pinto when O'Reilly's headlong charge slammed into him and they went crashing into some small willows just short of the pine trees.

They rolled and thrashed on the ground again. The brave lost hold of his rifle while he grappled with the Mountie. O'Reilly wrestled him until he had him over on his stomach. Straddling him, O'Reilly jammed his face down hard into the grass with one hand while he reached with his other hand and grabbed his right wrist. Then he forced the brave's right arm up against his back and held it there while he sat drawing in great gulping drafts of air into his lungs. A moment later, having regained some of his breath, he released his hold on the Indian's head while he reached into his pocket for his handcuffs.

"Christ!" O'Reilly muttered. The handcuffs weren't there. He must have lost them during the struggling. He looked quickly around, spotting them black and heavy on the grass a dozen or so yards behind him. Muttering another oath, he got his hand around the brave's chin, pulled upward and got to his feet without releasing his hold on his captive. He dragged him across the grass to where the handcuffs lay. He had just got him there when the brave suddenly tensed and twisted himself free.

"Son of a bitch!" O'Reilly swung his fist but the brave darted out of reach. Even so, O'Reilly's fist caught his shoulder and spun him around, although the coppery young brave was unhurt. They hurled themselves at each other and the fight started all over again.

The sun was setting behind the mountains as they stood face to face trading blows, O'Reilly fighting with fists, the Indian using the heels of his hands and his feet. They were both tiring, but both were too stubborn to give in. O'Reilly wanted to make his first arrest, and this Indian was wanted for horse theft, a serious enough offense in a land of stock-raising. As tough as the fight was, O'Reilly couldn't help but admire the young brave's determination and stamina, his spirit and his fighting ability.

They fought and struggled, throwing one another to the ground and wrestling wildly. O'Reilly felt a button ripped from the shoulder of his stable jacket. The brave carried a knife at his breechclout but made no effort to use it. Similarly, the flap on O'Reilly's revolver holster remained closed.

In the gathering darkness, O'Reilly could see the glistening sweat on the brave's coppery body. They were each growing more tired, and when O'Reilly threw the buck to the ground for the umpteenth time, losing another button from his jacket in the process, he was almost too exhausted to follow up. He dropped to one knee, bent over and drew in gulps of air, filling his lungs as the young brave lay on his back looking up at the Mountie.

Finally the brave struggled to his feet. Picking up his handcuffs from the grass, O'Reilly got up also. He held up the handcuffs and dangled them in front of the brave's eyes. The Indian's dark eyes locked onto them, staring intently, seemingly mesmerized by them. But when O'Reilly made a move to clap them on the brave's wrists, the brave resisted and the fighting resumed once more. They stood and grappled, and once again O'Reilly threw the brave to the ground. He followed up by dropping down on top of him, rolling him over onto his stomach and holding him there with a knee pressed into his back. He grabbed the brave's right arm and twisted it around behind him. Then he transferred his grip to the Indian's right wrist, holding it firm while he locked the handcuff around it. This time the brave was too exhausted to resist, and O'Reilly had the satisfaction of hearing the metallic click as the handcuff snicked into place and he turned the key.

With the one wrist locked, O'Reilly shifted his position and grabbed the brave's other wrist, jerking it around behind his back. He clamped the other handcuff into place and locked it. Then he turned the Indian around and pulled him up into a sitting position. A smile pulled at the corners of O'Reilly's mouth.

"Well, bucko, you put up quite a fight, but it's finished now. You're my prisoner and you're under arrest."

The young Indian sat looking steadily, unblinkingly, back at him. The sun had dropped farther beyond the mountains and it was almost dark.

It had been a good fight, one of the best O'Reilly had had in his life. It had been a fair fight. Both young men were of much the same build. The young brave was a splendid figure of Indian manhood. They were about the same age. It had been a clean fight, apart from the Indian using his feet, and that had simply been his way of fighting, not being versed in the ways of boxing or the white man's inclination of fighting with closed fists. In the eyes of an Indian, it had been a fair and acceptable way of fighting.

As they looked at each other, O'Reilly felt himself developing a reluctant liking for the brave. The Indian's eyes . . . he remembered the eyes of the Blood at the cell block window back at Standoff. Sergeant Hannan would be pleased with him, O'Reilly thought, now that he had arrested this young Blood horse thief. But slowly the smile faded from O'Reilly's face as Sergeant Hannan's words that day came back to him . . . *"They don't see anything wrong in running off someone else's horses. For generations they've been brought up to believe the more horses a brave runs off, the bigger warrior he is. How do we bring a race of warlike warriors to understand a law that's alien to everything they've been brought up to revere? They were born to ride and fight. I reckon half the time they get into trouble is because they're bored. How the hell do we expect 'em to be content to raise stock and grow crops? That buck in there, he'll go to the penitentiary at Stony Mountain. That's bad medicine to an Indian. They go there expecting to die. More often than not, that's exactly what happens. They pick up tuberculosis or some damn thing like that in the white man's prison and die."*

On feet spread apart, hands planted on his hips,

81

O'Reilly stood looking down at the Blood brave, staring into the black eyes. The Indian continued to look silently back at him, no expression on his face at all. Yet he must realize, O'Reilly thought, that he'll be going to the white man's prison eight hundred miles away in Manitoba. *"That's bad medicine to an Indian. They go there expecting to die. More often than not, that's exactly what happens. They pick up tuberculosis or some damn thing like that in the white man's prison and die."*

Suddenly — and inexplicably — O'Reilly stepped forward, pulled the Indian to his feet and turned him around. Without a word, he inserted the handcuff key into the lock and undid first the one handcuff, then the other. The handcuffs removed, he gave the Indian a rough push forward.

The brave turned and stared back at him. They faced each other for a long moment, neither speaking. There was just enough light for them to look into each other's eyes.

O'Reilly inclined his head toward the black and white pinto. For a minute or so it seemed the Indian didn't understand. But then he turned and walked toward the pony. He passed by his rifle lying in the grass. He stopped and looked back at O'Reilly, then glanced down at the rifle. O'Reilly nodded. The Indian bent down, picked up the rifle and continued to his pony. He jumped up onto the pinto's back. With a final backward glance at O'Reilly, he flicked his reins and rode away.

O'Reilly watched him. The next instant the brave was gone, swallowed up in the blackness.

Chapter 8

O'Reilly was lost. He had mounted up and ridden off in the same direction he had come, back toward the prairie. But the night-shrouded mountains and their treed slopes pressed in on him. He couldn't find his way out.

He pushed his horse on, hoping to stumble onto the way out. Occasionally he glanced up at the black sky, vainly searching for a moon, but he realized there wouldn't be one.

"Christ," he muttered, looking around. Dark shapes towered on all sides. There wasn't even enough sky above for him to recognize any stars.

He rode for a couple of hours, trying to find his way out of the wooded slopes. He wondered about Constable Wise. Had he followed and also become lost? Had he apprehended one or two of the other Indians or rounded up some of the horses?

At last O'Reilly reined to. He didn't know where the hell he was. The only logical thing to do was wait for morning and then find his way out, when he could at least see where he was going. Reluctantly he swung down from his saddle and prepared to make camp.

He spent an uncomfortable night. Although he was able to find some wood and get a fire going, his bedroll, together with his rations, was back among the poplars where Sergeant Hannan had left him and Wise to watch for Gus Breen and his whisky running outfit. So he stretched out beside the fire and tried to sleep, after having picketed his horse to graze on the grass nearby.

The next morning, hungry and unshaven, he saddled up and climbed back onto his horse. Guided by the sun rising over the walled ridges to the east, he found his way out through the mountain pass into the foothills. After little more than an hour of riding, he sighted familiar landmarks.

After another hour he saw riding toward him three horsemen spread out about a half a mile apart. It took only a moment to recognize them . . . Sergeant Hannan, Constable Scott and Constable Wise. Upon sighting him they started to converge. As they got closer, O'Reilly could see Sergeant Hannan glowering angrily under the wide brim of his tan-colored hat.

O'Reilly's appearance in uniform, be it scarlet tunic for parade or brown stable jacket for patrol, was generally immaculate. He had that Depot Division spit-and-polish shine, and Sergeant Hannan quickly observed the difference. He noted the ground-in dirt on O'Reilly's breeches and stable jacket, the missing buttons off his jacket, the skuff marks on his gun belt and boots.

"Where the hell have you been? Fall off your horse again?"

O'Reilly colored. ". . . er . . . saw some —"

"You disobeyed orders!" Sergeant Hannan snapped, cutting him off.

O'Reilly's guts sank as he tried to explain. "I saw some Indians running off horses —"

Sergeant Hannan cut him off again. "I don't give a damn what you saw! You had one hell of a nerve disobeying my orders. I left you and Wise to watch for Gus Breen and his outfit! Now, because of you, we've probably missed him. You left Wise in one hell of a bind. He had to make a decision whether to stay where he was, like he was ordered to do, or chase after you. He got worried that you might have run into trouble, so he rode off after you. He spent the rest of the night looking for you." The hard-faced sergeant sat his saddle glaring at the younger man. After a short pause, he said, "I ought to send you back to Fort Macleod with all your kit, O'Reilly, telling Inspector Cavannagh I don't want you. I need men who'll do what they're told."

O'Reilly wilted under the sergeant's scrutiny. He had disobeyed orders. There was no justification for him having done so. He had started to defend himself. Yet he had no defense. Even if he hadn't let the Blood go. Orders were orders. That's what sergeants and inspectors were for, to give orders. That's why they held their rank. And constables were in the Mounted Police to obey orders. He had been given specific instructions, clear-cut orders. He should have carried them out.

Sergeant Hannan jerked his head over his shoulder. "Let's get back and watch for Breen—*if* he hasn't already gone."

The reined their horses around and rode back to where they had been.

When they got there, Sergeant Hannan looked hard at O'Reilly. "Do you think you can stay here and watch for whisky runners this time?" His voice was heavy with sarcasm.

O'Reilly cringed under the red-headed sergeant's burning stare.

When Sergeant Hannan and Constable Scott rode off to the southeast to scout the coulees and rolling hills along the Montana border, O'Reilly and Wise dismounted and settled down to watch.

O'Reilly hungrily devoured cold rations—beef jerky and a couple of mouthfuls of water from his canteen.

"By the time I got my horse saddled," Roy Wise told him as he ate, "you were halfway to the God damn mountains. I didn't know whether to chase those Indians or go after you. Or stay where I was and do what the sarge told us. In the end I went after you, in case you got into

85

trouble. But you were riding so fast, I lost sight of you by the time you got into the foothills.

"I came back here in case Sergeant Hannan was looking for us. When he came back I told him what happened. We all three of us started searching for you. We looked as much as we could, until it got dark and we had to give it up until morning. At first light we started looking again. That's when we ran into you."

"Did you see any of those other Indians?"

"I was too busy looking for you. How about you? You didn't catch that buck on the pinto?"

O'Reilly shook his head.

They didn't talk much the rest of the day. They simply watched and waited. O'Reilly watched, fervently hoping they would sight Gus Breen's whisky wagons, and that Sergeant Hannan's prediction that Breen had already crossed would prove to be wrong. At least it would ease O'Reilly's guilty conscience.

Toward the afternoon Sergeant Hannan and Constable Scott rode up to the clump of poplars O'Reilly and Wise watched from.

"Any sign of Breen?" Sergeant Hannan asked, his face still hard.

O'Reilly swallowed and shook his head. "No, Sergeant."

"Well, keep watching."

Sergeant Hannan and Constable Scott then wheeled their horses around and rode off again. O'Reilly didn't see them again until the next morning.

All night O'Reilly and Wise watched and waited in vain. So anxious was O'Reilly to sight the whisky running outfit that he stayed awake all night, not even resting when Constable Wise was on watch. But no whisky-laden wagons rumbled by their poplar clump.

Sergeant Hannan and Constable Scott returned the next morning. Sergeant Hannan's face was tight and his tone of voice bitter. "Breen didn't show. He must've gone through earlier." Accusation glittered in his eyes as he fixed them on O'Reilly. "He must've gone through while you were off on your God damn jaunt into the mountains."

"Maybe we could go looking for him, Sergeant," O'Reilly replied quietly. "Maybe we could—"

Sergeant Hannan cut him off. "Christ! He could be anywhere by now. There's hundreds of square miles between here and the Old Man's River, and hundreds of God damn coulees. Breen could be in any one of them."

He pulled savagely on his reins. "Mount up," he snapped. We're going home."

Chapter 9

Sitting on an upturned bucket outside the Standoff barracks, O'Reilly held a riding boot in one hand and a brush in the other as he polished vigorously. On the ground beside him stood the other boot, glistening in bright morning sunshine, and over his knees rested his revolver holster and belt. He was engaged in covering up the scuff marks and nicks that covered them from his fight with the young Blood brave two days earlier. Every stroke of the brush reminded him of the tongue lashing Sergeant Hannan had given him.

He didn't blame the sergeant, but he was damned mad at himself for having chased off after those Indians. He should have known better. He had been in the Mounted Police thirteen months, most of them at Depot Division, where rigid discipline and strict obedience to orders were as sacred as the Ten Commandments. And he particularly, having been an assistant riding instructor, whose duties included instilling in recruits the virtues of discipline and compliance with orders, should have known better. Sergeant Hannan had given him clear orders to watch for Gus Breen, and now because of him Gus Breen had slipped across the border with his contraband shipment of whisky.

It had been his damned impetuousness to blame. It was

his principal character flaw as far as he was concerned. It had landed him in trouble before, going back to his boyhood. It wouldn't have been quite so bad if he had brought that Blood buck in. Then at least he would have had a horse-thief prisoner to show for it. But he had returned empty handed. If Sergeant Hannan only knew what really happened—that he had caught the young Blood but then let him go . . . well, he didn't like to think about that.

At that moment the sound of drumming hoofs drew O'Reilly's attention. Looking up from the boot he was polishing, he saw a red-coated horseman approaching from the south at a gallop.

O'Reilly lowered his boot and watched. As the rider got closer, he could see the flash of the sun's reflection on the brass buttons down the front of his scarlet tunic, the tan-colored felt hat, the yellow stripes down the sides of his blue breeches. Minutes later the Mountie galloped into the yard and reined his horse to a haunches-sliding stop, throwing up a shower of dust and gravel that threatened to cover the shine on O'Reilly's freshly polished boots.

"Where's Sergeant Hannan?" the constable asked excitedly as he jumped down from his horse.

O'Reilly pointed his boot at the barracks door. "Inside."

The constable dropped his reins and ran through the low gate to the front door. An instant later the screen door slammed shut behind him. O'Reilly stood watching the closed door. Something was obviously up, and a touch of excitement gripped him.

A few minutes later the screen door was thrown open and Sergeant Hannan appeared, looking smart and soldierly in scarlet tunic, despite his apparent disdain for spit-and-polish. Buckling his gun belt around his waist, he gave O'Reilly and his upheld riding boot a quick glance. "You can quit polishing those things, O'Reilly, and pull them on. We're going riding." Then he turned his head and shouted over his shoulder. *"Flying patrol! Turn out! Red serge and sidearms. Bandoliers as well."*

"Red serge?"

"That's right, O'Reilly. Trouble at the Blood reserve. There's a sun dance ceremony going on. The bucks will be pretty worked up. I hope none of Breen's whisky found its way onto the reserve. If it did, all hell could break loose. Now get into red serge and breeches and boots. We usually wear red for duty on the reserve."

Grabbing his boots and gun belt, O'Reilly raced into the barracks and quickly changed from brown duck fatigues into breeches, boots and scarlet tunic. He buckled on his gun belt and ammunition bandolier, adjusted his lanyard, then pushed shiny brass cartridges into the empty cylinders of his Enfield service revolver. Finally he put on his hat, pulled on his white gauntlets and picked up his Winchester. A moment later he was out in the stables with Scott, McCormack and Wise slapping saddles onto their horses.

"There are three wanted Indians who've just turned up on the Blood reserve," Sergeant Hannan told them as soon as they were mounted. "They're wanted for a couple of killings that took place two years ago. They hit out and crossed the border into Montana and they've been down there since. They just came back for the sun dance ceremonies. They probably figured the heat has died down and it's safe. We have a two man temporarily detachment on the reserve, watching to see that the Bloods don't get too carried away with the festivities. Constable Harry Davies here"—Sergeant Hannan inclined his head at the constable who had moments before ridden in, now sitting on his horse beside him—"and another man, Constable Jim Collins. But two men aren't enough to make an arrest, not the way the Bloods get when the sun dance is on. They get pretty fired up, so we'll have to be careful. But if we don't take those wanted bucks now, they'll disappear like they did before and Christ alone knows when or where they'll turn up again."

They rode out of Standoff, crossed the Belly River and cantered onto the Blood reserve.

They rode hard. The Blood reserve covered a lot of ground, fifty miles long and thirty wide. It was early afternoon when they heard the beating of drums.

They heard the drums over the hammering of their horses' hoofs. It was the first time O'Reilly had heard Indian drums and their sound sent a chill running through him. He thought of what those rawhide drums might have meant twenty years ago. Less. Even eight years ago, back during the Northwest Rebellion of '85.

Following the east bank of the Belly, they cantered around a bend and saw in front of them, on a broad flat of grassland fringed on three sides by clumps of cotton-woods, a sea of tepees pitched in a wide circle. In the center of the circle stood a large ceremonial lodge made of buffalo skins and green-leafed tree boughs. It was higher than the tepees and measured a good sixty feet across. Columns of smoke rose from dozens of fires in front of the countless tepees.

Sergeant Hannan hand-signaled his men and they reined their horses down to a smart trot, riding toward the camp in half-sections — a short column of twos — Sergeant Hannan and Constable Davies leading, with Scott and McCormack forming one half-section, and Wise and O'Reilly another, behind them.

O'Reilly had never seen so many Indians. They were everywhere. There were several hundred braves alone, not counting women. Within the center of the circle of tepees, in front of the big ceremonial lodge, sat chiefs and head-men of the Blood tribe, alongside elder councillors. A score or more older Indians sat cross-legged beating stone-headed sticks against drums of stretched rawhide. In front of them danced a mass of painted warriors, dressed in all their finery — feathered headdresses, buffalo head war bonnets with eagle tails, beautifully tanned deerskin shirts and breeches with leggings and moccasins richly decorated with hundreds of red and blue and yellow beads. They danced and whirled, stamping their moccasined feet on the grassy ground, cavorting and twisting, throwing back

91

their heads and uttering weird, high-pitched cries and whoops that sent tingles running down O'Reilly's back.

The dancing warriors shook feathered lances or tasseled tomahawks above their heads. Others waved rifles. A scalp swung suspended by a horsehair thong from a war lance, a relic from days not yet forgotten. The smell of incense and burning sweet grass filled the air.

Sergeant Hannan led his scarlet riders in among the tepees. Their Winchesters rested see-saw fashion in the slings across the pommels of their saddles. Afternoon sunlight glinted on burnished brass buttons and the embroidered crown and three gold chevrons on Sergeant Hannan's tunic sleeve.

A solitary white bell tent, together with a wagon, stood on the far side of the camp, pitched by the shade of the cottonwoods for protection from the heat of the June sun. Sergeant Hannan led them toward it. Painted faces stared at them as they rode by, but the dancers did not stop and the drums kept up their monotonous throbbing. Sergeant Hannan's eyes narrowed as he noticed some Indians tottering and swaying drunkenly. One fell down but then staggered back up onto his feet.

Constable Jim Collins stepped in front of the bell tent to greet the patrol as they rode up.

"Sure glad to see you, Sergeant."

Sergeant Hannan nodded to him. "I wasn't surprised when Harry here rode in to say you needed help, Jim. What's the situation?"

"Lame Bear is back, with Prairie Wolf Man and Black Cloud. There's a warrant out for Lame Bear's arrest on a charge of murder. Prairie Wolf Man and Black Cloud helped him escape and lit out across the line with him. There are warrants out for them, too. They just came back from across the line yesterday. Came back for the sun dance. If we don't arrest them while they're here, we mightn't get another chance. They'll pull back down into Montana as soon as the ceremonies are over. But the Bloods are all worked up from the dancing and ceremonial rituals and all that rehashing of the old days of the warpath. They're likely to turn ugly. And as if that weren't bad enough, some of them are all likkered up. Someone's been trading them firewater. Probably your old friend, Gus Breen."

"Where are they now?"

Constable Collins looked over in the direction of the dancing Indians. "In amongst that bunch, dancing."

"You can identify them?"

Collins nodded. "I know them, even under all the paint. They probably reckoned, with them being all painted up, they wouldn't be recognized. Not by us, anyway. I got the word from a buck who's jealous of Lame Bear because of some affair with a squaw."

"We better act right away," Sergeant Hannan said. "The longer we wait the harder it'll get." He turned in his saddle and looked at his men. "Dismount. Roy, you take the horses. Hold them ready in case we have to move out in a hurry. The rest of you come with me."

They dismounted, handing their reins to Constable Wise.

"Where's Red Crow?" Sergent Hannan asked.

Constable Collins pointed to the row of Indian chiefs, sitting on buffalo robes spread around the dancing Indians. "Over there, on the far side of that circle."

"All right. We'll tell him what we want."

They strode across the grass, wending their way among the tepees toward the center of the camp. The ceaseless beating of the rawhide drums throbbed in their ears, mixed with weird, chantlike cries and occasional piercing whoops. The very ground under their spurred boots trembled from the constant pounding of hundreds of mocassined feet. Bone whistles added flute-like sounds to the eerie, pagan atmosphere.

The Mounties pushed their way through the thronging Indians to reach the inside of the circle. Black heads turned as red coats and Stetsons pushed past. Emboldened by the ritualistic ceremonies of a warrior race that still remembered the glories of the warpath, several braves jeered at the Mounties. More vociferous Indian women shouted shrill abuse.

Once they were through to the interior of the circle, Sergeant Hannan led his five men to where Red Crow, aging chieftain of the Bloods, sat on a buffalo robe spread across the grass watching the dancing.

Reaching Red Crow's side, Sergeant Hannan raised a gauntleted hand in greeting. He bent forward so the Blood chief could hear him above the din and spoke in the Blood tongue. "There are three braves who have broken the White Mother's law, O Chief Red Crow. We have come to take them away to be judged by *Stamix-Otokan*."

The old Blood chieftain looked up at him. "You do not choose a good time. My people are excited."

"We did not choose the time. They did. We will require your help."

"There is little I can do, but I will do what I can."

Sergeant Hannan nodded. "That will do."

They left Red Crow's side and walked slowly around the dancing braves, Constable Collins searching the painted faces bobbing around in front of them. The cavorting Indians stared back, some sullenly, some defiantly, some simply curiously. Others paid the redcoats no attention at all.

They had paced a quarter of the way around the dancing ring when Constable Collins pointed to a big warrior with streaks of red and yellow ochre painted across his face. "That's Lame Bear," he shouted over the noise of the throbbing drums and bone whistles.

Sergeant Hannan snapped an order. "McCormack, O'Reilly. Arrest him!"

Eager to redeem himself after what happened over Gus Breen, O'Reilly stepped quickly among the dancing braves and grabbed Lame Bear's arm, pulling him from the dancers. McCormack grasped Lame Bear's other arm before the big Blood realized what was happening.

Immediately Collins pointed into the ring of dancers a

second time. "That's Prairie Wolf Man."

Sergeant Hannan snapped another order and Constables Scott and Davies moved in among the dancing braves and grabbed the second wanted Indian.

Constable Collins stood peering at the painted faces cavorting by in front of him. Suddenly, farther around the dancing circle, a paint-daubed brave broke from the dancers and darted away.

Collins shouted. "There goes Black Cloud!"

Collins raced after him. Black Cloud pushed his way into the watching Indians. Collins pushed his way after him, but the thronging Indians closed in on Collins, jostling and pushing him backward and forward while their tribesman disappeared among the tepees.

"Get those two prisoners over to the police tent!" Sergeant Hannan shouted, trying to make his voice heard above the noise.

O'Reilly and McCormack hustled Lame Bear away from the circle of dancers, while Scott and Davies followed right on their heels with Prairie Wolf Man. But Lame Bear suddenly decided he didn't want to go and he tried to pull away, shouting and digging his heels into the ground.

His struggles struck a responsive chord among his brothers. Shouting and jeering erupted all around the Mounties and several braves stepped out of the circle of dancers, shaking tomahawks or clubs at the redcoats as they advanced toward them.

O'Reilly wrapped an arm around Lame Bear's neck and pulled hard, almost lifting the painted warrior off his feet. He and McCormack dragged him shouting through the mass of Indians toward the police tent just beyond the edge of the camp, ignoring the jeering and yelling rising ever louder in their ears.

They were halfway there when a roar erupted from a hundred copper-hued throats. The next instant a wave of buckskin, paint and feathers swept across the grass after them.

"Get the prisoners over to that tent!" Sergeant Hannan

shouted again, turning to face the rush of redskins. "Quick!"

O'Reilly and McCormack started running, dragging Lame Bear with them. Scott and Davies, with a less recalcitrant Prairie Wolf Man, were slightly ahead of them. With outstretched arms, Sergeant Hannan tried to hold back the surging Indians but they swarmed all over him.

O'Reilly and McCormack were almost to the edge of the camp—the white bell tent was only forty yards away—when the Indians were upon them. O'Reilly felt clawing hands trying to prise his arm from around Lame Bear's neck, but he hung on all the harder. Drums and shouting filled his ears. He could smell whisky breaths as wild-eyed coppery faces milled around him. Hands grasped at his revolver holster. He slapped his free hand over the holster flap. As he did so, Lame Bear was dragged from him but he jammed an elbow into the midriff of an Indian grappling him from behind. The brave grunted and the grappling hands let go. The next instant O'Reilly swung a mighty fist and felt it crunch against a nose. Painted faces of red and yellow and blue and white swarmed all about him.

The shouting and war whoops were deafening. Rifle shots exploded into the air, while the rawhide drums continued their pounding and bone whistles kept up their hollow fluting.

Among the bobbing faces O'Reilly caught another glimpse of Lame Bear. He forced his way through the seething Indians and reached out, grabbing Lame Bear by the hair and yanking him back to him. The next instant O'Reilly felt himself losing his balance and he went down onto one knee. But he dragged Lame Bear down with him. Panic washed over him as an image of being trampled into the ground by hundreds of moccasined feet, of his life and breath being stamped out of him, flashed before his eyes.

O'Reilly was on the verge of being kicked right down onto the ground when a hand gripped his arm and pulled

96

him to his feet. Still holding onto Lame Bear, O'Reilly caught a glimpse of a crown and three gold chevrons and he realized Sergeant Hannan had somehow fought his way over to his side.

Bodies surged everywhere. Painted faces, flashing black eyes, buckskin and feathers. Then a roar engulfed them as the Indians wrenched Prairie Wolf Man from Scott and Davies.

"Get Lame Bear over to the tent," Sergeant Hannan shouted above the din. "We'll keep him, by Christ!"

His arm around Lame Bear's neck again, O'Reilly wrestled the struggling Blood toward the police tent. Constable McCormack pushed through the Indians to help O'Reilly. Constables Scott and Davies, no longer encumbered by Prairie Wolf Man, joined Sergeant Hannan in trying to hold back the engulfing tide of buckskin and ochre.

Although O'Reilly held a viselike grip around his neck, Lame Bear struggled violently. Tom McCormack tried to grab one of his arms, but Lame Bear aimed a vicious sideways kick that caught McCormack in the groin. McCormack doubled over. *"God damn you!"* he cursed.

O'Reilly released his grip. Thinking himself free, Lame Bear went to run but he had barely moved when O'Reilly swung a powerful fist that hit him in the side of the head and sent him reeling. The next instant O'Reilly had his arm twisted behind his back. Lame Bear let out a howl of pain.

"Now get moving!" O'Reilly said. "Over to that tent."

Lame Bear might not have understood O'Reilly's words but he certainly understood their message. And just in case he didn't, O'Reilly gave his arm another twist that brought Lame Bear dancing on his toes as O'Reilly propelled him toward the tent.

Still bent double, Tom McCormack staggered along behind them, while Sergeant Hannan and Constables Scott and Davies fought with their fists to hold back the engulfing tide of Indians.

Tossing a glance back over his shoulder, Sergeant Hannan saw that O'Reilly had at last got Lame Bear over in front of the white bell tent. "Fall back," he shouted to the other two.

Still facing the surging Indians, they moved backward to the tent. They reached it just ahead of hundreds of shouting Indians. At the same time, Constable Collins—hatless—broke through the Indians to join them.

"Black Cloud got away, god damn it," Collins shouted breathlessly.

Sergeant Hannan was too busy looking quickly around him to answer Collins. He was sizing up the situation. The tide of buckskin threatened to trample them all and the tent underfoot. Constable Wise stood beside the tent, holding the reins of the police horses as they snorted and pranced, frightened by the shouting and whooping, and threatening to pull free. Eyes catching the wagon, Sergeant Hannan's finger jabbed at it as he shouted. "Pull that wagon in front of the tent and turn it on its side. We'll make a stand behind it."

While O'Reilly handcuffed Lame Bear's wrists behind his back, Scott and Davies grabbed the wagon shafts and pulled the heavy vehicle in front of the tent, Collins pushing it from behind. Then they put their shoulders against its side and pushed, straining to tip it over on its side. Tom McCormack, his face pale and drawn, stepped over beside them and helped. With a heave they pushed it crashing onto its side amid a cloud of rising dust.

Sergeant Hannan sprang to his horse and slid his Winchester from its sling. "Get the prisoner down behind the wagon," he shouted as he threw himself against the overturned wagon and leveled his carbine across the wood and pointed it at the Indians.

"Get your rifles!" he snapped at his men.

The thronging, yelling Indians were little more than a dozen yards from the tent when the six redcoats stood shoulder to shoulder behind their overturned wagon barrier with Winchester barrels pointing over the top.

"No one pull a trigger unless I give the order," Sergeant

Hannan told his men. "They'll try to bluff us. They'll try to force us to start hostilities."

Then he called out at the oncoming Indians, only yards away, in their own tongue. "That is far enough."

At that moment shouted words, also in the Blood language, rose above the noise. The Bloods stopped, and Red Crow, his arms held high above his head, stepped out in front and turned to face his tribesmen.

"Stop this! We want no trouble. Go back to your dancing. Let the redcoats take their prisoner."

But a big lantern-jawed brave with red and blue zigzag marks that failed to hide the pock marks on his face, stepped from among the mass of Blood warriors and faced Red Crow.

"No!" he shouted. "We have had enough of the redcoats and the white man's law. Ever since we listened to white men, bad days have come upon us. Before white men came, buffalo covered the prairie for as far as the eye could see. When the white men came, they took away our land and put us on reservations. Then the buffalo disappeared. More white men came. They brought their iron horse, which brought more and more white men. Now the white man's government tells us we can no longer leave the reservations unless we have a piece of paper signed by the agent. They say that without it we can no longer ride across the land that used to belong to us. What will it be that they will let us do next? They try to take our brothers away when they are celebrating the Sun Dance. Will it be that next they will try to stop us from celebrating the Sun Dance altogether? Already they have tried to stop us doing it. That is why the redcoats are here. We have had enough of them."

"Lame Bear broke the White Mother's law." Red Crow replied. "The redcoats must take him to *Stamix-Otokan* to be judged for breaking the law. Lame Bear knew it was wrong to do what he did."

A rifle shot suddenly exploded in the air. *"Aiiyaah!"* shouted a brave as he held a smoking rifle high above his head and shook it vigorously. He grinned, as he looked around at his fellow braves. Then he staggered drunkenly out from among them and lurched forward to stand beside the big, lantern-jawed Blood. Next he looked over at the redcoats behind the overturned wagon and shook his rifle at them. "Down with the redcoats!" he shouted as his finger tightened around the trigger again. But he had forgotten to reload and the hammer clicked on the empty case.

"Aiieee!" yelled another brave. "Don't let the redcoats take our brother. We know what happens when our brothers are sent to the white man's jail. They get the coughing sickness and we never see them again."

A great roar sounded from the Indians. Wild shouting and blood-curdling war whoops filled the air. Another rifle exploded and a bullet whip-cracked across Constable Collins's hatless head. Collins involuntarily ducked. More shots erupted from the Indians' rifles, and more bullets cracked over the heads of the Mounties standing behind their barricade. Wide-eyed with terror, the police horses reared and kicked in a frenzy to pull away and escape the noise. Constable Wise dug his boots into the ground to brace himself as he tried to hold them. Constable Davies levered a cartridge into the chamber of his Winchester.

Sergeant Hannan saw Davies's movement. "Hold your fire," he shouted. "They're trying to provoke us into starting it."

Christ, thought O'Reilly. *It looks to me like it's already started.*

Sergeant Hannan shouted out in the Blood dialect again. "Red Crow, tell them to get back to their dancing."

Red Crow held up his hands and tried to make himself heard. But belligerent young braves shouted him down. A fusillade of rifle shots erupted, bullets cracking over the Mounties' heads. The terrified police horses almost pulled Wise off his feet.

Sergeant Hannan's voice shouted above the racket. "Hold steady! Hold your fire!"

100

Standing behind the overturned wagon, with Sergeant Hannan on his right and Constable Scott on his left, O'Reilly watched the excited Bloods shouting and jumping around. Red Crow tried to calm them but the younger braves, some inflamed by liquor, had already worked themselves into a frenzy. Many glared across the few yards between themselves and the overturned wagon, uttering fierce war whoops as they shook rifles or knives at the Mounties; sunlight flashed off the blade of a tomahawk as a brave waved it threateningly. O'Reilly watched the agitated faces, searching for one in particular, glad when he didn't find it.

The noise increased in intensity. The tide of indians started to surge toward the barrier. The distance between them and the wagon narrowed. O'Reilly could see the bloodshot whites of their eyes. Sergeant Hannan's order to hold steady ringing in his ears, he gripped his Winchester and wondered what the hell to do next.

Then suddenly, above all the noise and excitement, rose the urgent hammering of hoofbeats. The next instant a party of horsemen galloped into the camp. The drums stopped. Bright scarlet tunics, vivid in the afternoon sun, swept around the teepees and headed toward the overturned wagon. Almost onto it, the Blood braves stopped in their tracks. Silence descended, broken only by the sound of hoofbeats and the jingle of accoutrements as the tall, straight-backed figure of Inspector Cavannagh led a troop of Mounted Police right up alongside the wagon. The Mounties rode their horses into the narrow space between the wagon and the Indians, forcing the braves to scramble back out of the way.

"Troop — *halt!*"

Inspector Cavannagh's voice snapped out in rapid Blood dialect. The Bloods, visibly shocked by the unexpected arrival of a troop of redcoats, shrank back even farther.

Red Crow stepped forward and replied to Inspector Cavannagh. Then the inspector engaged in a ten minute harangue of the massed Bloods.

A single derisive yell rang out from among the Bloods. Inspector Cavannagh whipped back a reply as he calmly sat his saddle, staring them down with his steel-blue eyes. A hushed silence followed. Even the women, standing in a group behind the ranks of braves, kept quiet. Inspector Cavannagh resumed talking. When he had finished, the Indians turned around and started walking away, back toward the center of the camp.

Inspector Cavannagh reined his horse around and walked it over to the wagon. Sergeant Hannan called his men to attention and saluted.

Returning the salute, Inspector Cavannagh sat his saddle looking down at them. "How did all this start, Sergeant?"

Sergeant Hannan told him.

When Sergeant Hannan had finished, Inspector Cavannagh said, "It's a good thing you held your fire. Had any of you fired a shot, we could have had an Indian war on our hands."

Sergeant Hannan grinned. "We're lucky you turned up, sir."

"You can thank the agent at the Lower Agency. He found out that whisky had been smuggled onto the reserve. He was worried that it would fire up the young bucks attending the sun dance ceremonies. I decided to bring a troop along just in case."

"What will we do with our prisoner, sir?" Sergeant Hannan asked, inclining his head at Lame Bear, sitting handcuffed on the grass behind the wagon.

"You and your patrol can return to Standoff. I'll remain here with the troop to assist Constables Collins and Davies until the sun dance is over. You take Lame Bear with you and lock him up for the night. Tomorrow morning escort him to Fort Macleod and turn him over to the guardroom NCO. You had better report to Major Steele as soon as you get there. He'll want a full, firsthand account of what happened here. We'll look for Prairie

102

Wolf Man and Black Cloud while we're here, although I expect they'll be far away by now."

Sergeant Hannan and his men prepared to mount up. O'Reilly caught the sergeant's eye over the top of his saddle as he stood beside his horse about to thrust his boot into the stirrup. The sergeant's eyes were hard.

"You've just seen how firewater riles up Indians, O'Reilly. Now maybe you can see why I want Gus Breen so bad."

O'Reilly's mouth tightened into a thin, straight line beneath his moustache, but he said nothing.

Chapter 10

Watching from the barracks door, O'Reilly noticed the shinier than usual gleam of Sergeant Hannan's boots and belt as he swung up onto his saddle, and the extra glint of the brass buttons of his scarlet tunic. The sergeant was taking care that when he reported to Major Steele, the commanding officer would not find fault with his appearance.

Gathering his reins, Sergeant Hannan legged his horse into a trot. Constables Scott and McCormack followed, with a handcuffed Lame Bear riding between them.

O'Reilly was disappointed Sergeant Hannan hadn't taken him along as one of Lame Bear's escorts. He would like to have availed himself of the opportunity to visit Ruth Baker. However, Sergeant Hannan had done no such thing, leaving O'Reilly and Wise behind at the outpost. They had sat up all night guarding the prisoner.

Sergeant Hannan hadn't been gone an hour when a horseman rode into the yard. O'Reilly was alone in the general office. Wise, tired from his night of guard duty, lay sleeping in the barrack room

O'Reilly recognized the fox-faced man as soon as he went to the screen door in answer to the knock.

"Sergeant in?" the man asked.

"He left for Fort Macleod an hour ago."

"When'll he be back?"

"Tonight, or possibly not until tomorrow."

The man's fox-like face showed disappointment. "I've got something to tell him."

O'Reilly decided he didn't like the man. "I can pass it on."

The man hesitated, looking at O'Reilly with cunning eyes, then said, "The word is out that Gus Breen is making another whisky run across the border."

O'Reilly was instantly interested. "When?"

"Tonight."

"Tonight?"

The man nodded quickly.

"Where?"

"He's usin' the same route he used last time."

Thoughts went whirling through O'Reilly's mind. Could he mount up and overtake the sergeant before he reached Fort Macleod? How far ahead would he be? Would there be time for the sergeant to turn around and ride back and reach the Montana border by sundown and in time to catch Breen? But hell! Inspector Cavannagh ordered him to report to Major Steele and give him a firsthand account of what happened at the Blood reserve. That would have to take precedence.

O'Reilly nodded. "All right. We'll look after it."

The fox-faced man was no sooner back in his saddle and riding away from the barracks when O'Reilly went into action. He buttoned on his brown duck jacket, strapped his revolver around his waist, stuffed field rations into his saddle wallets and took his bedroll and Winchester. He left the barracks and quickly crossed the yard to the stables, where he saddled his horse. He was swinging up into his saddle when the screen door slammed and Constable Wise half-ran through the gate and across the yard toward him.

"Where are you going?"

"A man just brought in word that Gus Breen is making another whisky run across the border from Montana. I'm going down there to bring him in."

Wise screwed up his face. "You're crazier than hell."

Gripping his reins, O'Reilly looked down at Wise from the height of his saddle. "Maybe, but it'll be too late by the time Sergeant Hannan gets back. If I ride hard, I should be able to reach the border in time."

Shaking his head, Wise said, "The sarge'll have your guts when he gets back and finds out where you've gone."

"Not if I bring in Breen."

O'Reilly kneed his horse and it trotted off. Still shaking his head, Constable Wise stood watching him go.

O'Reilly rode steadily, following the high banks of the Belly, his eyes occasionally wandering across the river to the Blood reserve on the other side, the events of the previous day on his mind.

He pushed his horse hard all day, spurred on by hopes of single-handedly capturing Breen and seizing his wagons of contraband whisky. He was spurred on by playing over in his mind his version of Sergeant Hannan's anticipated reaction, the expression on the sergeant's face when he brought in his prisoner.

The sun still had two hours to go before dropping down behind the mountains to the west when O'Reilly found the poplar clump where he and Wise had hidden while watching the trails from Montana. He reined in and dismounted. He didn't know how long he would have to wait. He didn't know whether Breen would cross during the last hour of daylight or whether he would wait until nightfall. But he was confident he would spot Breen; there would be close to a full moon this night and there wasn't a cloud in the sky. In the stillness of the night, he would be bound to hear the movement of wagon wheels, the crack of whip.

As he unsaddled his horse and gave it a rubdown, O'Reilly tossed around in his mind just how he would tackle arresting Breen. It wouldn't be all that easy, one man alone against two or three, especially not at night. But he would worry about that when the time came. It

106

would have been better if he had stopped at one of the outposts on the way to the border, such as Kootenai or Big Bend. He hadn't done so because he would have had to detour and he hadn't wanted to lose time when every minute was precious.

After attending to his horse, O'Reilly positioned his saddle where he could readily sweep it up from the grass and slap it onto the dark bay the moment it was required. He ignored the field rations in his saddle wallets, and his bedroll. He didn't want to relax and he didn't want to take the time to eat. Not even so much as dry beef jerky. He wanted to give his undivided attention to the trails from Montana.

He took his Winchester, levered a round into the chamber and sat among the trees with a pair of binoculars. With a touch of impatience, he glassed the country to the south but saw not sign of movement.

As he watched and waited, it crossed his mind that when Sergeant Hannan returned to Standoff and found out where he was, the sergeant would be damned angry with him for having acted without instructions. However, O'Reilly reasoned, this time he wasn't disobeying orders. Sergeant Hannan had left him at the outpost with Constable Wise without giving him any specific instructions. Therefore, he was simply exercising his own initiative, as a Mounted Policeman was supposed to do. Anyway, if he arrested Breen . . . ah, he could picture it, riding into the yard back at Standoff single-handed with Gus Breen and his outfit under arrest.

A smile tugged the corners of his mouth as he sat thinking about it, how sweet it would be.

He woke with a start. He had dozed off. He didn't know for how long. Looking up at the sky, he saw the top of the bright golden ball sinking down below the mountains.

He scanned the country to the south. Still no sign of

movement yet . . . He felt someone was around, he sensed a presence. Picking up his binoculars, he was about to raise them to his eyes when he heard a faint rustle behind him. He was turning his head when a heavy weight hit him in the back, knocking the wind out of him. The ground hit him with a jarring thud. Something was gripping his neck at the back, forcing his face into the grass. Almost at the same time a hand grabbed his right wrist and twisted it hard against his back.

He realized a man was on his back. He could hear the breathing. He tried to twist his head around to see who but the hand on the back of his neck held his head rigid as he was forced into the ground. *Breen? One of his men?* He could smell woodsmoke on the man, or on his clothing. He fought to get free but the man was too strong. All he could breathe was earth. He felt himself suffocating. A wave of panic surged over him and he struggled harder. But the more he struggled, the more the pressure on his neck was applied.

Slowly O'Reilly felt his breath being forced out of him. A few seconds more and he would have no breath left at all. He *had* to get free. Tucking his left arm close against the side of his chest, he used it as a lever to lift his chest up off the ground. His assailant responded by twisting his right arm further up his back. But desperation lent O'Reilly strength and he managed to slowly turn his right arm back. His assailant exerted more pressure on O'Reilly's neck, pushing his face deeper into the grass, trying to force out of him what little breath he still had. For a moment he felt as though his neck would break. Then he became aware of his assailant's knee pressing into the small of his back, and an excruciating pain stabbed into him, gradually increasing in intensity.

Using his left arm as a lever once more, O'Reilly was able to lift his chest up again, this time further than the first time. At the same time he exerted the muscles of his right arm. Veins stood out on his forehead as he fought against his assailant's grip and slowly but surely twisted his right arm free. Blood pounded through his veins and his heart hammered against his chest. But the grip on his right arm weakened. His assailant was now fighting desperately to hold him down

With a tremendous effort, O'Reilly suddenly threw himself sideways, at the same time pulling his right arm free. But his attacker stayed with him, clinging to his back, and a buckskin-covered arm went around his neck from behind, while buckskin-clad legs wrapped themselves around his waist. The arm tried to choke him as O'Reilly was pulled backward, his assailant now under him. O'Reilly found himself staring up at the darkening sky as the attacker's arm tightened around his throat.

O'Reilly prepared himself for another effort to break free. Lying on his back like an overturned turtle, his attacker holding him from underneath, O'Reilly doubled his knees up in front of himself, tensed, then coiled himself like a giant spring. The next instant he unwound, flinging out his booted feet as he threw his chest and shoulders forward.

In one smooth movement O'Reilly landed on his feet, bringing his clinging assailant with him. Immediately he whipped both arms up over his head, reached behind him for the man on his back, his hands closing on a pair of ears. He pulled savagely. He heard a subdued grunt of pain. Then he threw himself forward. The buckskin-covered legs loosened around his waist, the arm around his throat was torn loose as his assailant went sailing over his head. The buckskin-clad figure slammed against a poplar, slid down the trunk and landed in a heap at its foot.

O'Reilly stared at the body of an Indian.

"You ungrateful son of a bitch!"

The young Blood rider of the pinto pony.

After he had taken pity on him, or out of admiration — O'Reilly wasn't sure which it had been — and released him when he should have taken him in and locked him up. Well, this time it would be different. This time he wouldn't show any compassion. This time he would take the young Blood under arrest back to Standoff.

The brave was winded but by no means out of action. Black eyes glittering, he suddenly sprang to his feet to face the Mountie. He dropped into a crouching position, legs spread apart, arms out in front of him, hands open, ready to grapple. O'Reilly stood straight, facing him. An instant later the brave flung out a moccasined foot, aiming for O'Reilly's abdomen. O'Reilly remembered the last time the young Blood did that and saw it coming. Like lightning he reacted, grabbing the Indian's ankle, wrenched hard and flipped him off his remaining foot over onto his back. The brave landed heavily on the grass. Before he could move, O'Reilly was on him. The air went out of the brave's body with a great rush. But the brave threw an arm around O'Reilly's neck, swung his hip and catapulted O'Reilly sideways. In that instant O'Reilly realized this wouldn't be an easy victory, any more than it had been on that earlier occasion. He had beaten the Blood that time, but only just. He intended doing so again.

O'Reilly rolled away just as the Blood flung himself out to grapple with him. In an instant they both sprang to their feet and stood facing each other once more.

The Blood's eyes glittered hard, black and unfathomable. His face was expressionless, his lips pressed together. He wore a knife at his waist. O'Reilly's arm brushed his revolver holster as he stood and readied himself to grapple with the brave again. Thinking briefly about it, O'Reilly was mystified by the attack, but he brushed the mystery of it quickly aside in his determination to make up for his misguided generosity the last time.

The Blood started circling to his right, moving in closer to come in at O'Reilly's left. O'Reilly circled warily to keep facing him. The Indian feinted with another kick. O'Reilly's hands shot out to grab the brave's ankle but the young brave danced back out of reach. He repeated the tactic. O'Reilly reacted again, but not quite as readily. When the Blood tried it a third time, O'Reilly didn't react at all. But the fourth time was for real and the moccasined foot flew out hard at him. O'Reilly had anticipated such a tactic and his hands closed around the brave's ankle again. This time, instead of wrenching him sideways off his feet, O'Reilly charged forward and bent the Blood's leg back hard against his body, sending him sprawling onto the ground. The Blood was just getting to his feet when O'Reilly caught him with a fist that lifted him off the ground and sent him crashing into a tree again.

It was a blow that would have put most men out of action, and O'Reilly was confident the Indian was winded. Pulling handcuffs from his pocket, he moved in on the young buck. He didn't intend spending the next half hour fighting. He was going to subdue this Blood brave as fast as he could and get the handcuffs on him. Then he would be able to turn his attention back to Breen.

As O'Reilly stepped forward with his handcuffs, the Indian unexpectedly jumped up in front of him. In a lightening move he snatched the front of O'Reilly's jacket, lifted a leg and jammed the sole of his foot on O'Reilly's chest, then threw himself backward, pulling the Mountie with him. They somersaulted through the air, O'Reilly landing jarringly on his back, the air knocked out of him with the power of the impact. The next instant the brave's body thudded on him with rocking force. The brave pulled the knife from his sheath and drove the blade at O'Reilly's throat.

O'Reilly saw the flash of the blade poised dangerously at his throat. He gripped the brave's wrist and pushed the blade away, but the Indian pushed back. Beads of sweat popped out on the coppery forehead as he pushed against the power of O'Reilly's arm. O'Reilly's eyes widened as the blade got closer and closer to his throat. The next second he felt a sharp pain as the knife nicked his throat just above the collar of his jacket. *Christ! This is it!* Straining mightily, O'Reilly slowly forced the knife back. But the brave's downward pressure had the advantage and the knife pressed back closer and closer to O'Reilly's throat. Looking into the Blood's face, O'Reilly saw the glittering

111

black eyes, saw the triumph in them. Then the knife blade nicked his throat again.

Suddenly the Blood's teeth flashed against his dark face and he laughed. An instant later the knife was pulled back from O'Reilly's throat and the weight on his chest lifted as the Indian sprang back up onto his feet. Thrusting the knife back into its sheath, he stood looking down at the Mountie, laughter still on his face.

Dumbfounded, O'Reilly lay where he was, staring up at the young brave. He felt the warm trickle of blood on his throat, trickling down his collar. He was still alive. Yet he could just as easily have had his throat cut.

The Indian unexpectedly held out his right hand, palm open. Looking up in amazement, O'Reilly realized he wanted to shake hands. Slowly, O'Reilly reached up his hand and they shook. It was a strong grip as O'Reilly lay on the ground, propped up on his left elbow, the young brave standing above him smiling down.

They looked into each other's faces the young Blood still with laughter in his eyes. Gradually it dawned upon O'Reilly. He had beaten the brave in combat the first time, now the brave had beaten him and evened the score. They were two young men who had contested one another and each had won a round. Now they were friends.

O'Reilly lifted a hand to the warm trickle on his throat, held it there for a moment, then withdrew it. He looked at the bright red blood — his blood. The Indian could have killed him. He could have scalped him for that matter. The Indian wanted O'Reilly to know he could have killed him but instead had returned the favor O'Reilly had done him by letting him go when he could have arrested him, locked him up and sent him to the white man's prison in Manitoba. The Mountie had given him his life. The Indian had done the same in return. Now they were even.

The Indian offered his hand to O'Reilly again. Reaching up, O'Reilly took it and the young Blood hauled him to his feet.

They stood looking at each other. The brave was still

grinning. A grin spread across O'Reilly's face.

"Do you speak English?"

The brave nodded.

"What's your name?"

"Porcupine Quill."

"Porcupine Quill?" O'Reilly's grin widened.

The brave nodded. "What is yours?"

"O'Reilly."

"O-rile-ee?" The brave laughed. *"O-rile-ee."*

O'Reilly laughed with him. He found himself liking the Blood brave.

"You ride with the red-headed sergeant, the grumpy one called *Han-nan?"*

Laughing, O'Reilly nodded. *The grumpy one.* He liked that.

The Indian frowned. "But *Han-nan's* yellow-legs all ride together. Why are you alone?"

"I'm waiting for Gus Breen, the whisky runner."

"Why alone?"

"I got into trouble for chasing you that last time when I was supposed to be watching for Breen. We missed him because of what I did, not staying where I was supposed to be. I decided to try to catch him this time. The sergeant had to go to Fort Macleod with two of the men, so I came alone."

"You would not have found the whisky trader that time if you had waited. He had already gone."

"But we were told he was making a run that night or the next."

Porcupine Quill laughed. "That is why yellow-legs not catch him. Someone tells you that so that you come and look for him while he takes another trail and trades blaze-belly at the same time you waste looking in wrong place."

"You mean someone's been making monkeys out of the Mounted Police?"

Porcupine Quill frowned. *"Mon-kees?"*

"Yes . . . speaking with the forked tongue . . . telling lies."

113

Porcupine Quill nodded. "Telling lies . . . yes."

"Do you know the trail Breen uses?"

"Yes. He is cunning like the prairie wolf. I will show you the trail he follows."

O'Reilly looked hard at the young brave. "Why should you do that?" Suspicion edged his voice.

Porcupine Quill's eyes held O'Reilly's. "White whisky trader cheat Indian. He charges us more than he charges white men, and the stuff he trades us is not as good." The Blood screwed up his face.

Satisfied, O'Reilly nodded.

Porcupine Quill looked up at the sky, rose-pink from the reflection of the setting sun. The mountains were throwing purple shadows across the foothills. "Tonight we sleep here. Tomorrow I show you."

Chapter 11

O'Reilly got back to Standoff late the next night. He expected a roasting from Sergeant Hannan, but he reasoned that the information he had would appease him. To O'Reilly's relief, Sergeant Hannan was still at Fort Macleod. Although Scott and McCormack had returned, Major Steele had ordered Sergeant Hannan to remain at Fort Macleod an extra day because he wanted to question him at length about the incident on the Blood reserve.

When Sergeant Hannan returned late the following afternoon, he appeared to be in a bad mood, so O'Reilly decided to keep his new found information to himself. It wasn't until two days later, when they were on patrol, that he mentioned it.

Sergeant Hannan's reaction was disappointing. Riding alongside O'Reilly, he scowled. "What the hell would he be telling you that for?"

O'Reilly shrugged. He did not tell the sergeant about the fight, or that he had caught Porcupine Quill on that earlier occasion. Nor did he tell him Porcupine Quill was one of the Indians who ran off the rancher's horses the day O'Reilly first arrived at Standoff.

"I can't see a Blood buck showing you a whisky runner's trail. Indians will sell their souls for a whiff of rotgut."

O'Reilly felt deflated. They rode for a distance in silence before Sergeant Hannan said, "I don't want you riding out on any more one-man patrols again unless I tell you."

The patrol cantered along the banks of the Belly. Everything was quiet on the reserve across the river. The rawhide drums were silent, the sun dance ceremonies over. Inspector Cavannagh and his troop had returned to Fort Macleod.

They crossed the Belly below the reserve and rode east across undulating prairie. They rode farther east than O'Reilly had been before. He could see off in the distance three hills rising out of the prairie. Roy Wise told him they were the Sweetgrass Hills, just below the border in Montana.

On the second day out of Standoff, the patrol sighted two wagons moving slowly across the prairie from the direction of the border. Suspicions alerted, they legged their horses forward. Wagons could mean whisky runners, especially when off the regular trails. But these two turned out to be immigrant settlers traveling north to find open homesteading country.

They checked them and itemized their belongings, calculating customs duties from a schedule Sergeant Hannan carried. After collecting customs duties and noting down immigration information, Sergeant Hannan gave them advice and directions and allowed them to proceed. The patrol then continued on its way.

On the third day they patrolled along the Milk River Ridge, a height of land that separated waters flowing south into the Gulf of Mexico from those flowing north to Hudson Bay. Toward evening they were looking for a place to camp when they noticed a campfire flickering in the purple dusk.

"Let's take a look," Sergeant Hannan said, and they rode toward it.

When they were closer Sergeant Hannan waved the patrol from a trot down to a walk. "Better approach easy.

Never know what you're going to run into. Could be more settlers on their way up from the States. If they are, we'll camp with 'em and socialize. Then again, they could be a camp of cowboys looking for lost stock. Or they could be rustlers for that matter."

Sensing the end of the day's journey, the horses walked quickly forward. Soon they were no more than two hundred yards from the campfire. Suddenly the gathering dusk exploded into a blaze of gunfire.

"*Scatter!*" Sergeant Hannan shouted, putting spurs to his horse. One of the patrol groaned and toppled from his saddle. The riderless horse galloped wildly away into the purple shadows, Winchester carbine swaying from side to side as it rocked from its sling across the saddle pommel.

Sergeant Hannan swung his horse around wide, riding closer to the campfire as he pulled his Winchester clear of its sling and levered a cartridge into the chamber. Flashes of fire erupted from the vicinity of the campfire and Sergeant Hannan fired a shot at them as he rode.

O'Reilly wheeled his horse around and was about to scatter when he saw Roy Wise fall to the ground. Amid a hail of lead, O'Reilly jumped down from his saddle, taking his Winchester with him. He dropped to a knee, lifted the Winchester to his shoulder and snapped a shot at the flashing red stabs near the campfire. Then he flung himself sideways as more bullets came his way.

Reaching the fallen Mountie, O'Reilly rolled him over on his back. "Where are you hit, Roy?"

Roy Wise didn't answer. He was dead, staring up lifelessly at the darkening sky.

Scott and McCormack had moved away the instant the shots erupted, a split-second ahead of Sergeant Hannan's shout. There was little cover on the grassed prairie, other than the rolling hills. Stabs of rifle fire flashed back at the camp from either side of O'Reilly, and he knew Scott and McCormack had also dismounted and were returning the fire.

117

Sergeant Hannan's voice rang out from somewhere in the shadows. "You in the camp—this is the Mounted Police! Put up your weapons."

The answer was a renewed burst of rifle fire from the camp. O'Reilly flattened himself into the ground, lying over Wise's body, instinctively trying to protect it from being hit again; it hadn't quite dawned upon him that Wise was dead.

Stretched out on the prairie grass, his horse lying prone beside him, Sergeant Hannan looked around, trying to spot the positions of the patrol. He didn't know Wise had been killed. It was too dark to see shapes but he could see the muzzle flashes from their rifles as they fired back at the camp.

Looking back at the camp, Sergeant Hannan counted the muzzle flashes, spread around the fire but beyond its illumination. "Five . . . six . . . seven . . . eight." Then two more. "Christ," he muttered. "They outnumber us two to one."

Who the hell were they? Cattle rustlers? Not likely. They would have no need to open fire on a Mounted Police patrol unless they were caught in the act of rustling, and this was just a campfire. There was no stock out there. If there had been, they'd be stampeding like mad with all the shooting. Whisky smugglers? Not likely. Indians? Maybe, if they thought they were being approached by a war party from a rival tribe. Despite the best efforts of the Mounted Police, different tribes still sent war parties to steal horses from one another. With their warrior instincts barely suppressed, they weren't averse to fighting each other. Many of them were still hereditary enemies. But he had called out to identify himself and the patrol.

Sergeant Hannan shouted to his men. "Move in on them, but be careful." He didn't shout out that they were outnumbered. He didn't need to give that information away. Besides, his men could count muzzle flashes as well as he could.

118

Finally realizing that Wise was dead, that there was nothing he could do for him, O'Reilly gripped his Winchester and crept forward. He too had counted the muzzle flashes and knew they were outnumbered two to one. More than that, now that Wise was dead.

A further fusillade of shots erupted from the camp and O'Reilly ducked low. A horse whinnied and screamed behind him and he knew that his horse had been hit.

A savage sense of rage swept over O'Reilly. Wise dead, now his own horse was hit. Raising himself to a kneeling position, he pulled his carbine into his shoulder and fired five shots in rapid succession at the camp, levering a fresh round into the chamber each time. After the fifth shot he threw himself to his right as far as he could and rolled over and over in the grass to put as much distance as he could between himself and where he had been when he fired the shots. A second later bullets whizzed across the prairie, speeding to the place where he had been. He shouldered the Winchester again and returned the fire.

Over to O'Reilly's right, Bob Scott poured a fire into the camp. To his left, Tom McCormack did the same. They heard a cry of pain from the camp and knew they had hit one of them.

More shots rattled backward and forward between the two sides as the Mounties gradually advanced toward the camp.

Sergeant Hannan was the closest. He counted only six muzzle flashes from the camp. Elated, he jumped to his feet and shouted. "Come on, boys!" He raced forward, firing his Winchester from the hip as he ran.

O'Reilly was almost as close but off to Sergeant Hannan's right. Scott was farther to the right again, while McCormack was to O'Reilly's left but a little back. Upon hearing the sergeant's shout, they all rose and ran forward, like the sergeant firing their Winchesters from the hip and levering as they ran.

Long-legged, O'Reilly reached the camp first. He

charged into the circle of light, leaping over a pile of blankets on the ground. The flickering flames illuminated scurrying shadows just beyond the camp. One of the shadows turned around, swinging a rifle pointed straight at O'Reilly's guts. In an instant O'Reilly recognized the buckskin body and painted face of an Indian. Still running, he swept his rife barrel into the Indian's face. The Indian pulled the trigger and a tremendous explosion and a stab of red erupted in front of O'Reilly. In a split-second O'Reilly waited for the bullet to tear into his body. But miraculously he felt nothing. The sudden movement of his swinging rifle had caught the Indian's rifle, knocking the barrel upward. The bullet singed O'Reilly's cheek, running a red furrow along the flesh above bone. O'Reilly didn't feel it, not yet; later it would sting like hell. But it left his ears ringing like church bells.

O'Reilly's rifle barrel struck the Indian's face a glancing blow but it didn't put him out of action. The Indian quickly levered another cartridge into the chamber, but O'Reilly brought his rifle barrel back. This time the muzzle whacked the brave on the ear, almost tearing it off. The brave howled in pain and dropped his rifle. Taking one hand off his Winchester, O'Reilly swung a mighty fist that crunched against the Indian's nose. The Indian went flying backward.

All around him O'Reilly saw activity . . . the glitter of Mounted Police brass buttons and belt buckles in the firelight, yellow-striped blue breeches and spurred boots. Shouts from Sergeant Hannan and Constable Scott, the metallic levering of Winchesters, shots, guttural shouts, the jingle of spur rowels. Running feet carrying Indians somewhere out in the darkness, pounding hoofbeats as they urged their ponies away.

Sergeant Hannan looked quickly around, seeing O'Reilly, Scott and McCormack. "Where's Wise?"

"Dead," O'Reilly answered.

"*Son of a bitch!*" Sergeant Hannan's bright blue eyes

120

fixed Scott and McCormack. "Get our horses. Quick! Before the Indians decide to circle around and try running them off."

O'Reilly glanced around the camp. Four buckskin covered bodies lay on the ground. Three had been shot; the fourth was the one O'Reilly had knocked down.

Sergeant Hannan rolled two of the dead Indians over onto their backs. They too had paint on their faces.

"War party."

O'Reilly's brow furrowed. "*War party?*"

"War parties steal horses from other tribes. To Indians, running off horses is part of warfare." Sergeant Hannan kneeled down beside one of the dead Indians and peered into the painted face. "Hey . . . wait a minute." Grabbing the Indian's ankles, he dragged the body close to the light of the campfire. Then he rubbed red ochre from the face. "This is Black Cloud, one of Lame Bear's friends, one of those two who got away from us down on the Blood reserve. Probably Prairie Wolf Man was with him. Some of those others could have been wanted as well. Likely that's why they opened fire on us."

He stood up, walked over and examined the others. "They're from across the line. Probably planning a raid on Crees or Assiniboines."

A shot cracked out on the darkened prairie. It was the heavy, punch-like sound of an Enfield. O'Reilly jumped; he knew his wounded horse had just been put out of its misery. A few minutes later Scott and McCormack rode up to the flickering campfire, towing two horses. The body of Roy Wise lay across the saddle of one.

Scott sat his saddle, expectantly awaiting the order to go after the escaping Indians. Sergeant Hannan shook his head. "No use chasing 'em in the dark. They've got too much of a head start."

While O'Reilly handcuffed the Indian he had knocked down, Sergeant Hannan and Tom McCormack lifted Wise's body off his horse's back and laid it on the ground

121

beside the light from the fire. They took off their hats and stared grim-faced at their late comrade.

"I'd like to know which son of a bitch it was who fired that shot," Sergeant Hannan said.

No one else spoke. They stood for a moment longer, then Sergeant Hannan said, "We'll bury the Indians and move out. What's left of that war party might get the idea to come back and snipe us from out on the prairie."

Chapter 12

The trumpeter was sounding the call for morning parade when Sergeant Hannan's patrol, with their Indian prisoner, rode into the Northwest Mounted Police barracks at Fort Macleod two days later. They had stopped at a ranch along the way and borrowed a wagon to carry Constable Wise's body.

Sergeant Hannan glanced at O'Reilly, riding Wise's horse. The furrow mark on his cheek was covered with congealed blood; it looked red and angry. "You'd better report to the surgeon at the post hospital and get that attended to."

Although saddened by the death of Roy Wise and his own horse, O'Reilly was pleased to be back at Fort Mcleod. It was the first time he had been back since he had left on transfer weeks earlier. It wasn't the post hospital he was interested in visiting, however. It was a certain young lady staying with her aunt and uncle at the officers' quarters.

They rode around the parade square, keeping clear of the lines of red-coated men forming up under the watchful eyes of Sergeant Major MacGregor. Sergeant Hannan, Constable Scott and O'Reilly took Constable Wise's body to the post hospital, leaving Tom McCormack to turn the Indian prisoner over to the guardroom NCO.

The post surgeon examined O'Reilly's cheek, then ordered the hospital sergeant to clean and dress it while he wrote out a death certificate on Constable Wise.

"There you are," the hospital sergeant said when he had finished. "Near as good as new."

O'Reilly left the post hospital and marched smartly around the parade square toward the officers' quarters on the west side of the square. Arriving at Inspector Cavannagh's house, he raised his fist and rapped firmly on the door. Then he stood with his breath held for fear that Ruth Baker would not be there, that she might have gone back home to New York.

The door was opened less than a minute later. Ruth, looking delightfully gorgeous in a yellow gingham dress, stood there, bathed in morning sunlight. Her violet eyes sparkled the instant she saw him.

"Hugh!" she said, smiling radiantly. Then the smile disappeared as she noticed the dressing on his cheek. "What happened? Are you all right?"

He grinned. "Just a bit of trouble with an Indian war party," he said as nonchalantly as he could manage. "A bullet nicked me."

Concern leaped into her eyes, and she asked a second time, "Are you all right?"

The grin on his dark face widened. "Right now, I've never felt better."

He stood on the porch step, his flashing dark eyes taking her in. It was the first time he had seen her without a hat and he liked the smooth chocolate-brown waves of her hair, which was brushed back from her brow and clipped in loose waves down the back of her neck.

She smiled again. "Won't you come inside? Do you have time to stay for a cup of coffee?"

"I'd be pleased to . . . if Inspector Cavannagh won't mind."

She stood aside to let him enter. "Of course he won't. Anyway, he's not at home at the moment. He's over at

124

headquarters. But he told me to invite you to dinner the next time you came to Fort Macleod. I've looked for you almost every day, but I haven't seen you until today. I was afraid you would never come."

O'Reilly stepped into the house and followed her into the parlor. The house was neatly furnished with what looked to O'Reilly to be good quality furniture. There were several pictures on the walls, some of Eastern scenery, some of ships at sea, which interested him, and two or three were photographs of earlier days in the Mounted Police taken at old Fort Walsh in the Cypress Hills. One of these he recognized from having seen it at Regina.

"Please sit down, Hugh. I'll put some coffee on. My aunt had to go into town. She does volunteer work for the Anglican Church."

They sat in the parlor drinking coffee. O'Reilly sat on the edge of his chair, balancing a delicate cup and saucer on his knee in a situation he was entirely unfamiliar with. But it didn't matter. He felt as though he was only one step down from heaven. They talked and laughed together, enjoying each other's company, two young people talking about the weather, the countryside, cowboys and Indians, the snow-crowned Rockies off to the west. Ruth asked him about his patrol, and how he had come to be wounded. Because he didn't want to think about the death of Roy Wise, whom he considered a friend, he talked only briefly about the patrol. He didn't mention the death of his horse, which had upset him just as much. So he pressed Ruth to talk about herself and to tell him about her own activities. She told him her aunt — Aunt April — planned to take her to Calgary to go shopping and sight-seeing, and on by train to the new but growing tourist resort and mineral hot springs at Bannff, eighty miles into the Rockies from Calgary. Ruth asked O'Reilly to tell her about some of the places he had seen when he was sailing the seas.

They were still talking happily, with O'Reilly onto his

fifth cup of coffee and his third buttered cake when the sounds of boots on the front porch announced the arrival of visitors.

"That will be Uncle Jack," Ruth said.

The front door opened and seconds later the tall, blue-uniformed figure of Inspector Cavannagh stepped into the parlor. By his side stood the beautiful, golden-haired woman O'Reilly had seen at the front door that day when he first arrived at Fort McLeod. Ruth rose, while O'Reilly stood up and stiffened to the closest approximation of attention that he could while holding a delicate china cup and saucer in front of him.

"Hello, Uncle Jack," Ruth said. "Aunt April."

"Hello, Ruth," Inspector Cavannagh and the woman beside him chorused together. The inspector's steel-blue eyes looked at O'Reilly. "Good morning, O'Reilly."

"Good morning, sir."

Inspector Cavannagh turned to the woman beside him. "April, this is Constable O'Reilly, the young man Ruth met on the train from Calgary." Inspector Cavannagh turned to O'Reilly. "Constable O'Reilly, I'd like you to meet my wife."

Still holding his cup and saucer, O'Reilly clicked his spurred heels together and inclined his head forward slightly. "Mrs. Cavannagh. I'm honored."

"Good morning, Constable O'Reilly," she said smilingly. She had the bluest eyes O'Reilly had ever seen. "I'm pleased to meet you. I've heard so much about you."

O'Reilly reddened under his tan.

Ruth said, "Would you like some coffee, Uncle Jack, Aunt April? I put on a fresh pot just before you arrived."

"That will be nice, Ruth," Mrs. Cavannagh said. "I'll help you."

"Oh, that won't be necessary, Aunt April. You sit down. I'll get it."

Inspector and Mrs. Cavannagh sat down, the inspector signalling O'Reilly to do the same. He glanced at O'Reilly's cheek. "You had some excitement the other night, O'Reilly. Bit of a wound?"

Subconsciously, O'Reilly's had went up to the dressing on his cheek. "Just a bullet graze, sir. The bandage makes it look worse, but the surgeon thought it might become infected if it wasn't dressed."

Inspector Cavannagh raised a finger to a scar on his right temple. "I know what you mean. I had one like it back in '75, eighteen years ago."

April Cavannagh smiled at her husband. "That's how Jack and I met. He had just ridden into old Fort Macleod. It was the original log fort built by Colonel Macleod and his men the year before. It was on a sort of isthmus running into the Old Man's River. I was an Anglican Mission nurse working with the Mounted Police to help the Indians. Jack had just left the American cavalry to come up here to join the Mounted Police. The doctor was busy at the time so I dressed his wound."

Inspector Cavannagh turned his head and looked into his wife's eyes. An expression came over the officer's face that O'Reilly hadn't seen before. It was a tender look, belying the legend of the steel-nerved man who had helped tame the Sioux warriors responsible for the annihilation of Colonel Custer and part of the Seventh United States Cavalry. Inspector Cavannagh said, "I fell in love with her then, but not long after that the Church transferred her and I didn't see her again for years."

Ruth returned with two cups of coffee and the four of them sat talking. O'Reilly had another cup—his sixth—before getting that edgy feeling that Sergeant Hannan would be looking for him. He stood up.

"If I may be excused, I should be getting back. Sergeant Hannan will probably be wanting to head back to Stand-off."

Inspector Cavannagh also rose. "I'll walk around the square with you, O'Reilly. It's time I was getting back to headquarters."

127

Ruth and Mrs. Cavannagh saw them to the door. Ruth held out her hand to O'Reilly. He took it and they shook politely. "It was nice to see you again, Mister O'Reilly. I do hope we meet again before I return to New York."

"I hope so too, Miss Baker."

O'Reilly and Inspector Cavannagh walked around the parade ground toward the headquarters building.

"We're holding our annual regimental ball next month, O'Reilly," Inspector Cavannagh said. "My niece would like to attend. She will find it colorful. I can arrange, of course, that she be escorted. There are single NCOs on the post. However, she likes you. I happen to know she would rather go with you than anyone else. I would appreciate it if you could see your way clear to escorting her."

O'Reilly jumped at the invitation. He couldn't dance, but he'd worry about that when the time came. "I'd be most pleased to do that, sir."

"I will, of course, pay any expenses you incur," Inspector Cavannagh added quickly.

"That won't be necessary, sir."

"Constables don't make much money, O'Reilly."

"That's all right, sir. I don't have much place to spend money down at Standoff."

They reached the headquarters building. Inspector Cavannagh paused before turning to enter. "Well, carry on, O'Reilly."

O'Reilly saluted and marched quickly away to find Sergeant Hannan.

On the ride back to Standoff, O'Reilly reined his horse alongside Sergeant Hannan.

"The annual regimental ball is coming up at Fort Macleod next month, Sergeant," O'Reilly said. "Any chance I might have a pass to attend?"

Sergeant Hannan didn't take his eyes off the trail ahead. "How long have you been on the flying patrol now,

O'Reilly?"

"Five weeks."

"Then you know better than to ask me that. How the hell am I expected to know whether I can spare you that far in advance? You know damn well how quickly things happen with us. We never know from one day to the next what might come up. Besides, you're junior man on the patrol. Scott or McCormack might want to go. They're senior. I'll have to give them first choice."

O'Reilly's spirits dropped and he rode in silence for the remainder of the trip.

O'Reilly returned to Fort Macleod two days later, when they buried Constable Wise with full military honors in the Mounted Police cemetery. He paraded with Sergeant Hannan, Scott and McCormack and the Fort Macleod command, and listened to Major Steele and the Anglican minister from the town conduct the service. It was a touching scene of regimental splendor . . . a full dress parade under clear blue skies, review order uniforms of scarlet and gold, white helmets with burnished brass spikes glinting in the sunshine, men on foot and men on horses, the Union Jack flying at half-mast, a trumpeter sounding *Last Post*, a firing party discharging volleys from their carbines over the open grave as Constable Wise's body in its flag-draped casket was lowered to its final resting place.

It was a parade that would have done justice to St. James's Palace at London, and O'Reilly reflected that it deserved a better setting than out in the middle of the wind-blown prairie.

They rode back to Standoff in silence as soon as the parade was over, each man's heart heavy with the loss of their late comrade.

* * *

129

The day following Constable Wise's funeral, Sergeant Hannan and his men patrolled from Standoff and were gone a week. When they got back, Constable Wise's replacement, a red-faced young man with blond hair, was waiting for them. His name was Clarence Dempsey.

During the next two weeks they patrolled backward and forward across the rolling prairie between Standoff and the Montana border, from the St. Mary's River on the eastern boundary of the Blood Indian reserve to the Rockies to the west. They rode up and down rolling hills, probed hundreds of coulees, splashed across river fords. They fought a prairie fire and turned back a raiding party of South Assiniboines intent on running Blood horses back across the border into Montana.

No further reports of cattle rustling were received by the Mounted Police, and Major Steele and his officers began to breathe easier. It looked as though the ceaseless activity of the flying patrols had brought some success. They hadn't caught the perpetrators, but they had seemingly checked their activities at least.

The fact that no further complaints of cattle rustling had been received hadn't escaped Sergeant Hannan's attention, and he and Constable Scott were discussing it as they rode side by side across the rolling prairie east of the St. Mary's on their way back to Standoff after a seven day, wide-ranging patrol.

"Could have been some gang of rustlers from below the line," Scott was saying. "Maybe they reckon they've made a good enough haul while they were doing it and decided to quit before they got caught."

Sergeant Hannan shook his head. "I don't reckon they'd have known the country well enough. All that rustling that went on for so long, without anyone getting caught, and no trace of the cattle . . . uh-uh, that would've taken some organizing, too much organizing for a gang that didn't know the country damn well."

O'Reilly, McCormack and the new man, Dempsey, rode

along behind Sergeant Hannan and Constable Scott. They weren't talking, each man lost in his own thoughts. Dempsey, not fully broken in to the rigors of patrolling, was almost asleep in his saddle. O'Reilly was thinking about Ruth and the forthcoming regimental ball at Fort Mcleod, which he had all but given up hope of attending.

While they were riding, they came upon a set of wagon tracks stretching across the prairie.

"That wagon's carrying a heavy load," Sergeant Hannan said, staring down at them from his saddle.

"Another settler, maybe," Scott suggested.

"Could be," Sergeant Hannan agreed. "Anyway, we'll have a look."

They followed the tracks. They had ridden several miles when they sighted a covered wagon climbing a long hill off in the distance. Legging their horses into a canter, they rode to overtake it. Suddenly the wagon bolted.

"He's trying to run," Sergeant Hannan shouted exultantly. "That's no settler. That's a whisky runner."

"He hasn't got a hope in hell of getting away from us," Constable Scott shouted back over the noise of the horses as they cantered across the rolling prairie.

But they had only covered a third of the distance when the wagon topped the hill and disappeared down the other side. They put their horses into a gallop. Saddles creaked as the Mounties leaned forward, hoofs pounded, the horses breathed heavily. The top of the hill came closer as they skimmed across the grass.

Moments later they crested the top of the hill and thundered on down the other side. The wagon tracks went down to a dip between two rolling hills. Off to the left ran a deep gulch. Farther down, the tracks led away from the gulch. Down in the dip was the wagon. As the patrol galloped down on it, the wagon slowed. Escape had been hopeless. A moment later they reined in to a trot alongside it.

"Pull up," Sergeant Hannan shouted at the driver.

131

The bearded driver pulled on the reins and stuck a boot up on the brake handle. The wagon ground to a stop.

"What's your hurry?" Sergeant Hannan growled.

The driver glared at him. He didn't look happy and he did not answer.

Sergeant Hannan said, "Let's see what's in the back of your wagon." He reined his horse over beside the wagon, leaned from his saddle and peered over the driver's shoulder into the canvas-covered back. To his astonishment, the wagon was empty.

"*What the hell* . . . ?"

He sat back in his saddle and looked hard at the bearded face of the man sitting on the driver's seat. Were the man's brown eyes mocking him? "Why were you running?" The sergeant's voice was taut with suspicion.

The driver licked his lips. "I . . . I thought you was Indians."

Sergeant Hannan scowled. "Dressed like *this?*" He jabbed a finger at his brass-buttoned jacket.

The bearded driver squinted his eyes up at the sky. "The sun was behind you. I couldn't see your uniforms."

Sergeant Hannan inclined his head at the wagon. "You always travel with nothing in your wagon?"

"I come up here from Fort Benton lookin' for a place to homestead. I figgered on findin' a place first. Then I'll go back and bring up my wife and our things."

Sergeant Hannan stared at the driver. He didn't believe him, but he had no proof that the man was lying. "All right, mister," he said, reining his horse away. "You can go on your way."

"Thanks," the driver said sarcastically. He kicked the brake handle free, flicked the reins and the wagon rolled on its way. The patrol sat their saddles watching it go. They watched for a long while, the wagon jolting along on its way, growing smaller and smaller in the distance to the north. Finally Sergeant Hannan reined his horse around.

"Let's go," he said and they rode back the way they had

132

come, Sergeant Hannan staring down at the wagon tracks beside them as they rode. Then his eyes narrowed and he stared harder. After a moment he legged his horse into a smart trot as it made its way back up toward the top of the hill. The gulch yawned deep just off to his right, its bottom covered with long grass and brush.

The constables jogged along in their saddles beside him. As they neared the top of the hill, Sergeant Hannan's freckled face creased into a grin. Turning in his saddle, he looked back over his shoulder. The wagon was a tiny speck in the distance. "You cunning son of a bitch!" Then he led his men up over the top of the hill in the direction they had come from.

But they didn't go all the way. Several miles off to their right rose a plateau. Sergeant Hannan swung off to his right and led them toward it. They reached it almost an hour later. The sergeant wheeled his horse around and raised his hand.

"We'll make a dry camp here."

"*Dry* camp?" Constable Scott glanced up at the afternoon sun, then he looked at Sergeant Hannan. "*Now?* What's doing, Sarge?"

Sergeant Hannan grinned. "You notice something strange about those wagon tracks?"

Neither Scott nor the other three said anything.

Sergeant Hannan said, "They were deep until they got close to that gulch. Then they suddenly got light."

Understanding crept over Scott's face. "You mean . . . ?"

Still grinning, Sergeant Hannan nodded. "That's exactly what I mean. Now, we'll just set down on top of this ridge. From up here we'll be able to see that gulch real good through field glasses. We'll just watch and wait."

Only his head showed as Sergeant Hannan lay flat on his stomach on top of the plateau and held a pair of

133

binoculars to his eyes while he watched the country to the northeast. Two hours passed before his patience was rewarded. A covered wagon crawled across the distant landscape, heading for the dip below the hill they had ridden over earlier.

Sergeant Hannan watched patiently as the wagon drew closer. He held his breath momentarily when the wagon veered over beside the deep gulch. Then it stopped. The driver climbed down off his seat. He stood there for several minutes, looking around in all directions before he walked to the edge of the gulch and stood looking down. A moment later he climbed down into it and disappeared.

Sergeant Hannan watched intently. The man was gone for quite a while before his head appeared at the edge of the gulch, then his shoulders, then his body. He carried something. Sergeant Hannan strained his eyes to see what it was. It looked like a jug. And it looked heavy. The man carried it to the back of the wagon and loaded it aboard. Then he returned to the gulch and disappeared again. After a further interval he reappeared carrying another jug, which he also placed in the back of the wagon.

Several more times he repeated the process, until he had loaded nine jugs. Then he climbed back up onto the driver's seat, wheeled the wagon around and drove back toward the north.

Moving back from the edge of the plateau, Sergeant Hannan stood up and ran a few yards to where his patrol waited. "Mount up," he said.

They swung themselves up into their saddles and were soon cantering their horses in pursuit of the wagon a second time.

They made a wide swing down from the plateau and came around several miles on the far side of the hill. The wagon was lumbering slowly along a low depression when the patrol topped a slight rise and saw it no more than three hundred yards away. They cantered their horses toward it, approaching it from its side. They were a hundred

134

and fifty yards away when the driver heard them and looked up. This time he made no attempt to escape.

When they pulled up alongside the wagon, Sergeant Hannan grinned at the bearded driver. "It didn't take you long to find a place to homestead on. Now I suppose you've been back to Benton, collected your wife and belongings, which are in the back of your wagon, and returned."

The driver's face was like a thundercloud.

Reining his horse over to the wagon, Sergeant Hannan reached out, grabbed the canvas flap and threw it back. He looked in over the driver's shoulder and counted nine cream-colored earthenware jugs with black lettering which read *Coal Oil*.

"Coal oil, huh?" He reached in and lifted one of the jugs out. He pulled the cork and put his nose over the neck.

"Some coal oil! It mightn't start a fire in a pot belly stove, but it would sure as hell set flames to an Indian's belly."

Avoiding Sergeant Hannan's eyes, the man sat on the wagon seat and stared morosely down at the cracked leather of the traces in his hands.

"That was some cunning trick," Sergeant Hannan said, "throwing those jugs down into that gulch after you saw us, then going back to pick them up again after you thought we were gone. Only trouble was, we were a little smarter than you reckoned on. And now, mister, this outfit is seized in the name of the Queen and you're under arrest for the unlawful importation of liquor into the Northwest Territories."

They were sitting around their campfire, their prisoner handcuffed by the wrist to one of the wheels of his wagon. O'Reilly smoked his pipe. Sergeant Hannan got up from where he was sitting, walked around the fire and kneeled down beside O'Reilly.

"That young Blood buck who showed you Gus Breen's whisky running trail . . . you reckon he was telling you the truth?"

Turning his head toward the sergeant, O'Reilly took the pipe out of his mouth and nodded. "I reckon he was, Sergeant."

"Reckon you could find it again?"

O'Reilly nodded a second time. "I could find it."

The ghost of a smile lit up on Sergeant Hannan's face. "Good. I have a feeling Breen is going to make another run any time now. But this time we're going to get the son of a bitch."

Chapter 13

From a shale-littered slope just above the pointed green tops of pine trees running up the lower side of a mountain, O'Reilly and Sergeant Hannan watched a trail that led from Montana.

It wasn't much of a trail, little more than the bottom of the valley what wound its way between the mountains towering above. About thirty yards wide, it was covered with small rocks and was fringed on both sides by pine trees. It was the trail that Porcupine Quill had shown O'Reilly, telling him it was the one Gus Breen used.

Sergeant Hannan expressed his doubts. "This is too far west. It's well hidden, but it would take Breen too long to get around this way. He'd be hauling the stuff from Benton, and he'd have to haul it into these mountains and up through the passes all the way. That's a long trip, too long. It'd be closer and easier to run straight across somewhere over the prairies. Whisky runners like a fast, easy trip."

O'Reilly had given the matter a lot of thought. "But it would be worth it. This way he might make fewer trips because they take longer, but he doesn't get caught. He doesn't lose whisky, outfits or men. He doesn't have to pay fines. Each trip he makes is a profit."

Sergeant Hannan merely grunted.

They sat among the shale and waited, watching all the time. Their brown duck stable jackets blended in with the color of the rock, and they had replaced their yellow-striped blue breeches with fatigue trousers the same color as their jackets. Also, they hadn't polished their brass buttons for several days, allowing them to tarnish and grow dull so the sun wouldn't reflect off them. Down below, hidden among the pines fringing the trail, the other members of the patrol waited.

It was afternoon of the second day when they spotted movement down the trail. Through binoculars Sergeant Hannan saw two horsemen riding side by side. They carried rifles cradled in the crook of their arms and wore belted pistols around their waists with bullet loops full.

Shortly after, two canvas-covered wagons in tandem followed around a bend.

Sergeant Hannan said, "That's a whisky peddling outfit, sure as hell. Look at those mules, pulling hard." He ignored the fact that O'Reilly didn't have binoculars. "But I don't see Gus Breen. He's not driving that outfit, and he's sure as hell not either one of those two lookouts.".

They watched the mule-drawn wagons crawling along the trail. The two armed lookouts, riding half a mile ahead of the wagons, were nearing a second bend, after which the trail led in a more or less straight line past where Scott, McCormack and Dempsey waited.

Sergeant Hannan's red brows met above the bridge of his nose in a severe scowl. "Too damn bad that's not Breen down there." His voice carried an unmistakable tone of disappointment, even resignation. "Anyway, let's get down into position to take 'em."

He was about to slide down the shale into the cover of the pines when O'Reilly grabbed his shoulder. Excitement

138

edged the younger man's voice. "Wait, Sarge!"

Sergeant Hannan stopped. O'Reilly was pointing farther along the trail. The NCO lifted the binoculars again. A lone horseman was riding around the first bend, about half to three-quarters of a mile behind the wagons.

Sergeant Hannan watched for a long moment. Then he muttered, "That's Breen, by Christ! That's him."

He handed the binoculars to O'Reilly. "Take a look, young O'Reilly. That's the most wanted whisky runner in the Northwest Territories. He's been peddling firewater since back in the days before there were any Mounted Police in the country. He's an old Fort Whoop-Up man. Knows the country inside out and backward. That's why he's lasted this long. Speaks the Blood and Blackfoot dialects real good, too."

O'Reilly saw a squarely built man with a black beard and a black hat. He carried a rifle in a saddle scabbard, butt protruding upward just in front of his right leg.

Sergeant Hannan said, "Let's get down to the trail."

Sliding down the shale-covered slope, they made their way in among the pines until they reached the edge of the trail below. Quickly Sergeant Hannan told his men what he and O'Reilly had seen, then he explained his plan.

"Bob, you and Tom get across into the trees on the other side of the trail. I want to take those two lookouts without any fuss. I don't want any shots fired, neither by them nor us. I don't want Breen getting any warning, any hint that anything's wrong. Tom, you go down the trail a piece, stay mounted in case one of them tries to make a run for it. Both of you muzzle your horses so they don't give the game away. Now, hurry, before they come around the bend."

Bob Scott and Tom McCormack led their horses and hurried across the trail and into the trees beyond, where

McCormack mounted and guided his horse through the pines until he was farther down alongside the trail. Scott pulled his Winchester from his saddle and waited.

Sergeant Hannan had selected a spot where there was a small clearing about twenty yards long with grass as high as a horse's belly. O'Reilly and Dempsey, both mounted, waited beside the clearing. Sergeant Hannan positioned himself among the pines and some underbrush, where he could watch the trail without being seen.

It was only moments later when the two lookouts rounded the second bend and walked their horses along the rock-littered trail, heading toward the hidden Mounties. Sergeant Hannan watched them ride closer.

Still cradling their rifles, they rode side by side, talking and laughing as though they didn't have a care in the world. Scowling, Sergeant Hannan thought, *they're not earning their pay.*

Soon he could hear the ring of shod hoofs on rocks as well as voices and laughter.

As the two lookouts rode unconcernedly by, Sergeant Hannan and his men emerged on both sides of the trail, Winchesters pointed.

Sergeant Hannan's voice rasped out sharply. "Hold it right where you are! Drop those rifles and get your hands up. Don't make a false move and don't make a sound. If I have to drop you, I will."

Utter amazement spread across the lookouts' faces. They raised their hands, their rifles dropping to the stony ground with a clatter.

"Get down off your horses. Slow and easy."

Their eyes darting around wildly, the pair did as they were told.

"Now get over here. Dempsey, take their horses."

O'Reilly covered them from his saddle while Dempsey took their horses and Sergeant Hannan lifted their revolvers from their holsters and handcuffed their wrists behind their backs. Then Sergeant Hannan led them into the trees well away from the trail and sat them on the ground, where he tied rope around their ankles and stuffed gags into their mouths. Leaving Dempsey to stand guard over them as well as looking after the horses, Sergeant Hannan returned to the trees bordering the trail, where O'Reilly joined him to wait for the wagons and Gus Breen.

Before long the mule-drawn tandem of wagons rounded the bend, the mules plodding toward them. Sergeant Hannan and O'Reilly watched and waited. O'Reilly had patrolled with Sergeant Hannan long enough now to recognize the eagerness coiled up inside him. He was like a kid awaiting the arrival of Santa Claus, so anxious he was to get his hands on his long-time quarry. O'Reilly tried to suppress the smile pulling the corners of his mouth.

The wagons drew closer, their iron-bound wheels rattling on the rocky trail. The sound grew louder and louder, until the wagons were level with the waiting patrol.

Sergeant Hannan stepped out of the trees, revolver steady in his hand. "All right, sunshine," he said to the Negro driver. "Hold it right there." The Negro's eyes widened, white against his dark face. He made no attempt to reach the pistol at his waist.

"Drive the wagon over here," Sergeant Hannan said, pointing. Off the trail."

Frightened, the Negro steered the mule team off the trail into the long grass of the clearing. Sergeant Hannan made sure he drove it far enough off the trail so the wagons couldn't be seen by the lone horseman following until he was almost on the spot.

"Get down," Sergeant Hannan ordered.

Under the intimidating barrel of O'Reilly's Winchester,

the Negro complied with the order. Sergeant Hannan climbed up onto the seat of the lead wagon and unlashed the canvas flaps. Impatiently jerking them aside, he peered into the back. His face lit up when he saw the contents—kegs of whisky packed solid on the deck. He climbed down and walked alongside the tandem to the second wagon, where he did the same. It was also fully loaded. Then he retraced his steps and climbed back up onto the seat of the first wagon.

He spoke quickly to O'Reilly, stepped into the back and pulled the canvas flaps back into place. That done, he sat down on one of the kegs and waited. O'Reilly pushed the prisoner ahead of him into the trees to join the two handcuffed lookouts.

Sitting in the stifling interior of the front wagon, the sun beating down on the canvas covering, it seemed an eternity to Sergeant Hannan before he heard the clip-clop of horse's hoofs coming along the trail.

Gus Breen's eyes narrowed when he saw the tandem of wagons sitting in the bright sunshine in the high grass beside the trail. Momentary suspicion twisted his face as he sat stock-still in his saddle. He stared fixedly at the wagons for a moment, then he cursed.

"Ebenezer, God damn you! You've been swiggin' on the whisky again and gone to sleep. You careless son of a bitch! Drive them wagons back onto the trail and get movin'. We ain't got time to waste!"

He gave his horse a couple of angry kicks and rode it toward the wagons.

"Ebenezer, you hear me, damn you?"

Breen pulled alongside the driver's seat of the front wagon. *"Ebenezer!* Where the hell are you?"

Standing in his stirrups, Breen reached out for the canvas flap, pulled it savagely aside and looked in. To his astonishment he found himself staring into the black muzzle of a .476 Enfield.

142

"Good afternoon, Gus. You're under arrest."

"What the hell is this?" Breen demanded, his voice echoing with righteous indignation. "You got nothing on me. I don't know anything about these wagons. They ain't mine."

Sergeant Hannan stepped forward and climbed out of the wagon, his revolver pushing Breen back onto his saddle. "This is your outfit, Gus, and I'll prove it in court, even if I have to ride down to Fort Benton myself and dig up the evidence. Now climb down off that saddle. I'll just slap a pair of handcuffs on you. Then we'll take you and your outfit to Fort Macleod. You're out of business, Gus. And you're going to stay out of business for a long time."

The neat gray buildings of the Mounted Police barracks at Fort Macleod stood on the flat in the distance, the prairie wind whipping the Union Jack at the top of the flagpole.

O'Reilly and Sergeant Hannan rode at the head of the small cavalcade traveling along the trail to the barracks. The mule-drawn tandem of wagons followed, with Gus Breen and his three accomplices sitting handcuffed on them, their horses towed behind. Constable Scott rode alongside the wagons, McCormack and Dempsey brought up the rear.

Sergeant Hannan looked extremely pleased. "You still want a pass to attend the regimental ball?" he suddenly asked.

Surprised by the complete unexpectedness of the question, O'Reilly stammered a reply. "Ah . . . yes, Sarge . . . sure."

"Got your eye on a pretty young lass, eh?"

"Yes . . . yes, I have." O'Reilly didn't want to tell him she was Inspector Cavannagh's niece. The sergeant might get the wrong idea. After all, he had spoken with her before he knew she was an inspector's niece.

An uncharacteristically benevolent smile on his face, Sergeant Hannan nodded. "Well, you can have your pass. In fact, I might even go to the ball myself. Not that I'm a dancing man, mind you. But I can watch the dancing, and perhaps have a drink or two with some of the other sergeants in the Sergeants' Mess."

Chapter 14

The sun was about to set behind the Rockies to the west as Hugh O'Reilly marched around the barrack square. Fort Macleod was alive with activity . . . officers and NCOs and their ladies, the regimental guard, the orderly officer, the color party standing beside the flagpole in the middle of the square, the trumpeter ready to sound *Retreat*.

O'Reilly wore his dress uniform. He felt nervous. It was the evening of the annual Fort Macleod regimental ball. He had half-hoped Ruth would have turned down his offer to escort her. He would have been hurt and disappointed, but at the same time he would have been relieved. It would have been simpler. At least he wouldn't have felt nervous. He was nervous because he couldn't dance.

He was halfway to Inspector Cavannagh's house when the trumpeter commenced to blow *Retreat* and the color party started lowering the Union Jack. The orderly officer saluted and the regimental guard presented arms. O'Reilly slammed to a halt, executed a left turn and stood at attention facing the flag. He remained that way until the trumpeter had finished and the color party untied the flag from the halyards and began folding it. Then he resumed his journey around the square.

Reaching Inspector Cavannagh's house, he turned in

and walked along the boardwalk to the front door and knocked. Inspector Cavannagh, wearing mess regimentals, opened the door. O'Reilly saluted.

"Good evening, Constable O'Reilly. I'm glad you were able to make it. Come in."

"Thank you, sir." O'Reilly stepped in past him and took off his pill-box. Inspector Cavannagh led him into the parlor. "Sit down, O'Reilly. The ladies will be down shortly. Drink?"

"Yes, thank you, sir."

"Scotch, brandy?"

"Scotch, please."

The inspector poured drinks and handed O'Reilly a glass. They raised their glasses. "The Queen," Inspector Cavannagh toasted.

"The Queen," O'Reilly repeated.

"God bless her and the Royal Family."

The scotch tasted good and O'Reilly felt his nervousness slipping away a little.

"How are you liking the flying patrol, O'Reilly?" Inspector Cavannagh asked conversationally.

"Fine, sir."

"Are you and Sergeant Hannan getting along well together?"

"Yes, sir."

Inspector Cavannagh stood in front of O'Reilly, holding his drink in one hand, his other arm behind his back. "A good man, Sergeant Hannan. A bit of a rough diamond at times, but a good man."

"Yes, sir."

"Doesn't always see eye to eye with divisional headquarters over certain matters, but a good man all the same. Knows his work, and he's a good man in a tight situation. A bit hot tempered at times, but that seems to be an Irish characteristic, eh, O'Reilly?" The inspector smiled.

O'Reilly smiled also and nodded. "I suppose so, sir."

The women came downstairs a few moments later, Ruth wearing a dove-gray gown that suited her complexion and chocolate-brown hair. Her violet eyes sparkled as she gave him a smile that instantly sent him head-over-heels in love with her. Mrs. Cavannagh looked charming in a pale blue off-the-shoulder gown and pearl necklace.

They engaged in polite conversation while the men finished their drinks. Ruth sent shivers of delight down O'Reilly's spine when she reached up and touched the bullet scar on his cheek.

"Is it sore at all?" she asked, still concerned.

"No," O'Reilly replied, his face flushing, conscious of the presence of the legendary Inspector Cavannagh.

They left the house and walked around the barrack square. It was a delightful, warm July evening, but the wind was blowing as usual. The two nine-pounder field guns, shells stacked beside them in pyramid shapes, stood sentinel around the square as if on guard to protect the Force's hallowed traditions. The white flagpole rose empty against the darkening sky. On the far side of the parade ground, carbine carrying sentries in scarlet tunics and white Wolseley-pattern helmets marched around the barracks.

A wing of the barracks had been converted temporarily into a reception area and a dancing room for the regimental ball. NCOs and men had worked assiduously to disguise the spartan appearance of the place, varnishing floors and decorating walls with steel-tipped bamboo lances and red and white pennons, steel spurs and bits, curb chains, crossed swords and rifles, draped Union Jacks flanking the portrait of Queen Victoria on one wall and pictures of Colonel Herchmer, the Force's Commissioner, and Major Steele on another. Boughs of spruce and pine had been placed around the walls, and tables and benches had been pushed against the far wall, the tables to host a fine meal of roast beef, chicken, asparagus, lettuce, baked potato, curry and salad. The place smelled of soap and leather, and a fine covering of dust lay on everything, a reminder that they were out on the wind-blown prairie frontier hundreds of miles from civilization.

Major Steele and his wife met the incoming guests at the head of a reception line, while the Mounted Police band played martial music. An inspector introduced each guest or couple to Major and Mrs. Steele.

When Inspector Cavannagh arrived at the head of the reception line he shook hands with Major and Mrs. Steele. Then he said, "Sir, you already know my niece, Miss Ruth Baker, but may I introduce Constable O'Reilly. He arrived here on transfer from the Depot Division at Regina two months ago."

Major Steele shook hands with Ruth, then turned to O'Reilly. O'Reilly stiffened to attention before shaking hands with the commanding officer. The officer's hand-shake was like iron. He smiled slightly behind his wide moustache.

"Good evening, Constable. Nice that you were able to join us."

"My pleasure, sir," said O'Reilly, then he and Ruth fol-lowed Inspector and Mrs. Cavannagh into the "ballroom."

The band changed to popular pieces as color filled the long room. Mounties in scarlet dress tunics and long blue over-alls with wide yellow stripes down the legs, the ladies in long gowns of pink and blue and green and orange, civilian men in dark dinner jackets or white ties and tails, and one or two simply wearing dark suits. They were the district's leading citizenry—ranchers, merchants and busi-nessmen. O'Reilly noticed Iron-Fist Taggart among them.

When all the guests were in the room, the band broke into a march and Major and Mrs. Steele led the couples into a grand march. They marched and promenaded around the floor until they were a mass of colored move-ment, and then the finale came when the couples broke off into a short but whirling dance. O'Reilly was able to handle that because the dance was indeed short and the floor crowded. Everyone was too busy taking part to notice that he couldn't dance.

But when it came to the next dance, really the *first* dance, O'Reilly's knees felt as though they would buckle underneath him, they turned to water. He did not want to get out on the floor, but Ruth was so enthusiastic to enjoy the evening, and her smile was so inviting, that he didn't have the heart not to.

However, first he had to confess.

"I should've told you . . . I can't dance."

"Not at all?"

"No," he answered miserably.

She looked up at him through her violet eyes and smiled. "Well," she said, taking his hand and leading him onto the floor, "just watch what everyone else does and do the same."

She slipped in close to him, and he placed an arm around her and held her hand in his.

"Just follow me," Ruth said, "and move your feet with the music."

And onto the floor they went, mixing with the dancing couples.

Despite the sweeping and cleaning and washing and painting, the boots of the men and the ladies' shoes ground a fine covering of dust into the varnished floor. They knew they were not in the plush ballroom of the Dominion Hotel or the Grand Trunk Pacific or the Royal Alexander of the cities back east, but hundreds of miles away in a converted Mounted Police barracks at Fort Macleod, Northwest Territories. However, for the moment that didn't matter. The music reminded them of other places and other times.

The ladies wore gowns that hadn't been worn since New Year's Eve, or gowns they had spent months making for

149

this occasion. If O'Reilly had thought about it at all, he would have presumed that Ruth had brought hers with her from New York in anticipation of just such an occasion to wear it. The men's uniforms and the ladies' gowns made whirls of color down the length of the room.

O'Reilly lost some of his nervousness. His greatest fear, that he would step on Ruth's toes, didn't eventuate. As they danced, she gazed up into his eyes and he smiled down into hers.

The long room was full to bursting, and with so many people it became warm, especially after the heat of the long midsummer July day.

O'Reilly managed the first few dances with Ruth, then Inspector Cavannagh danced with her and O'Reilly dutifully escorted Mrs. Cavannagh to the floor.

"I'm not very good at this," he apologized.

Mrs. Cavannagh smiled reassuringly. "The most important thing is that you enjoy yourself. And I know Ruth is having a wonderful time in your company."

After the next dance, O'Reilly led Ruth outside, where it was cooler in the evening shadows. The strains of the band followed them.

"It's a beautiful evening," Ruth said. "Warm, but not stifling like it sometimes is back home at this time of the year. Yet I like the heat and the smells of summer."

"Out here you smell mostly dust," O'Reilly said. "I know what you mean about the humidity of Eastern summers. I'm an Easterner, remember? What we call Maritimers in Canada."

She smiled, her teeth showing white in the shadows. "I remember. I love the beauty of the mountains out here in the West. Look," she said, pointing, "you can see them tonight, even in the dark, that long line of white over there."

"That's because you know they're there."

"No. I can see them. Look. They're there, almost as

150

plain as in the light of day."

He made a pretense of peering where she pointed. "So they are," he said, grinning.

"Oh, you're fooling with me," she said, shaking his arm playfully.

"We can see them because there's a full moon tonight."

Looking up at it, he suddenly felt a moment of foreboding, and then it passed, as quickly as it came. It was unexplainable, and he could not imagine why he had felt that way. Then Ruth's voice broke into his half-formed thoughts.

"It's marvelous what they do out here on the frontier. The ball has all the atmosphere of a formal ball back in New York."

A pang of jealousy stabbed through O'Reilly at the thought of Ruth attending a formal ball with some eligible young man down East.

When they returned to the ball, O'Reilly led Ruth over to the punch bowl and found her a glass. As they sipped, O'Reilly glanced around. The band was playing a sonata. In the entranceway leading to one of the adjoining rooms where the unattached men could stand around or sit while smoking or watching the dancing, he noticed Iron-Fist Taggart talking with Major Steele. Further into the room he saw Inspector Cavannagh and Sergeant Hannan engaged in conversation. He noticed that Sergeant Hannan, although listening to Inspector Cavannagh, had his eyes riveted on Taggart's back. Sergeant Hannan's words as they rode out to Taggart's ranch came back to O'Reilly . . . "*He drifted up this way from down south of the border years ago . . . he owned nothing more than a horse, saddle, rifle and the clothes he was wearing. Now he's an aspiring cattle king with one of the largest leases in the district. I've even heard he's planning to run for election as local member of Parliament.*"

Just then that sense of foreboding returned to him.

Again it passed just as quickly. And again he couldn't explain it.

A moment later the band started up with a lively two-step, and Ruth took O'Reilly's hand and led him onto the floor, where they whirled and twirled with the other couples.

After three more dances, which he miraculously stumbled his way through, O'Reilly returned to the punch bowl for two more glasses. He was about to take one to Ruth when Inspector Cavannagh approached him.

"Sergeant Hannan told me about the part you played in the apprehension of Gus Breen, O'Reilly. Good work."

"It wasn't my doing, sir. It was an Indian, a young Blood. He showed me the trail Breen used."

"So Sergeant Hannan informed me. But congratulations are in order, all the same. It's the sort of cooperation we like to see between Indians and the Force. That young Blood sounds as though he would make a good Mounted Police scout. We use them, you know. They work out well. You might consider asking whether he'd like a job when you see him again. All he has to do is provide his own horse. We supply the rest—saddle, weapons, rations and twenty-five dollars a month."

O'Reilly nodded. "I'll do that, sir." But he wondered whether the offer would still hold if Inspector Cavannagh knew Porcupine Quill was a horse thief.

The bandsmen perspired in the closeness of the room as they played a reel. Couples danced by on the floor in front of them . . . flashes of scarlet and gold, of pink and blue and green, of black and white. Dance followed dance and the evening moved quickly.

As he held Ruth in his arms, O'Reilly thought that he could be content to spend the rest of his life like that. It was his momentary version of heaven. Then he became sad as he realized that this night could be the last time he would see her. He didn't know when he might get into

Fort Macleod again. And she couldn't remain indefinitely.

As if the same thoughts were going through her mind, Ruth asked, "Will you be sorry to see me go home to New York, Hugh?"

Even though he had been thinking something the same, her question took him by surprise and he didn't answer immediately. "Yes," he finally said. "Will you be sorry to go?"

"Yes." She paused as they danced. Then quickly, eagerly, she said, "I really don't have to go back just yet. I can stay for a little while longer—as long as Uncle Jack and Aunt April will have me."

O'Reilly smiled down at her. "If it was up to me, I'd let you stay forever."

O'Reilly enjoyed the rush of cool mountain air fanning his cheeks as he rode steadily through the night back to Standoff. It was three o'clock in the morning and after the closeness of the crowded dancing room, the coolness of early morning was refreshing.

It was a two hour ride to Standoff. Once the ball was over, he had taken Ruth home to Inspector Cavannagh's house and said goodnight. Then he had saddled up his horse, ridden out of the barracks and headed out along the Standoff trail.

Sergeant Hannan's horse was still in the stables when O'Reilly left. He didn't know whether his sergeant would be following shortly. He had seen Sergeant Hannan and Sergeant Major MacGregor together, and it had looked as though they had been imbibing. Sergeant Hannan might remain at Fort Macleod for the night. But he was a senior non-commissioned officer, and O'Reilly just a constable. The sergeant had given him a pass to attend the regimental ball but he hadn't said anything about dallying overly long at Fort Macleod. O'Reilly's pass expired at *Reveille*, which was five-thirty in the morning, just two and a half hours away, so he had decided he should get back.

The moon still rode high in the sky, and O'Reilly had no trouble following the trail. The miles passed by as he posted to the movements of his trotting horse, his mind on the ball and the pleasant evening he had enjoyed. Then, without warning, that sense of foreboding returned once more. He tried to fathom it, tried to reason why. The only answer he could come up with was that he had become melancholy over the thought of Ruth's inevitable departure back to New York.

As he rode, he wrestled with that thought. *I shouldn't have let myself get so hung up on her. I knew she was only out here for a visit, that she'd eventually go back. I should've known better. Anyway, I'm out here to be a Mounted Policeman,* he told himself with forced resolve, *not a lovesick dandy.*

Suddenly his horse stumbled and O'Reilly somersaulted through the air. After what seemed an eternity, he landed on his shoulder in the grass beside the trail.

It took him a moment to realize what happened. His shoulder hurt and at first he thought he had dislocated it. Then he got dazedly to his feet and shook his head to clear the swimming sensation. He breathed a sigh of relief as he realized he was only winded.

The next instant alarm filled him as he looked for his horse, the same horse Roy Wise used to ride. It stood, head lowered, the reins dangling freely over its head. It stood with one hoof held gingerly just above the ground.

He hurried over to the animal. "Are you hurt, boy?" The horse lifted its head and looked at him. Its eyes glistened in the moonlight. Kneeling down beside it, he ran his hands down its legs.

While he was kneeling he suddenly stiffened, cocking his head. *What the hell's that?* He listened intently for several seconds. Drumming, a distant drumming . . . then

154

he heard faint bellowing. He listened further. Now he could no longer hear it. Lowering himself flat on the grass, he pressed an ear against the ground. A distant, muted thunder . . . a rumbling. It seemed to shake the ground. *Christ!* Hoofbeats! Hundreds of them. Then vaguely, almost so indistinct that he wasn't sure whether he was hearing it or imagining it, he heard—or thought he heard—high-pitched yells carried in the night air.

O'Reilly got up off the ground and finished examining his horse. He checked the one leg particularly thoroughly, pressing the tendons gently, but couldn't find anything wrong. He breathed a sigh of relief.

"Must've hit a gopher hole, boy. But it scared hell out of you, didn't it? Scared hell out of me, too."

He climbed back up into the saddle, gathered his reins and gently urged the animal into a trot. It seemed none the worse for the experience. O'Reilly legged and reined it into a canter, then pulled it off the trail and across the prairie in the direction of the sounds he had heard.

He rode for several miles, stopping half a dozen times to listen. He could still hear occasional faint rumblings. Wondering whether it could be distant thunder, he peered up at the night sky, looking long and hard toward the distant line of mountains, still slightly visible and white against the dark blue to the west. But the sky was clear of cloud wherever he looked. No, it wasn't thunder. It sounded like cattle on the move. But the middle of the night was an odd time to be moving cattle. Unless—?

O'Reilly pushed his horse on farther. A mixture of curiosity and instinct lured him on. But after a half-dozen miles he was no nearer to the sounds. If anything, they seemed farther away, still only indistinct. He reined to and stood in his stirrups, peering across the moonlit-bathed shadows of the rolling prairie, but seeing nothing unusual, nothing moving.

Slowly, reluctantly, he reined his horse around and

155

headed back toward the Standoff trail. It was useless to continue chasing a ghost. For that matter, he wasn't sure he had been chasing anything at all. And anyway, what was he going to do about it if it was cattle or horses being run off? He was alone and unarmed.

But the foreboding feeling remained in him. It was still with him as the first gray streaks of dawn lightened the eastern sky and the outpost buildings at Standoff came into view.

Sergeant Hannan returned to Standoff in the afternoon. He had just stabled his horse, crossed the yard and gone into his office when a second horseman clattered up to the outpost. Iron-Fist Taggart.

His face a thundercloud, the big, burly rancher swung down from his saddle and stalked toward the main building containing the offices and barracks. He almost kicked the fence gate open. Without pausing to knock, he slammed open the screen door and barged in. Sergeant Hannan stood inside his office removing his pill-box and his shiny dress belt.

"While you redcoats were all at Fort Macleod dancing around like a bunch of gigolos," Iron-Fist's gravelly voice thundered, "those bloody rustlers ran off half my cattle. Why the hell weren't some of you out on patrol protecting the interests of hard working cattlemen instead of waltzing around a bloody dance floor?"

Sergeant Hannan glared back at Taggart. "We have a habit out here in the Territories. It's called knocking on a door before trying to pull the thing off its God damn hinges. It seems people don't practice it in England or Australia or wherever you come from."

"Don't try and fob me off with that kind of bullshit, Hannan!"

"I seem to recall seeing you at that dance, Taggart."

156

"It's not my job to be patrolling the prairies protecting the lives and property of decent, law abiding citizens. That's your job." As he said that, Taggart poked a hard finger into Sergeant Hannan's chest.

"Get your finger out of my chest, Taggart." Sergeant Hannan's voice was deceptively soft. Even so, O'Reilly heard every word spoken as he listened from the barrack room at the rear of the building.

"What are you going to do about it, Hannan?" Taggart said, but he dropped his hand.

Holding his belt in his hand, Sergeant Hannan said, "You're not fooling anyone with that decent, law abiding citizen talk, Taggart. How the hell is it that you came into this part of the country a few years back with nothing but a horse and saddle, and now you're a big-time rancher?"

"Don't talk to me like that, Hannan. I could make things bloody tough for you. All I got to do is make a complaint to Steele about you and you won't be wearing those stripes on your arm."

"Like I told you the last time you said something like that, Taggart, the day you can swing that sort of weight with the Mounted Police, I'll turn in my uniform. Your kind is what's spoiling this country. I'd rather see the Indians have it back than the likes of you."

Sergeant Hannan rolled his belt loosely and laid it on the table he used as a desk. Taggart watched him, his big fists clenched.

"I could take you apart, Hannan."

Just then the barrack room door opened and O'Reilly stepped into the hallway and strolled along the hallway until he stood in the doorway of Sergeant Hannan's office. Thrusting out his jaw, he looked Iron-Fist Taggart squarely in the eye as Taggart turned his head at the sound of O'Reilly's footsteps. O'Reilly didn't say anything; he simply stood in the sergeant's doorway staring Taggart down. At six-two and a hundred and ninety pounds,

157

O'Reilly was a magnificently proportioned young man with wide shoulders, deep chest and lean waist. But Taggart was bigger and heavier, standing two inches taller and outweighing O'Reilly by a good twenty pounds.

Taggart stared back at O'Reilly for more than twenty seconds, neither man saying a word. Then Taggart suddenly snapped his head back to look at Sergeant Hannan.

"I want action on my rustled stock, Hannan. You and your men better get your arses onto your saddles and out lookin' for rustlers. Otherwise, I'll be riding into Fort Macleod and giving Steele an earful."

Taggart spun around on his heel to leave. O'Reilly stepped aside to let him pass. Without giving O'Reilly another look, Taggart stormed by him, barged his way out through the screen door and along the pathway to his horse.

During the next two days, complaints of rustled stock poured into Mounted Police divisional headquarters at Fort Macleod and to the outposts at Standoff, Kootenai, Pincher Creek and Big Bend. It was the same story. Rustlers had struck, running off large numbers of cattle, while the Mounties entertained at their regimental ball.

At Fort Macleod, Major Steele's face was red. He was furious to think that while his officers, NCOs and men hosted a fine summer ball and dinner for the enjoyment of the people of the district, rustlers had taken advantage of the occasion to run off hundreds of head of cattle.

Major Steele had no doubt that it was the work of the same rustlers. Obviously they had been planning it all along.

Orders went out to all detachments and flying patrols that every effort was to be made to recover the stolen stock. Every man was to be out in the saddle until the rustling was thoroughly investigated and the rustlers cooling their backsides in the Fort Macleod guardroom. Every square mile from Fort Macleod to Montana was to be patrolled. Every rancher and cowhand was to be questioned for anything out of the ordinary that they might have seen or heard. Every square mile of the Blood and Peigan Indian reserves was to be searched. The stolen stock was to be recovered and the rustlers brought to justice. Major Steele ordered it so.

Chapter 15

Standing in his stirrups, O'Reilly gazed around at the rolling hills and coulees of the Upper Agency. Off to the southwest he could see, in all its snow-crowned majesty, Chief Mountain rising square and dazzling white against the blue sky.

The civilian sitting his saddle beside O'Reilly gazed around with him. "We've ridden over every one of 'em, Constable. The only cattle we seen belongs to the Indian Department or to the Bloods. None of it is stolen stock."

O'Reilly sat down in his saddle. "I appreciate your help, Mister Jeffers. Good of you to take the time from your duties."

The civilian grinned. "T' tell the truth, I found it a right pleasin' change from what I'm usually doin' all day long. Teachin' agriculture to the Bloods can be plumb tiresome at times, especially when so many of 'em ain't interested. They'd rather be out ridin' around or huntin'. Trouble is, there ain't much for them to hunt any more. Which is the main reason I'm here, I suppose. At least, it keeps me employed."

They reined their horses around and headed back toward the Upper Agency headquarters. "What'll you be doin' now, Constable?" the agricultural instructor asked as they walked their horses steadily across the undulating prairie.

"Report back to Sergeant Hannan at Standoff. Maybe he'll then send me out searching somewhere else. A couple of others are searching the Lower Agency, doing the same as you and I have been doing up here. The detachments over at Pincher and Kootenai, and across at Big Bend, they'll all be looking. I daresay Major Steele at Fort Macleod will be anxious to hear if any of us have found anything."

O'Reilly roamed his eyes around the rolling hills as they rode. "He'll be disappointed if we don't find anything. I hope some of the other patrols have had more luck than we have."

The agricultural instructor shook his head. "It's a bad thing, all this rustlin'. I've been out here in this part of the Territories five years now. Never heard of anythin' like it before. Oh, sure, there was always the odd bit of stock bein' run off. Usually some small band of rustlers from down in Montana runnin' off stock across the border before you fellers could stop 'em. And occasionally an Indian war party—usually Gros Ventres or Crows—stealin' the odd few head here and there. But it never lasted long, and most of the time you redcoats put a stop to it right smart-like. But this spate . . ." He shook his head and left the remainder of the sentence unsaid.

After a while they kneed their horses into a trot, and the miles clicked by underneath their horses' hoofs. When the buildings of the Upper Agency hove into view, O'Reilly said goodbye to the agricultural instructor and continued on toward the Standoff and Fort Macleod trail.

He rode another two miles and reined his horse back down to a walk. Standoff was only a short distance away. He was in no real hurry to get back. He had enjoyed these last two days, riding freely across the Blood reserve looking for the herds that had been stolen the night of the regimental ball. He hadn't expected to find any of them, not after what the agricultural instructor had told him, that if there had been more than a few head of stolen stock on the Upper Agency, he—the agricultural instructor—would have known about it. In retrospect, it seemed to O'Reilly that the two days he had just spent riding around had been a waste of time and effort, except that he had enjoyed it. He had enjoyed the aloneness of it, just he and the agricultural instructor, who had been largely a taciturn man only occasionally given to saying more than a few sentences at a time.

What he had enjoyed most of all, O'Reilly reflected, was the relative independence, being free of the restraints imposed by the disciplinary presence of Sergeant Hannan. It wasn't anything personal against his red-headed sergeant; actually, O'Reilly had developed a liking for him. He didn't think of Mike Hannan as a disciplinarian in the usual sense of the word, not in the parade ground sense. It was the rank that O'Reilly felt, the confinements imposed by non-commissioned rank. O'Reilly accepted the fact that he had a lot yet to learn before he could be considered to be a valuable Mounted Policeman. But it was nice to be out on his own, his own boss in a way, even if only for a couple of days. For a moment he found himself looking forward to the future, to the time when he would wear gold chevrons on his tunic sleeve, when he would be an NCO in charge of a detachment or a flying patrol.

As those thoughts were running through his mind, a steady drumming sound broke into his momentary daydream, chasing away the fleeting vision of a set of gold corporal's or sergeant's chevrons. The drumming of hoofbeats.

Turning in his saddle, O'Reilly looked back over his shoulder. A black and white pinto was cantering across the prairie behind him. A smile spread on O'Reilly's face as he recognized the slouched figure of Porcupine Quill, riding Indian-style after him. Reining to, he turned his horse around and waited.

The Blood's white teeth flashed against his copper-colored face as he pulled his pinto to a stop beside O'Reilly.

"You catch whisky runner," Porcupine Quill said matter-of-factly.

"That's right. I want to thank you for showing me the trail he used."

"You look for cattle stole from ranches."

"That's right."

"I help you."

O'Reilly frowned. "How?"

"You get me job as Mounted Police scout, I help you."

Inspector Cavannagh's words the night of the regimental ball came instantly to O'Reilly's mind. *That young Blood sounds as though he would make a good Mounted Police scout.* But so did the realization that if the Force knew about Porcupine Quill's past involvement in running off horses it would never take him on as a scout. O'Reilly had never told Sergeant Hannan about that. He had never mentioned Porcupine Quill's name, and Sergeant Hannan had never asked him. But if Sergeant Hannan knew him . . .

The frown on O'Reilly's brow deepened beneath the brim of his hat. "But you've stolen horses. It might be hard getting you a job as a scout."

To O'Reilly's surprise, the young Blood grinned. "Because I have done that, I know how to find men who run off cattle."

O'Reilly couldn't help grinning with him. The old saying entered his mind, *Set a thief to catch a thief.* He nodded. "I will speak for you. I can not make a promise, but I will speak for you."

Porcupine Quill looked into O'Reilly's eyes for a moment, then he thrust out his right hand, palm open. O'Reilly reached across his horse and they shook firmly.

"Come." Porcupine Quill tugged the pinto's reins and turned the animal around, then pushed it into a canter back across the prairie in the direction he had come from. O'Reilly followed.

After riding for two or three miles, the frown returned to O'Reilly's forehead. Porcupine Quill wasn't taking him toward the cattle ranges but deeper onto the reserve. Were the rustled herds hidden somewhere on the Blood reserve after all?

He was on the verge of asking Porcupine Quill where they were going when the Blood veered off in the direction of a line of trees screening the base of a hill a mile away.

When they reached the trees, Porcupine Quill rode into a clump of cottonwoods. They picked their way through until they emerged on the far side, where O'Reilly saw a solitary tepee standing at the foot of the hill. Porcupine Quill rode right up to it, dropped the reins over the pinto's head and slid down off its back.

Porcupine Quill glanced up at O'Reilly. Without a word, he inclined his head toward the tepee flap, which he reached for and pulled open. Then he stooped forward and disappeared inside.

Swinging down from his saddle, O'Reilly followed Porcupine Quill inside the tepee. There was no one else inside. On the ground was an old buffalo robe, a few neatly folded deer and antelope hides, and a buckskin bag. Hanging from one of the spruce poles that comprised the tepee framework were several strips of dried meat. The interior was clean and tidy. It obviously accommodated only one person, although it was large enough to take a family of three or four.

"Is this where you live?"

Porcupine Quill nodded. He lifted the buckskin bag and began pulling from it fringed buckskin clothing . . . shirts, breeches, moccasins, leggings. He shook them out and handed them to O'Reilly.

O'Reilly smelled woodsmoke on them. He stared at Porcupine Quill. "You want *me* to wear these?"

"Where I take you, you cannot look like that," Porcupine Quill said, pointing at O'Reilly's uniform.

Hesitating, O'Reilly stood staring at the buckskin clothing in his hands. Then he shrugged, unbuckled his belt and started unbuttoning his tunic.

A few minutes later he was attired in buckskin. It felt strange on him, the unaccustomed texture of the deerskin shirt and trousers, and the moccasins lacking the familiar support of instep and heel like his riding boots. And the buckskin clothing felt a little tight.

He folded his uniform neatly, his wide-brimmed hat on top, and placed it beside the buffalo robe. His gunbelt he strapped around his waist.

Porcupine Quill's face was expressionless as he looked at O'Reilly, but his black eyes glittered approval.

Minutes later they were riding southwest across the rolling prairie.

They rode until they reached the Belly, then swung south. Four or five miles before the Big Bend police outpost on the far side of the river, they veered more southerly. Several miles later they rode across the southern boundary of the reserve and cantered on across open rangeland. Chief Mountain loomed on O'Reilly's right, just over the border in Montana.

"Where are we going?" O'Reilly asked as they cantered their horses toward Lee's Creek.

But Porcupine Quill didn't answer. He just kept riding his pinto steadily southward.

At Lee's Creek they swung southeast and crossed at a low spot. A little farther on they splashed across Boundary Creek. Not long after that they were in Montana.

They cantered along the foothills that separated the rolling prairie to their left and the Rockies on their right. O'Reilly began to grow uneasy. It would soon be dark, and he would be expected back at Standoff. He remembered what Sergeant Hannan had told him several weeks ago about not going on any more one-man patrols without orders. And he vaguely remembered something in Mounted Police regulations that prohibited members of the Force from entering American territory without

165

proper authorization.

They were more than a dozen miles below the border when Porcupine Quill held out his arm, then pointed a finger to his lips. They slowed their horses to a trot. Off to the right stretched a long rise, the mountains behind it. Porcupine Quill led the way toward it.

There were scattered clumps of poplar and pine dotting the lower slope of the rise and they rode into one of them, where they reined to. Porcupine Quill made a half-fist of both hands, then held them up in front of his eyes for a second or two, then he pointed to O'Reilly's saddle wallets. O'Reilly frowned for a moment, then understood and reached into one of the wallets for the binoculars he carried. When the young Blood slid off his pinto's back, O'Reilly slung the binoculars around his neck and swung down from his saddle. They tied their horses to the trees, emerged from the clump and made their way up to the rise on foot. When they reached the top they dropped to their stomachs in the long, wind-blown grass and peered down into a wide grassed valley below.

O'Reilly's lips pursed into a long, low whistle of surprise. It was more like breath escaping from his body. Spread below were hundreds of grazing cattle.

"There must be well over a thousand head down there," he muttered.

On the far side of the valley a thin column of smoke rose lazily into the air, gray against the green of the hills and lower slopes of the mountains beyond. O'Reilly lifted the binoculars to his eyes, taking care to shield the lenses with his hands to prevent the sun's light reflecting off them. He thumbed the center focus wheel until the blurred image sharpened into a clear picture. Then he studied the scene below. The smoke led to a campfire and beside it stood two wagons, some crude log shacks and a number of saddled horses. Several men dressed as cowhands busied themselves around the fire. The bawling of cattle sounded from below.

"They're branding," O'Reilly said.

Porcupine Quill, lying in the long grass beside him, said nothing.

"How did you know they were here, Porcupine Quill?"

"One night of the full moon I hear cattle, many cattle, going past the reservation. It was strange for cattle to move like that at night. They were moving fast, so I ride out to see. I follow. They go all way, cross the medicine line. I follow. I follow them here."

"Why didn't you report this to the Mounted Police right away?"

Porcupine Quill did not answer. He simply lay in the grass and stared down at the valley below. O'Reilly did not press the point. He knew the answer. Porcupine Quill had already told him.

Turning his attention back to the valley below, O'Reilly wondered how the rustlers managed to drive the cattle all the way from the Fort Macleod country down across the border into Montana without at least one of the detachments or patrols running across them. They would have had to travel within easy riding distance of Big Bend detachment, and the Kootenai detachment as well. But then O'Reilly remembered having seen the men from both detachments at the regimental ball.

He studied the men down by the wagons and the log shacks. He counted a dozen or more, all wearing guns. A hard looking lot.

"They're either branding, or else they're changing the brands."

"They steal cattle from white ranchers," Porcupine Quill said as he also watched. "Then Indian people get blame."

Porcupine Quill had just finished speaking when movement off to the right caught O'Reilly's attention. He swung his glasses slightly and trained them on the movement. Riding down along the valley from the north was a solitary horseman. A big man. There was something familiar about him. He was riding a big horse. It had to be

big to carry such a big rider. Then O'Reilly stiffened.
Iron-Fist Taggart!

The big horseman rode on toward the group of men.
He was less than half a mile away from them. Surely he
must have seen them, must have seen the smoke from the
fire.

"What the hell's he doing down there?" O'Reilly muttered. "He must be looking for his own stolen cattle. He's
going to blunder right into that nest of rustlers."

O'Reilly tensed himself to move.

"We've got to do something to head him off, to warn
him. They'll probably shoot him if we don't."

O'Reilly had no love for Iron-Fist Taggart, but he didn't
want to see an innocent man, a man out trying to find his
own stolen cattle, gunned down by cattle rustlers, men
who were ruthless killers.

Porcupine Quill laid a restraining hand on O'Reilly's
arm. O'Reilly looked into the Indian's face. Porcupine
Quill's black eyes looked right back into his. The young
Blood shook his head. "Wait."

O'Reilly looked down on the valley again. He watched
Taggart's big frame sitting astride his horse continue on to
the rustlers' camp. The rustlers looked up. Expecting to
see them go for their guns and to hear the rattle of gunfire, O'Reilly watched in fascination. But to his surprise
nothing like that happened. As Taggart rode right up to
them, several of the men nodded to him. It went through
O'Reilly's mind that perhaps Porcupine Quill had made a
mistake, that those weren't stolen cattle down there at all,
that the men were legitimate ranchers and their hired
hands and had greeted Taggart as a fellow rancher from
north of the Canadian border.

Through the binoculars O'Reilly watched Taggart en-
gage in a lengthy conversation with the men. He climbed
down from his saddle and stood watching the branding,
then he was gesturing with his hands as though giving
them directions. After that Taggart reached into his

pocket, pulled out a sheet of paper and handed it to one of the men. They talked for several minutes, then Taggart pointed southward.

Sergeant Hannan's words about Taggart came back to O'Reilly. He looked at the hard-faced men down there and remembered the hard-faced hands he had seen on Taggart's ranch. Sergeant Hannan was right. *Taggart — he's behind the rustling!*

Sergeant Hannan alone among members of the Mounted Police had suspected Taggart all along. While Taggart hid behind a front of respectability and righteous indignation, his men systematically rustled cattle from the other ranchers, drove them down across the border where they kept them hidden and changed the brands, then probably herded them south to the closest railhead and sold them. That was how Taggart had built up one of the largest cattle spreads in the Fort Macleod district.

The sun was sinking down toward the far side of the mountains. There was less than an hour of daylight left. O'Reilly knew he had to do something about what he was seeing. That paper Taggart had given one of the men down there . . . what had it meant? A forged bill of sale? Taggart had pointed to the south. Were they preparing to drive the cattle south? O'Reilly realized he didn't have time to waste. He had to get word back to Sergeant Hannan.

Lowering the glasses, O'Reilly turned to Porcupine Quill. "We have to tell Sergeant Hannan about this. One of us has to ride back to Standoff right away and bring back the flying patrol and some cowhands to round up those cattle and herd them back to their owners. But one of us will have to stay here and watch in case those men down there decide to move the cattle first. Now, which one of us is to go?"

Porcupine Quill pointed at O'Reilly. "You go. You can say right things. I stay."

O'Reilly nodded. "Right. If they move the cattle before

169

I get back, follow them. But they're not likely to move them before tomorrow at the earliest. I should be damn near back by then."

O'Reilly backed away from the top of the rise, and when he was far enough he got to his feet and ran down the slope to his horse in the poplar clump. Untying his horse, he climbed up into the saddle, reined the animal around and cantered down the gradual slope, heading back north toward Canada.

He was back across the border not long after the sun went down. He rode hard all night, not slackening his horse's pace even in the dark. He knew that part of the country well enough now to find his way in the dark.

It was well past midnight when he arrived back at Standoff. Sergeant Hannan was sitting in his office, the light from the coal oil lamp throwing a patch of yellow from the window. At the sound of O'Reilly's horse, Sergeant Hannan appeared in the doorway. At first he didn't recognize O'Reilly dressed in buckskin. Then his eyes narrowed at O'Reilly, loping along the pathway, crossed into light thrown from the open door.

"O'Reilly! For Christ's sake! What the hell are you doing dressed like that? Where the hell's your uniform? And where the hell have you been? You should've been back hours ago."

Inside Sergeant Hannan's office, O'Reilly quickly told him where he had been and what he had seen.

Sergeant Hannan didn't interrupt, but as soon as O'Reilly had finished he threw a question at him. "How do you know the cattle that Blood friend of yours showed you is stolen, stolen from this side of the border?"

"It all fits, Sergeant," O'Reilly replied eagerly. "It fits with what you've said about Taggart."

"You said they were changing brands?"

"They were branding. I can't say whether they were changing brands, but all we have to do is get down there with some men and look for ourselves. Anyway, they're the same cattle my friend followed down into Montana the night of the regimental ball."

"Who is this young Blood buck, anyway?"

O'Reilly hesitated for a moment before he said, "His name is Porcupine Quill."

Sergeant Hannan's freckled face suddenly looked as though something had struck it. *"Porcupine Quill! Christ Almighty! That young buck!"*

Disappointment swept over O'Reilly at the sergeant's reaction to his friend's name, although he wasn't really surprised. He'd half-expected it.

"He's trouble, that buck."

"He showed me Gus Breen's whisky running trail."

Sergeant Hannan sat on the corner of his table, swinging a spurred and booted leg to and fro. He raised his hand to his jaw and rubbed it, his red-hued whisker stubble making a sandpaper-like sound. "We'll have to be sure we can prove those cattle were stolen from this side of the border. That's United States territory down there. I can't take men across the line. We don't have any authority down there. And I can't go getting US authorities to mount up a strong posse without being sure of my grounds."

Impatience and a growing feeling of exasperation goaded O'Reilly. "You're telling me all the things we *can't* do. There must be something we *can* do. If we wait too long, those rustlers are likely to start moving that stock. I think that's why Taggart is down there—he's overseeing the arrangements to herd that stock down to the nearest railhead or other buyer."

"By rights I should refer this matter to Fort Macleod. Let the high-priced help make the decisions."

But O'Reilly was anxious to get back to Montana. He'd given his word to Porcupine Quill that he'd be back shortly after sunup. "If we find Taggart down there with stolen cattle, that should be enough to charge him with complicity, at least."

"We can't touch Taggart as long as he's down in Montana, O'Reilly. They must have taught you that at Regina."

"But we could arrest him as soon as he crosses back into the Northwest Territories."

Chapter 16

The sun was well up in the eastern sky when O'Reilly and Sergeant Hannan crossed the border into Montana. The only recognizable items of Mounted Police uniform Sergeant Hannan wore were his riding boots, spurs, gun belt and wide-brimmed hat. In addition he had on a pair of light-colored moleskin breeches that had once been regular issue but had since been replaced by dark blue breeches with a yellow stripe, and a gray flannel shirt. O'Reilly rode a fresh horse. He had wanted to take along the other members of the Standoff flying patrol but Sergeant Hannan had said no. United States troops never crossed into Canada in pursuit of Indian war parties, and he wasn't going to risk creating an international incident by taking an armed party of police, even though a small one, into their country. As far as he was concerned, he and O'Reilly were on a scouting mission only.

They rode steadily southward. Another hour saw them within sight of the long rise that marked the valley where the stolen cattle were. But as soon as they sighted it, O'Reilly felt a sickening feeling grip his guts. Something was wrong!

O'Reilly slowed his horse. Sergeant Hannan glanced sideways at him. Before he had a chance to say anything,

O'Reilly saw it—a column of black smoke rising into the sky.

"That smoke . . ." O'Reilly left the rest of the sentence unsaid. He legged his horse back into a canter, then into a gallop up the long slope, past the clump of trees where he and Porcupine Quill had hidden their horses the previous day and on up toward the top of the rise. Sergeant Hannan rode right behind him.

As soon as he reached the top, O'Reilly reined to a stop. He stared down at the valley. The cattle were gone. The valley was empty, except for the two wagons the rustlers had used and the old log shacks. But they were blackened, smoking ruins. There was no sign of Porcupine Quill.

They reined their horses down over the top of the rise and rode down into the valley. They reined to when they reached the smoking ruins of the wagons and cabins. All that remained of the two wagons were the iron hoops, the metal frame and axles, and the iron wheel rims. The smell of charred wood and coal oil hung heavy in the air. Around the blackened remnants lay several bodies, all dead, every one with a missing scalp. Some had arrows embedded in their chests or backs, the others bullet holes.

O'Reilly and Sergeant Hannan sat their saddles staring down silently at the carnage. The scalped heads were quivering, bloody messes. O'Reilly had never seen a scalped man before. He hoped he would never see one again. Suddenly he leaned over in his saddle and retched violently.

Sergeant Hannan swung down from his horse and walked over to what had been the branding fire. A branding iron lay beside it. He picked it up and examined it. "The Circle T. Taggart's brand." He looked over to O'Reilly, still throwing up. "Looks like that Blood friend of yours was right. This iron sure links Taggart with the rustling. But there's no sign of Taggart himself." His voice changed tone. "You all right?"

After a moment O'Reilly cleared his throat and straightened in his saddle. He nodded. Reining his horse around, he walked it away from the bodies. Sergeant Hannan stepped back up into his saddle and rode along beside him.

"Where's Porcupine Quill?" the sergeant asked.

"Probably trailing whoever did all that," O'Reilly replied, jerking a thumb back over his shoulder at the bodies lying on the ground. "They must've run off the cattle."

Sergeant Hannan's face hardened. "Or else he rode back to the reserve and returned with some of his friends and did this themselves."

O'Reilly's head snapped sideways, his dark eyes flashing as he stared at the red-headed sergeant. "I don't believe that."

"You don't know him well enough to know what he'd do."

They rode back up to the top of the rise. O'Reilly reined his horse over to where he had left Porcupine Quill the previous evening. He looked for some message or sign that his Blood friend might have left. But there was nothing—except some flattened grass that looked as though it could have got that way from bodies thrashing around on it. Like bodies fighting. That sickening feeling gripped his guts again.

Then something on the ground caught his attention. Something dark against the sun-faded green grass. Jumping down from the saddle, he kneeled, his fingers closing around it, and scooped it up. It was an eagle claw on a rawhide necklace.

O'Reilly heard Sergeant Hannan's horse behind him and the creak of saddle leather as the sergeant leaned forward to look over his shoulder. O'Reilly held it up for him to see.

"An Indian's strong medicine charm," Sergeant Hannan

175

said. "Blackfoot or Blood, or it could be Peigan."

"It's Porcupine Quill's. I've seen it around his neck. The rawhide thong, it looks like it's been wrenched loose. He must've lost it in a struggle. They must have jumped him and taken him prisoner. If they'd killed him, his body would probably still be there."

O'Reilly stood on top of the long rise, looking into the distance along the valley. *Who the hell were they and where the hell have they gone?*

Sergeant Hannan's words cut into his thoughts. "We better be getting back. I'll report what's happened here to Fort Macleod. They can wire the United States authorities at Fort Benton. Seeing as how Indians are involved, they'll be able to call in the army."

O'Reilly whipped his head around and looked up sharply at him. "But those Indians have taken Porcupine Quill. They could kill him yet. We can't abandon him."

Sergeant Hannan stiffened in his saddle. "And just *what* would you suggest we do, Constable?"

"Go after them. Try and get him out of their hands. They haven't been gone all that long. That charred wood down there is still hot."

"Just the two of us! That was a war party that did that, without a doubt. There would've been at least twenty of them. Could have been a hell of a lot more. That's a job for the army."

"Getting the army would take too long. Those Indians could kill Porcupine Quill before the army could catch up with them."

Sergeant Hannan sat his saddle looking down at O'Reilly. There was a pleading expression in the young constable's dark eyes. "God damn it, O'Reilly! We can't go galloping all over Montana chasing Indians. We've got no authority down here. God damn it, we're not even supposed to *be* here."

O'Reilly remained standing where he was, dressed in his

Indian buckskin, still looking up at his sergeant. The pleading expression remained in his eyes. There was something else in them as well—determination.

Sergeant Hannan drew in a deep breath. "All right, God damn it! Don't stand there looking at me like that. Get your ass up into that saddle and let's move."

They rode back down into the valley and followed it southward. Foothills rose on either side. The grass passing beneath the hoofs of their cantering horses had been flattened by the passage of the large herd of cattle.

Sergeant Hannan shouted above the noise of the horses' pounding hoofs. "They'll stampede the herd for the first dozen or fifteen miles but after that the cattle will balk and they'll have to slow down."

O'Reilly and Sergeant Hannan rode steadily all morning. They stopped once to grain-feed their horses while they themselves munched on patrol hardtack. After that they were back in their saddles riding south again.

Sometime after midday they rode up out of the valley and paused on top of a hill while they glassed the country ahead. O'Reilly stifled the impulse to shout out jubilantly when they sighted a large brown dust cloud many miles to the south.

"That must be them," Sergeant Hannan said. "They're making better time than I would've reckoned."

The two Mounties, looking little like what they were, reined their horses down into the valley again and cantered onward at a good clip but taking care not to push their horses too hard.

The valley angled around to the southeast and after a few more miles the foothills became smaller.

The war party kept up the punishing pace, either not knowing or not caring that they were running the fat off the cattle, lowering the price they might get for them.

"I don't know where the hell they're taking 'em," Sergeant Hannan said as they rode. "But they sure can't take

177

a herd that size onto the reservation. The agent would spot it before long and call in the army."

By late afternoon O'Reilly and Sergeant Hannan spotted the herd in the distance.

The war party had slowed the herd down to a walk, and O'Reilly and Sergeant Hannan would have run into the tail end of it as they rode around a bend and saw, where the valley widened, the herd spread out ahead of them. But fortunately they were still two miles off.

They reined to quickly, pulled out their binoculars and studied the scene ahead.

"Can't tell how many of them there are," Sergeant Hannan said. "They're spread all around the herd. Let's take a look from the top of that bend we just came around. We'll see better from up there."

They rode up the side of the valley and around some hills until they reached the top of one from where they could see the herd spread out in the valley below.

They hobbled their horses just behind the brow of the hill, crawled to the top and stretched out on their stomachs, their elbows propping them up as they held binoculars to their eyes.

"They've stopped," Sergeant Hannan said.

"Maybe they're going to pull in and make camp for the night."

"No, they'd push on regardless of nightfall if they took a mind to. They've stopped for some other reason."

They watched several of the Indians riding around the herd to join together in a small group. O'Reilly looked anxiously for Porcupine Quill's pinto. A chill gnawed at his guts when he couldn't find it.

"I count fourteen, no . . . fifteen," Sergeant Hannan said. "There's a few more over on the far side of the herd, but I can't make them out. This is South Blackfoot country, but they're kin to the Bloods and Blackfoot up our way. They wouldn't likely take a Blood prisoner, and they

178

sure wouldn't kill him. They'd be more likely to invite him to join 'em."

O'Reilly sensed the accusation in Sergeant Hannan's tone. He reached down to his gun belt and lifted Porcupine Quill's eagle claw necklace, tossing it onto the grass in front of the sergeant. "Then why did they have to fight him?"

Sergeant Hannan took his eyes away from his binoculars for a moment and looked at the charm with its broken rawhide thong lying on the grass in front of him.

"Then they must be Gros Ventres," he said, looking through the binoculars again. "They'd sure as hell kill a Blood."

Silently O'Reilly cursed himself for having left Porcupine Quill behind. The two of them should have ridden back to Standoff together.

"One thing," Sergeant Hannan said, lying watching the activity in the valley below, "they don't seem to be expecting any pursuit. If they were, they'd have had a rear guard out and they'd have seen us. No scouts out now, either. In the old days that sort of carelessness would have cost 'em their lives. And we'll have to be more careful from now on. Our luck mightn't hold good a second time."

Sergeant Hannan watched without further comment for several minutes, then said, "There's a lot of arm waving going on down there. I reckon they're trying to figure out their next move. If that's a Gros Ventre war party, they were probably on the prowl for trouble, probably figuring on running off some South Blackfoot horses when they came across that herd of stolen cattle, more by accident than anything else. It looked too good an opportunity for them to pass up, so they killed and scalped Taggart's men and ran off the herd. The only trouble is, they didn't think the whole thing through. They didn't figure out just what to do with all those silver dollars on the hoof. That's what they're trying to figure out now." He added, "That's the

179

way I reckon it."

Sergeant Hannan had just finished speaking when O'Reilly, his voice tight with excitement, suddenly said, "There's Porcupine Quill. That black and white pinto — that's his horse."

Shifting his glasses slightly, Sergeant Hannah watched for a moment. "You're right. He's a prisoner, no doubt about it. They've got him tied onto his horse. Maybe they've got Taggart down there, too."

They watched as the war party continued their conference, waving their arms and gesturing excitedly with their hands. They appeared to be arguing and shouting among themselves.

"They're having a hell of a time trying to figure out what to do next," Sergeant Hannan said, without removing the binoculars from his eyes. He watched a moment longer, then said, "That valley keeps on going for a bit before it peters out onto open prairie. They'll have to stay in the valley at least that far. There's two rivers way off, one off to the left, the other off to the right. I reckon one of them flows on east until it empties into the Missouri."

"Then we can't be all that far from Fort Benton," O'Reilly said eagerly. "We can get help from the United States Cavalry."

Still looking through the binoculars, Sergeant Hannan said, "Fort Benton is all of a hundred miles away. Anyway, it isn't a military station. The closest troops that I know of are at Fort Shaw, southwest of Benton."

O'Reilly was becoming impatient. "Then we'll have to get Porcupine Quill away from them by ourselves."

Intent on what he was seeing through the binoculars, Sergeant Hannan didn't appear to have heard him. "They're getting off their horses. I think they're going to stop for the night."

The sun was dipping below the mountains behind them, throwing lengthening purple shadows across the rolling

180

hills and the prairie beyond.

"But if they're still in South Blackfoot country, wouldn't they be a bit shy of hanging around too long?"

"Depends on how real they reckon the danger is. Considering how careless they've been in not having any scouts out, I'd say not. But one thing Indians really like doing, next to fighting, running off an enemy's horses, and gorging themselves on buffalo meat or beef, is talking. They're going to sit down there and pow-wow. They'll smoke some tobacco and eat a little, but they'll talk. Then they'll decide where they're going to take that herd and what to do with it. After that, come first light, they'll do whatever it is they decide upon. And that's when we'll try and get that young buck friend of yours away from them."

Chapter 17

The sun rose in a burst of crimson across the eastern sky. From behind a rocky outcropping perched just above the valley, O'Reilly and Sergeant Hannan watched the cattle plodding toward them. Six painted warriors rode out in front. The sun was in their eyes. One, wearing a wolfskin cap, held a rope in his hand, the other end of which was looped around the neck of Porcupine Quill following behind. The young Blood was pulled forward over his pinto, his wrists tied together around its neck, his ankles bound together beneath its belly. The remainder of the war party were spread along both sides of the length of the herd.

"I count sixteen," Sergeant Hannan said. "There's probably a few more farther back where we can't see 'em because of the dust that herd's kicking up."

"They couldn't have got Taggart. If they had, they'd have him up front with Porcupine Quill."

"It's just as well. We're going to have our hands full getting Porcupine Quill away from them, let alone Taggart as well." Sergeant Hannan turned his freckled face, red from sun and wind, to O'Reilly. "You ready?"

O'Reilly nodded.

"Wait until they pass directly beneath us. Then go. I'll

cover you."

The war party was moving quickly, their ponies covering the distance in short, trotting, prancing movements, their heads bobbing up and down. The warriors sat their backs with heads held arrogantly high, rifle butts resting on bare thighs, barrels pointed to the sky. They had no scouts out and had no idea anyone else was within miles of them.

Sergeant Hannan had chosen the spot well. The war party would pass no more than twenty feet below the outcropping. The valley, although shallow, narrowed into a neck at this point before widening out again and going on until it flattened out onto the prairie beyond.

Behind the rocks, Cavannagh swung up onto his horse, while Sergeant Hannan levered a cartridge into the chamber of his Winchester and pulled the butt into his shoulder. As the six leading warriors passed below, O'Reilly reined his horse around the edge of the outcropping and down the shallow valley wall. Loose rock showered down with him. He reached the bottom a dozen yards behind the painted warriors and charged them.

A rifle shot cracked out from farther along the herd. One of the warriors back there had spotted O'Reilly and fired his rifle as a warning. Suddenly alerted, the leading warriors twisted around to look behind. But as they did so, O'Reilly smashed into them. He struck his fist at the warrior in the wolfskin cap. Startled, the warrior's pony leaped forward. The force of O'Reilly's blow sent him hurtling off the pony's back. He lost hold of both his rifle and the rope around Porcupine Quill's neck.

O'Reilly pulled his horse to a sharp stop, its hoofs skidding up a shower of dust and gravel. He leaped out of his saddle and pounced on the fallen warrior, yanking the Indian's knife from his belt. The warrior started to struggle but O'Reilly hit him on the side of the head with his fist and he slumped to the ground.

Shouting in startled surprise, the other five warriors swung their ponies around and around in wild confusion.

They saw the buckskin-clad intruder, with his short black hair and wind-tanned face, but everything was happening so fast they couldn't quite comprehend just what.

With knife in hand, O'Reilly reached for the black and white pinto's bridle. Alarmed, the pinto pulled back. It tried to veer away but it bumped into a warrior's pony and O'Reilly caught its reins, holding them with his left hand while he started cutting through the rawhide rope holding Porcupine Quill's wrists around the pinto's neck.

The din was terrific, magnified in O'Reilly's ears. Savage shouts, the scream of startled ponies as their riders cruelly jerked their reins and kicked their ribs as they wheeled them around and around, the stamping of unshod hoofs, clouds of choking, swirling dust.

As O'Reilly cut through Porcupine Quill's bonds, the warriors began to realize what was happening. One raised a rifle to smash the barrel down on O'Reilly's skull. A shot rang out from the outcropping above and the warrior spun from his pony's back.

Another warrior, carrying a lance instead of a rifle, drew back his arm to thrust the weapon at O'Reilly. Lifting his head, Porcupine Quill saw him and shouted a warning. Just in time, O'Reilly threw himself forward against the pinto, forcing it to prance backward. The lance thrust harmlessly by O'Reilly's spine. Before the warrior could pull it back for a second thrust, another shut rang out from the rocks above. The warrior toppled sideways.

Holding his rifle into his shoulder, a big scar-faced brave whirled his pony around as he tried to get into position to fire at O'Reilly. At the same time yet another warrior, hideously marked with yellow paint on his face, raised his rifle and pointed it up at the top of the outcropping, trying to sight Sergeant Hannan.

O'Reilly saw the threat from the rifle barrel pointed at him. Cutting through the last of the rawhide binding around Porcupine Quill's wrists, he handed him the knife. Then he darted around the pinto, drawing his Enfield at the same time. He came around the other side of the black and white. The scar-faced brave legged his horse sideways, bringing his rifle around to get a shot at O'Reilly. O'Reilly extended his pistol arm and pulled the trigger. The pistol went off with a deafening explosion, a stabbing red jet and gray smoke. The scar-faced brave was blown off his pony's back. The pony whinnied wildly and galloped away, reins flying behind it. Dust swirled up from the melee, almost blinding O'Reilly.

A rumble swelled from somewhere behind, rapidly intensifying into thunder. The shooting had startled the cattle, added to by high-pitched yells from some of the warriors farther back, who started galloping forward to join in the action.

Up on top of the rocks, Sergeant Hannan jumped up shouting and waving at O'Reilly down below. "Get the hell out of there! The herd's stampeding."

The warrior with the yellow paint snapped off a shot at Sergeant Hannan. He missed. O'Reilly killed him with a bullet from his pistol.

While Porcupine Quill was busy cutting the rawhide rope from around his ankles, O'Reilly bent down and picked up a fallen rifle from the ground. He thrust it out to Porcupine Quill. Although still leaning over cutting, the Blood took the rifle eagerly.

Amid excited ponies rearing and prancing around, billowing dust, shouts, shots and falling bodies, everything had happened very fast. The remaining warrior of the war party's advance guard, riding his pony around and around in confusion, finally decided what to do. He reached out and grabbed the reins of O'Reilly's horse just as O'Reilly was about to mount from the other side. The warrior pulled the horse away. O'Reilly snatched at a stirrup and pulled back. Bewildered and frightened, the horse shook its head and tried to draw back. It gave O'Reilly time to get around in front of it and reach up to grapple with the mounted warrior.

With his arms around the warrior, O'Reilly pulled him

185

off his pony and threw him violently to the ground. Then he spun around and hauled himself up into the saddle. But the warrior leaped back up off the ground and grabbed O'Reilly's leg. With his horse prancing and rearing, anxious to get away from all the noise and wild activity, O'Reilly hung onto his reins and saddle as he tried to kick the warrior clear.

"O'Reilly! Stampede, God damn it! Get the hell out of there!"

Too busy trying to kick the warrior away, O'Reilly didn't hear Sergeant Hannan's shouting.

But Porcupine Quill sensed the urgency of the situation. He pointed the rifle O'Reilly had handed him at the warrior and fired. The warrior jumped, then went limp. At the same time O'Reilly's startled horse leaped into the air and kicked out with its hind feet. One of its shod hoofs struck the warrior's body and sent it flying.

Porcupine Quill shouted at O'Reilly, but O'Reilly couldn't hear him. He couldn't hear the sound of stampeding cattle. All he could hear was the ringing in his ears from the exploding rifle.

Porcupine Quill rode his pinto alongside O'Reilly, reached out and shook O'Reilly's shoulder, at the same time flicking his head back over his shoulder. O'Reilly turned his head to look behind. He saw three painted warriors of the war party charging toward him, and behind them the stampeding cattle. Puffs of smoke erupted from the warriors' rifles. Bullets sang around O'Reilly's ears.

O'Reilly wasted no time. Leaning forward over his horse's neck, he kneed it into a gallop. He and Porcupine Quill raced for their lives along the valley toward the prairie ahead.

Up on top of the outcropping, Sergeant Hannan took aim at the foremost of the three pursuing warriors, led him a little, then squeezed the trigger. The Winchester bucked against his shoulder. The warrior rolled sideways off the pony's back.

One of the other two warriors veered his pony to one side to miss the falling body. Instantly he became aware of the danger from the marksman on top of the outcropping. Unconvinced that it was time for him to make the long ride to the happy hunting grounds, he abandoned the chase and galloped away to the far side of the valley. A moment later the third warrior, seeing himself alone, followed the example of the other one and followed him.

Galloping their horses along the valley, O'Reilly saw a slope they could ride up to get back up onto the higher ground and out of the path of the stampeding cattle. He veered off to the left, Porcupine Quill following.

The slope was only twenty feet high, at a forty-five degree angle, and they raced their horses up it. Seeing they were out of immediate danger, Sergeant Hannan withdrew from his position on top of the outcropping, swung up onto his horse and galloped away to join up with them. He had covered less than a mile when he heard rifle shots behind him. He looked back over his shoulder. A handful of the war party had ridden up out of the valley and were chasing them. Hannan had hoped they would have decided to cut their losses and drive off with the cattle, but the warrior instinct was too strong.

"Christ!"

Reining his horse to a stop, Hannan slid his Winchester from the pommel sling and swung down from his saddle. He pulled the Winchester into his shoulder and snapped off a shot at the oncoming Indians. A warrior fell from his pony. Hannan levered another round into the chamber and took aim and fired again. His horse, standing beside him, stamped a hoof but otherwise remained quiet. A second warrior slid from his pony's back.

The small knot of painted warriors slowed their ponies. Sergeant Hannan quickly mounted up again and galloped away, angling across the prairie after O'Reilly and Porcupine Quill. Bullets cracked past him as the warriors opened fire. Hannan crouched low over his horse's back. The animal streaked across the grass, Hannan zig-zagging to make his horse and himself as difficult a target as possible.

Ahead and over to the right, O'Reilly heard the shooting and looked back. He saw the war party, which had resumed the pursuit as soon as Hannan had ridden off. He saw the sergeant cutting across the prairie to join him. He saw the puffs of smoke coming from the Indians' rifles. He wasn't sure whether they were shooting at him and Porcupine Quill or at Sergeant Hannan, but as no bullets seemed to come his way he reckoned it was the sergeant they were shooting at. He was about to wheel his horse around to go to Sergeant Hannan's assistance and make a stand together when he saw the warriors pull their ponies to a stop, shake their rifles in frustrated anger at the three of them, then turn around and ride back toward the valley and the cattle. A moment later Sergeant Hannan thundered up alongside.

"Looks like they reckon there's more profit in that herd of cattle than in chasing us," Sergeant Hannan shouted as he reined down to a canter. "As for us, we did what we had to do. Now let's ride back where we belong."

Chapter 18

Iron-Fist Taggart paced backward and forward across the floor of his ranch house living room. He was furious. All his planning and organizing, all the hard work over the past few months—gone! Taken by an Indian war party that relieved him of well over a thousand head of cattle, killed his men and burned his wagons and equipment.

Damnation! Just when he had given orders to his men to drive the herd south to the rail head at Helena, a raiding party of Indians had to strike. His men were to have started herding the cattle out the next day. Taggart shuddered when he realized how close he had come to losing his own scalp. He would have lost it if he hadn't decided to leave camp early and head back to his ranch before sunup.

Lounging in a comfortable leather armchair, Slim Gude, Taggart's foreman, rolled a smoke.

"That's a hell of a lot of greenbacks those bloody Indians have cost me," Taggart said. "Now we've got to start all over again."

Gude stuck the cigarette in his mouth, lit a match on the sole of his boot and looked up at Taggart. "What you got in mind, boss?"

Taggart smacked a clenched fist into the open palm of

his left hand. "We've got to make another hit. Tonight! I've got to make up those losses, damn it."

"But the same thing could happen again if we run the stock down the same place."

"We're not going to run them down to the same place."

Gude dribbled smoke from his nose. "It'll be too dangerous to leave 'em anywheres around here."

"We're not going to leave them around here."

"Where the hell—?"

"I've already found a place. Over in the mountains west and a little north. There's a valley in behind the front range a day's ride. Lots of good grassed meadows. We can keep stock there until we've got a sizeable herd. Then we can drive 'em further into the mountains until we're out of the Northwest Territories and into British Columbia. From there we move 'em down through the mountains to Montana. It'll take longer but the Mounted Police can't touch us in British Columbia."

"What sort of law have they got in British Columbia?"

Taggart snorted. "Next to nothing. A provincial constable here and there. They won't be any problem. We'll blast 'em out of their saddles if they get in our way."

"So where do we hit?"

"The Stinson ranch has a large herd grazing out on the western edge of their lease. That's over in the foothills, in the right direction to the valley I've been telling you about. That'll make it easy. We haven't taken any cattle from out that far west, so they won't be expecting anything. We'll run off the whole lot, so get all the boys together. Right after that we'll hit the Mackenzie spread, then the Easthill ranch. They've both got big herds out. That way we'll clean up fast. Now, you'd better move. I want to get this thing rolling right away—tonight."

Gude looked down at his burning cigarette. Taggart noticed the mannerism. "What's the matter with you?" he asked.

190

Gude said, "Don't you think it would be better if we run off just a few head each night? That way the losses won't be too noticeable."

Taggart scowled down at his foreman. "Are you losing your nerve?"

"No, but the Mounted Police have reinforced their detachments and brought in Indian scouts. I don't see any point in pushing our luck."

"The Mounted Police are concentrating their patrols between Fort Macleod and the Montana border. They're still spread pretty thin toward the mountains. Dress some of the boys in buckskin again so they can be mistaken for Indians. When the losses are discovered, the Mounted Police will waste their time searching the Peigan reserve and Porcupine Hills. By the time they get finished doing that, we'll have damned near a thousand head ready to move into British Columbia and down the mountains."

"That's another problem we're gonna have. Seein' as how we lost a dozen men to that Indian raiding party, we won't have enough to run off cattle and watch the Mounted Police outposts and patrols as well."

Taggart's scowl deepened. "Forget about watching the Mounted Police. We'll get by with a couple of lookouts up on the high places. Now get your arse out of that chair and start organizing the men."

Gude unlimbered his long frame from the chair, crossed the living room floor and ambled on outside across the yard to the bunkhouse. Taggart watched him go. He hadn't told his foreman everything. He couldn't afford to. His ambitious plans and the considerable wealth he had accumulated were falling apart, all through a stroke of bad luck—a damned Indian raiding party. Who the hell would have dreamed that a bunch of ragged-arsed reservation Indians would've had the audacity to run off such a large herd of white man's cattle? A herd that size in the hands of Indians would attract attention. The army would be called in, rounding up the cattle, or what was left of them. If they did some investigating, and the cattle were returned to their rightful owners in the Northwest Territories, and some of those altered brands were looked at too closely, suspicion would fall on him. It was a good thing he had heard the shooting not long after he had left his men's camp in Montana and gone back to see what it was all about. Apart from finding out firsthand what had happened, it had given him the opportunity of retrieving that false bill of sale he'd written out and given one of his men when he was there before the attack. If that had fallen into the wrong hands, and the Mounted Police investigated, he would be faced with spending the rest of his life in Stony Mountain Penitentiary, and the gallows if they investigated far enough. It was too damned bad he had overlooked that branding iron. He had the uncomfortable feeling that things were getting too hot. But he still had time to recoup his losses and get out from under it all.

He would make a few more raids on his neighbors' cattle, big raids, and when he had enough he'd drive them south and sell them to Eastern interests at a good profit. It would be risky. Time was of the essence. He would have to abandon some of his other ambitions. But he would make up his losses, then get the hell out of the country. What was left would tumble down around Gude's ears. But by then, Iron-Fist Taggart would be gone. The Scarlet Riders would not get him.

"The Stinson ranch lost five hundred head of cattle last night," Major Steele said, looking across his desk at Inspector Cavannagh and Inspector Ainsworth, sitting on chairs opposite. "They were rustled, there's no doubt about that."

The two inspectors maintained a respectful silence.

192

"Indians were seen in the distance where the herd had been grazing," Major Steele added. He said nothing further as he continued looking at his two officers.

Inspector Cavannagh felt the major's silence was an invitation to comment. "That has a familiar ring."

Major Steele's big moustache bristled. "Yes, it does. I thought we were finished with this sort of thing, after reading Standoff's report about finding the bodies of dead rustlers who were apparently scalped by an Indian war party not far from the international boundary in Montana."

Inspector Cavannagh said, "It was interesting to read in that report, sir, that Constable O'Reilly recognized Iron-Fist Taggart talking with those rustlers before they were attacked and killed."

"Yes," Major Steele replied, nodding. "I'm tempted to call Taggart in here and ask him to account for his activities in Montana with those men. However, he could give a number of explanations that, in the absence of proof to the contrary, I would have to accept."

Sitting straight-backed on his chair, Inspector Cavannagh crossed one leg over the other, careful not to nick his polished riding boot with the spur on the other. "There is that branding iron Sergeant Hannan and Constable O'Reilly found at the remains of the rustlers' camp, sir. It carried the Circle T brand — Taggart's brand."

"True, but that's only circumstantial. Taggart could explain that away, also. We would not necessarily have to believe him, but neither would we be justified in laying charges against him on the basis of it. I can't bring Taggart in here because of it, or because of what Constable O'Reilly and an Indian saw, or thought they saw."

Inspector Cavannagh's steel-blue eyes locked onto his superior officer. "O'Reilly seemed to be quite sure, sir."

Major Steele didn't comment.

Inspector Ainsworth, a slight, sandy-haired officer with

a neatly trimmed moustache, cleared his throat. "Any word from the United States marshal at Fort Benton yet, sir?"

"No, but I have wired the United States military at Fort Shaw for assistance. In the meantime, gentlemen, I suggest you send some men to the Peigan reserve and the Porcupine Hills to search for the Stinson cattle. Alert Standoff, Kootenai, Pincher Creek, Big Bend and Boundary Creek detachments and flying patrols of the Stinson losses. They're to be particularly on the lookout for cattle being driven toward or near the international boundary."

As Sergeant Hannan read aloud Inspector Cavannagh's message a second time, O'Reilly's mind raced. He and Sergeant Hannan were alone in the sergeant's office. The rest of the patrol, including three additional men Fort Macleod had transferred to Standoff to increase the strength, were out on patrol under Constable Scott. Sergeant Hannan and O'Reilly had stayed behind to compile a comprehensive but carefully worded report on their exploits in Montana. Sergeant Hannan had already sent a report to Fort Macleod, but Major Steele had pressed him for more detail.

"We know Taggart is responsible for the rustling, Sarge," O'Reilly said. "How about letting me and Porcupine Quill watch his ranch? That hasn't been tried. Patrolling hasn't stopped him. If we watch long enough, we might be able to follow Taggart's men when they make their next move and catch them in the act."

Tilting his chair back dangerously on its two back legs, Sergeant Hannan looked across his table at O'Reilly. "You mean, act as detectives, sort of?"

"I guess you could call it that."

Sergeant Hannan thought about it for a moment, then nodded. "All right. It's worth a try. You and Porcupine

Quill did all right before. But this had better be unofficial. I don't know whether Fort Macleod would authorize it, so I reckon we just won't tell 'em."

Chapter 19

A butte, about seventy feet high, stood a few miles to the southwest of Taggart's ranch. O'Reilly remembered having seen it in the distance that day he rode with Sergeant Hannan to the ranch. It was ideal for what O'Reilly wanted. Although it showed signs of crumbling at its base, it was partly hollow and allowed easy access to the top without exposure to the ranch buildings or anyone riding by. A hundred yards away ran a clump of cottonwoods, with good grass for grazing, where they could hide their horses. The only drawback was that it didn't afford much visibility to the north of Taggart's ranch, and even less to the east. O'Reilly didn't worry about the northeast, in which direction lay Fort Macleod, because he didn't think Taggart would be stupid enough—or even greedy enough—to risk running off cattle right under the noses of Mounted Police divisional headquarters.

O'Reilly and Porcupine Quill approached the butte under cover of the darkness, and by sunup were well hidden on top of it, with O'Reilly's binoculars trained on Taggart's ranch buildings.

O'Reilly had again adopted Porcupine Quill's buckskin trousers, shirt and leggings. With his black hair and wind-tanned face, added to by his moustache and a chinful of growing black whisker stubble, he could at a quick glance pass as a halfbreed, and at a distance with Porcupine Quill, as just another Indian. Only his military seat in his saddle would give him away, and he did his best to affect a casual slouch when riding.

With some misgivings, Sergeant Hannan had accepted Porcupine Quill as a Mounted Police scout on a temporary basis, pending approval by Fort Macleod, which didn't seem to be in much doubt in view of Inspector Cavannagh's comments to O'Reilly on the night of the regimental ball. Sergeant Hannan had finally acquiesced, saying, "Well, they took on Star Child as a scout. At least Porcupine Quill didn't kill a Mounted Policeman. All he did was run off horses." Horse stealing was a serious enough offense, guaranteed to bring the perpetrator upon conviction a sentence of four or five years in Stony Mountain Penitentiary at Manitoba, and across the border in Montana it generally occasioned a necktie party. However, Sergeant Hannan didn't bother notifying Fort Macleod of Porcupine Quill's suspected involvement in such past activities.

Porcupine Quill proudly wore the silver star with the words *Mounted Police Scout* on his shirt and carried a government issue Winchester, Enfield revolver and gun belt, the same as his friend. But while they watched Taggart's ranch, O'Reilly convinced the young Blood not to wear his star pinned to his shirt. Somewhat reluctantly, Porcupine Quill wore it around his neck suspended from a rawhide thong, the star tucked below the V opening at his neck.

For two days they watched Taggart's ranch. They camped dry, munching hard tack and beef jerky, washed down by occasional mouthfuls of tepid water from their canteens. The August sun beat down warmly. O'Reilly didn't shave and his beard stubble grew thicker and blacker, and he came to look less and less like a Mounted Policeman. They saw occasional comings and goings of a

197

few of Taggart's men, but the movements weren't significant enough for O'Reilly to take any action other than continued watching.

On the morning of the third day they watched a large body of horsemen leave the ranch and head west. The riders passed within half a mile of the butte. Through his binoculars O'Reilly counted thirteen. Taggart wasn't among them.

"Taggart's lease runs south before it goes west," O'Reilly said, thinking out loud as much as talking to Porcupine Quill. "Why should they be riding west? Taggart doesn't graze any stock out there."

He lay on top of the butte watching them grow smaller in the distance. Then suddenly he jumped up, touched Porcupine Quill on the shoulder and together they climbed down from the butte, raced across the ground to the clump of cottonwoods and unhobbled their horses. A moment later they rode out of the trees and headed west-southwest, keeping the butte between themselves and Taggart's ranch buildings. When they were satisfied the contours of the rolling prairie hid them, they veered around to the west.

They cut the trail of the thirteen horsemen after an hour of cantering and then, Porcupine Quill leaning low over the side of his pinto to watch for hoofprints from time to time, continued on west. Once, they topped a hill and spotted Taggart's men not far ahead, and they reined to a stop until the thirteen got farther off. After that they stayed well back, watching through binoculars, and only riding on when they were satisfied there was enough distance between them and their quarry.

After several miles of riding they sighted a large herd of cattle grazing on the lifting uplands. O'Reilly studied them through his binoculars.

"They would be Mackenzie's cattle," he said. "Or Easthill's. Looks like they're untended."

He swung the binoculars onto Taggart's men, expecting to see them veer toward the herd. His spirits slumped when they continued riding westward, ignoring the herd. He had been sure Taggart's men were . . .

Then his spirits soared back up. Coming over a hill just short of the herd rode a handful of buckskin riders, seven of them, two or three with blankets over their shoulders despite the warmth of the August sun. They rode toward Taggart's men, who pulled to and waited.

They were west of the Peigan reserve. "Must be Peigans," O'Reilly said. He handed the binoculars to Porcupine Quill.

Porcupine Quill held the binoculars to his eyes and trained them on the buckskin riders. Then he laughed. "Not Peigans. White men, like you. Dressed to look like Indians."

O'Reilly took the binoculars back. Porcupine Quill was right. O'Reilly grinned at the clumsy attempt to make them look like Indians, wearing blankets on a hot summer day. Still, he ruefully reflected, it had fooled him.

The two groups of horsemen met. O'Reilly almost whooped for joy. They were all Taggart's men and they were going to rustle that herd.

After a few minutes of conversation, a rider detached himself from the group and rode off, making for a long, high ridge farther to the west. The others waited. O'Reilly watched him until he disappeared over a hill.

"Now, where the hell's he going? And what the hell are they waiting for?"

Doubts began to nag him when nothing happened for nearly an hour. Yet *something* was happening, or about to happen. Why else were Taggart's men, some disguised as Indians, hanging around a large herd of cattle belonging to the Mackenzie ranch?

Suddenly a hand clapped hard on O'Reilly's shoulder, knocking him clean out of his saddle.

"What the hell—?"

O'Reilly rolled to the ground, at the same time glimpsing Porcupine Quill leap from his pinto and grasp O'Reilly's horse's reins and his own and drag both animals down onto the ground.

Angry and confused, O'Reilly glared at Porcupine Quill, but the young Blood scout tossed a quick glance at the distant ridge. O'Reilly followed the direction of his glance. At first he saw nothing, but then caught a flash of light up on the ridge. It only lasted a second. But then it happened again. A few seconds later it flashed a third time.

As he crawled toward Porcupine Quill and lay his body over his horse to keep it on the ground, O'Reilly realized what the flashes were.

"I hope he didn't see us," he muttered.

Porcupine Quill didn't reply. They were just below the top of a small rise. But for the young Blood's quick response upon seeing the flash of the sun's reflection off the lenses of a pair of binoculars, they would have been in easy sight of the man who had ridden off and was now on top of the distant ridge, glassing the country to the east. From up there he would be able to see the rolling prairie for miles around.

While Porcupine Quill held the horses, O'Reilly bellied up to the top of the small rise and, his head hidden in long, wind-blown grass, watched Taggart's men. As he watched, a light flashed twice from the ridge, a much brighter light. Almost immediately Taggart's men broke into small groups and rode toward the herd.

O'Reilly fought to suppress his jubilation. The two flashes were a signal to Taggart's men, who were now on their way to carry out whatever plan Taggart had conceived. O'Reilly had no doubt they were going to rustle the herd. And it seemed the man up on the ridge hadn't spotted him and Porcupine Quill. If he had, he wouldn't

200

have sent the signal.

Now O'Reilly understood how Taggart's men managed to rustle cattle without being caught by the Mounted Police. Not only did they scout out the herds to make sure they were unattended, they posted lookouts to watch for the approach of Mounted Police patrols. O'Reilly remembered what Sergeant Hannah had said that day they visited Taggart's ranch, about the number of hired hands Taggart employed, more than enough to handle the operation of a ranch that size. With the number of men he had, Taggart was able to watch most of the Mounted Police outposts in that part of the country. And the country — buttes, foothills, high ridges and rolling hills — was ideal for that sort of surveillance. Hell, O'Reilly thought, the Mounted Police themselves often used those high geographical features as observation posts.

He grinned. If he and Porcupine Quill watched, they could catch Taggart's men in the act. If he could positively identify them — and the cattle as belonging to someone else — he would have enough evidence to convict them in a court of law. He needed evidence to clearly implicate Taggart himself — evidence beyond a reasonable doubt.

Then the grin slowly left O'Reilly's face. As long as that lookout was up on that ridge, he and Porcupine Quill couldn't move. With a growing sense of frustration, he watched Taggart's men riding around the herd. Then they disappeared over the next rise of the rolling prairie.

For the next two or three hours O'Reilly and Porcupine Quill could hear the shouting of men and the bellowing of cattle. The ground beneath him seemed to vibrate as the herd was driven off. The shouting and bellowing grew fainter and fainter until it finally stopped altogether. But O'Reilly's sense of frustration didn't. Mixed with a heightening impatience, it took all his self-discipline to remain where he was, pressed against the rise. He had the feeling that his hopes of getting evidence to convict Taggart and

201

his men were fading fast.

Many times over the next few hours, O'Reilly peered over the top of the rise, staring intently at the distant ridge, but he couldn't see a damned thing.

"We'll have to stay here until nightfall," he said disgustedly.

Porcupine Quill merely grunted.

They moved out after dark and rode west, in the direction O'Reilly believed Taggart's rustlers had gone. However, there was no moon and they couldn't see where they were going. The distant ridge wasn't even a faint shadow against the backdrop of the Rockies. They were left with little alternative but to pull into a sheltered dip and settle down until sunrise.

The next morning they found the ridge was closer than they had thought. With the sun rising behind them, O'Reilly and Porcupine Quill took turns studying the ridge through the binoculars. They studied every foot of it, every feature, until they were satisfied, or as satisfied as they could be, that there was no longer anyone up there.

Then they mounted up and rode toward it.

They reached the top of the ridge half a dozen miles later, the wind whistling in their ears, blowing their horses' manes and tails straight out, and rippling the long grass beneath O'Reilly's stirrups. Farther off to the west, balls of fleecy cloud bunched up over the snow-topped Rockies. Above the rolling prairie to the east behind them, the sky was a brilliant blue.

After a little searching, they found the spot where the lookout had been. There were blades of broken grass, where he had sat while watching the prairie below, and a little of it had been cropped by his horse. They dismounted and looked around but found nothing else except some ground-out cigarette butts.

"He could see a long way from up here," O'Reilly said as he stood staring down at the rolling prairie. "Nearly all the way to Fort Macleod, and down toward Standoff, too. If a patrol approached, he would have seen it."

Turning away, O'Reilly pointed at the cigarette butts on the ground. "At least he was careful with those. Had enough sense to put them out properly and not start a prairie fire." He raised his eyes and looked at Porcupine Quill. "He's probably ridden off to join the others. Can you trail him?"

Porcupine Quill bent down and examined the grass. After a moment he stood up, jumped up onto the pinto and rode off. O'Reilly stepped up into his saddle and followed.

They rode down the western side of the ridge, down onto a wide sweep of gradually rising upland. They saw no sign of the herd of cattle Taggart's riders rustled the previous afternoon. They rode steadily throughout the morning and before noon they neared pine-covered foot-hills, and beyond them the Rockies themselves. A few more miles they came to a river. On the far side stood fringe of pines. Behind it rose a small, craggy mountain.

O'Reilly was about to ride his horse into the river when Porcupine Quill, riding on O'Reilly's right, suddenly turned his pinto into O'Reilly's horse, forcing it to turn left and follow the bank of the river southeast instead of crossing.

Puzzled, O'Reilly rode alongside him for a while, then said, "Why did you do that? Why aren't we crossing the river?"

Looking straight ahead, Porcupine Quill replied, "Man up in rocks watching. We go this way, maybe he think we hunting."

O'Reilly resisted the temptation to turn his head and stare up at the small mountain rising above the pines on his right. Instead he dropped his shoulders, slouching

203

Indian-style on his horse, and pulled his rifle from its pommel sling, to carry it like the Gros Ventres he saw down in Montana, butt on his thigh, barrel pointed to the sky. What Porcupine Quill said made sense. Indians often rode off the reservations to hunt for food, and deer and wapiti elk roamed the foothills.

They rode southeast along the river bank for a long way, until it angled around the mountains, and they were well out of sight of the lookout up on the rocks. He was watching for a flying patrol, four or five riders wearing brass-buttoned brown duck jackets, dark blue breeches with yellow stripes down the sides, and wide-brimmed hats, not a pair of Indians out hunting. His presence assured O'Reilly they were on the right track.

As soon as they found a suitable fording spot they reined their horses into the glacial-fed river and splashed across to the other side. Once across they rode into the seclusion of the pine trees. Slowly they picked their way through the trees, following the river back upstream until they were opposite the spot where they had been when Porcupine Quill spotted the lookout.

Peering up through the spear-topped pines, they tried to spot him but he was up high, hidden from them by a rocky overhang. O'Reilly took some consolation from the fact that if the overhang hid him from their view, it also hid them from him. Nonetheless, he breathed easier once they got far enough around the north side of the mountain where they were completely out of his line of vision.

"I don't know whether he was the same lookout who was up on that ridge where we were this morning," O'Reilly said. "But he's not up there to admire the scenery. If we keep pushing west and maybe a little north, we should run into that stolen herd, or pick up their trail."

Porcupine Quill nodded agreement.

They stayed in the pines a little longer, letting their horses pick their way along the needle-covered ground, only guiding them with their knees or a touch of the reins if they showed signs of venturing out from the protection of the trees. Eventually the pines petered out and they walked their horses out into warm sunshine. But the country ahead was a maze of hills. They would have to find their way through them. As if that was not enough, the ground was covered with gravel and small rock.

"Not much chance of finding a trail on that," O'Reilly remarked, but Porcupine Quill, his keen dark eyes glued to the rocky ground, led them on. Several times he jumped down off his pinto and kneeled to examine the ground. Whether he saw an occasional mark where an iron horseshoe left a faint scar in its passage, Porcupine Quill didn't bother to tell O'Reilly.

As they rode, O'Reilly kept his eyes on the surrounding countryside. The sun was getting warmer, beating down on his head and shoulders, heating his body under his buckskin shirt. He understood why Indians so frequently rode around bare-chested or wearing only a breechclout. He glanced several times at Porcupine Quill. The young Blood didn't seem bothered by the heat, apparently too intent on what he was doing.

Pushing their horses through the hills, O'Reilly worried whether they were on the right track. How the hell could Taggart's men have driven a large herd of cattle through such a maze? Unless there was a way around them a little farther north . . . ?

After what seemed to O'Reilly a long time, they emerged from the jumbled hills. Ahead were mountains, mighty gray or brown peaks rising high in the sky, their lower slopes covered by pines. The cloud that had banked up over them earlier had gone. Off to the north ran a long gray escarpment, and pressing against its base was a wide green meadow that stretched over to the north side of the mass of hills they had just ridden out of.

"That must be where they drove the cattle through,"

O'Reilly said. There was jubilation in his voice, mixed with excitement. He was eager to catch up with the rustlers, to *know* they actually *had* rustled the herd, to be able to swear under oath in a court of law that they had rustled the herd.

The meadow swept ahead of them, west along the foot of the escarpment until it narrowed to form a passageway along the bottom of a pass between the mountains a few miles farther on. O'Reilly glassed it. Beyond the pass it widened out again to form a grassed valley between the mountains.

They legged their horses into a canter and quickly covered the distance to the pass. As the meadow narrowed closer to the pass, Porcupine Quill pointed to the ground. The trampled grass showed plainly the recent passage of a large herd of cattle.

Pines covered the lower slopes of the mountains forming the pass and spread out from both sides across the meadow, mixing with scattered clumps of birch and poplar, compressing the entrance to the pass to four, maybe five hundred yards wide.

They were just riding into the pass when they heard the bawling of cattle from somewhere not far ahead. O'Reilly and Porcupine Quill exchanged glances and, as though both arriving at the same decision together, they reined their horses toward the cover of the trees.

The trees forced their horses down to a walk, picking their way through the pines as O'Reilly and Porcupine Quill pushed them on in the direction of the sounds of the cattle.

They had gone perhaps half a mile when the valley opened out again. The sight that met O'Reilly's eyes as he sat his saddle peering out through the trees was enough to make him want to whoop for joy. Spread out before him, on a wide expanse of rich grassland, stood hundreds of grazing cattle.

"These trees run right up the side of the mountain," O'Reilly said. "Let's get up among them, up the slope. We'll be able to see better from up there."

They reined their horses around and moved them deeper into the pines, until the ground beneath the horses' hooves started to incline upward and they knew they were riding up the foot of the mountain.

Some eighty feet up they paused to look out. Below, spread out across the valley floor stretched the herd, two herds actually. From the advantage of height, they looked larger than they had from below. O'Reilly pulled out his binoculars.

He tried to keep his excitement in check. They had found Taggart's new hiding place. His suggestion had paid off.

"There must be eight or nine hundred head down there. The Stinson herd and the bunch they just rustled from the Mackenzie lease."

Men rode around the herd at intervals. Over on the opposite side of the valley a knot of men stood or squatted around a fire. A short distance away saddle and pack horses grazed and near them stood four dirty white canvas tents and a chuck wagon.

O'Reilly trained the glasses on the knot of men. He grinned, his teeth showing white against his whisker-blackened, weather-tanned face.

"Iron-Fist Taggart!"

O'Reilly could scarcely believe his luck. The big man himself. The man responsible for the murder of innocent cowhands and the near-ruination of several small ranchers. There he was, right at the scene of the crime, overseeing it. Irrefutable evidence of his guilt.

His eyes ablaze with exultation, O'Reilly lowered his binoculars and turned to Porcupine Quill. "I want you to get back and report to Sergeant Hannan. Bring him back here with as many men as he can find as quickly as

207

possible. Taggart got out from under the last time. Maybe it was just as well, because this time we can bring him before a court of law, where he belongs. But this time we've got to get him before he decides to slip away. If Sergeant Hannan's not at Standoff, send out some of your friends from the reserve to find him. Or report to Inspector Cavannagh at Fort Macleod. Watch for that lookout up on the mountain. You'll have to get around him. Warn whoever you bring back about him. They'll have to detour wide and come in from the north or south along the foot of the mountains so he won't see them."

Porcupine Quill opened his mouth to say something but O'Reilly silenced him with a raised hand. "It's my turn to stay and watch this time. You're a Mounted Police scout now. Pin your star on your shirt when you report in. They'll believe you."

This time Porcupine Quill nodded silently, then he was gone. O'Reilly swung down from his horse, gripped his Winchester and checked the magazine to make sure the weapon was fully loaded and ready for instant action. Then he settled down to wait.

Chapter 20

O'Reilly spent an uncomfortable night. He didn't sleep, he just dozed from time to time, but by morning he was stiff and cramped. He munched on beef jerky, which quelled the rumbling in his stomach, but he longed for a cup of strong black coffee or tea, even a smoke of his pipe.

Little had stirred during the night, just the occasional bawling of a cow, or a bit of stirring among the cattle at large. Taggart's hands kept watch over the herd, riding around it from time to time. Occasionally O'Reilly had heard the ring of a shod hoof on a rock or the snorting of a horse. Sometimes he had seen the glow of a rider's cigarette.

The mountains remained shadowed until the sun was high enough to warm the meadow. Men stirred around the campfire, and O'Reilly could almost smell the coffee as smoke from the campfire columned upward.

From his position up on the slope, hidden behind the thick green-needled boughs of the pines, O'Reilly studied the activity around the campfire through his binoculars. The rustlers were talking and laughing as they ate a hearty breakfast of beefsteak, gravy and beans from tin plates and drank their coffee.

"Laugh while you can, you bastards," O'Reilly muttered as he watched. "It's more than you deserve. You won't be laughing much longer."

Taggart and a tall, slim man stood apart from the others, talking in earnest. Taggart was making wide, sweeping motions with his arm, and pointing off to the south, while the slim man kept nodding his head.

"Christ!" O'Reilly muttered. "I hope they're not planning to move the herd out of here right now. Not yet. Not until Sergeant Hannan gets here with some men."

O'Reilly didn't know when Sergeant Hannan would arrive. That would depend where he was when Porcupine Quill reached Standoff, or whether the young Blood scout had had to ride on to Fort Macleod. Sergeant Hannan had told O'Reilly he'd try to keep the flying patrol close to Standoff, and would only leave the area if some sort of trouble broke out somewhere else. O'Reilly reasoned that Porcupine Quill, by riding all night, would reach Standoff in the early hours of the morning. If Sergeant Hannan was there, he would ride out within fifteen minutes. It would take the patrol six to eight hours—depending upon the condition of their horses—to reach the mountains where he waited. They would have to ride by a circuitous way to avoid being spotted by Taggart's lookout. They would have to send a couple of men forward to try and work their way around the mountain and take the lookout before he could sound the alarm. That could delay them an hour or two, perhaps even three. At the very earliest it would be at least noon before help would arrive, and probably later.

Shortly after breakfast several of Taggart's men mounted up and rode back out through the pass.

Where are they going? O'Reilly wondered as he watched them through his binoculars, anxious to make sure Taggart didn't ride with them. To his relief, he spotted the big man standing near the campfire, but the tall, slim man Taggart had been talking to rode with them. Perhaps they were going to rustle more stock. At least Taggart wasn't likely to move the herd out of the valley with some of his men away, O'Reilly thought consolingly. He would want as many men as he could get for that.

The sun rose higher, warming the pine-covered slopes. O'Reilly fretted restlessly. As his restlessness grew, so did his impatience. But there was nothing he could do except watch — and wait. And, as he watched, the sun's rays shafting down through the deep green pines and warming him, a sudden drowsiness washed over him. Leaning his back against a tree, he opened his mouth in a wide yawn. He rubbed his red-rimmed eyes, sore from lack of sleep, and yawned again. Slowly, he slid his back down the tree trunk until he found himself sitting on the needle-covered ground. The next minute he was asleep.

O'Reilly awakened suddenly in alarm and jumped to his feet, looking quickly around. He remembered the last time he had done that. But his rifle was beside him and his horse stood a few feet away where he had picketed it. Everything looked all right. The cattle were still spread across the valley, and there was no unusual activity going on. Yet . . . O'Reilly lifted the binoculars to his eyes and trained them on the camp below. *Taggart!* He couldn't see him anywhere. Where was he? O'Reilly wanted as many of Taggart's men as possible down in the valley with the rustled cattle when Sergeant Hannan arrived. Most of all he wanted Taggart down there — caught red-handed with the goods. There would be no denying their guilt, no denying Taggart's involvement.

O'Reilly glassed the area around the camp but couldn't see Taggart anywhere. The gang was busy with a variety of tasks, some riding around the herd, some cutting, others branding, while yet others were repairing equipment, shoeing a horse or sewing a tarpaulin.

From the men, O'Reilly swung his binoculars to the horses, looking for Taggart's big black. But trees hid some of them from view.

A sense of desperation gnawing at his innards, O'Reilly swept the glasses backward and forward across the camp.

"Christ!" He cursed himself for dozing off instead of watching the camp all the time.

Just then he spotted movement at one of the tents. Relief rushed over him as he recognized Taggart's big form step out into the sunlight. He *needed* Taggart down there when Sergeant Hannan and the patrol rode up.

He could do no more than wait. But he did not doze off again. He did not even sit down, nor even lean against a tree. He kept his eyes on the camp below. From time to time his mind wandered . . . to his training days at Regina, the time he spent at sea, his boyhood, to Ruth. Ruth . . . it seemed such a long time since he had last seen her. He hoped that as soon as this business with Taggart and his rustlers was over, as soon as they were rounded up and escorted to the guardroom at Fort Macleod to stand trial for murder, rustling, and other criminal offenses, he would be able to see her again before she returned home to New York.

He waited . . .

The sun travelled high across the sky . . . soon it was directly overhead.

As the afternoon lengthened, O'Reilly's impatience sharpened. *Where the hell are Sergeant Hannan and the flying patrol?*

High above the mountains, the August sun arced farther west across the blue sky.

There was not much difference in the activity around

212

the camp. Taggart had pulled the flaps of his tent back wide and rolled up the sides to allow ventilation during the heat of the summer afternoon, and O'Reilly could see him plainly enough all the time.

Time passed . . .

O'Reilly's impatience began to grow raw.

Come on, Sergeant. Get here!

By late afternoon O'Reilly heard shouting below. Craning his neck he saw the rustlers who had left camp early that morning returning with about a hundred head of cattle. More rustled stock, O'Reilly reckoned.

Through the glasses he saw the tall, slim man ride over to Taggart's tent. Taggart stepped out, a grin creasing his mahogany-colored face. As he watched, O'Reilly's impatience burned. *Hannan should be here by now, damn it all!* Then another thought jolted him. *What if Porcupine Quill didn't get to Standoff? What if something happened to him?*

O'Reilly was wrestling with that unsettling thought when a rifle barked. He stiffened. It came from somewhere to the east, from where Taggart's lookout was watching up on the rocks, from where Sergeant Hannan would come.

The shot drew instant attention from the rustlers below. They stood or sat wherever they were for several seconds, or perhaps a minute, as though waiting for something else to happen. Then shouts broke out.

"Someone's comin'!"

"It might be yaller-legs. Let's get the hell outta here!"

"Get your guns out, damn you! It'll only be a patrol—four or five men. We've got 'em outnumbered four to one."

Exhilaration surged through O'Reilly as he snatched up his Winchester and reached for his horse's reins. After all the pent-up waiting, he itched for action. Sergeant Hannan and a patrol were close by. It *had* to be them. The

213

rifle shot must have come from the lookout up on the rocks. No more shots followed, so he must have got off that one shot before Sergeant Hannan's men reached him.

Swinging up into his saddle, O'Reilly reined his horse down through the pines to the bottom of the slope.

The sudden rifle shot had taken Taggart and his men by surprise. It meant trouble. Someone had discovered their hiding place, the last thing Taggart wanted or expected. His men stood around arguing among themselves, or heading for their horses, while others pointed to rocks or trees from where they could make a stand.

Reaching the bottom of the slope, O'Reilly impatiently reined his horse through the trees until they thinned and he could peer out across the valley. He was in time to see Taggart holding a rifle and shouting orders at his men. O'Reilly grinned. *You might as well save your breath, Taggart. It's just about all over for you.*

At that moment yellow-striped blue breeches swept into view as horses galloped into the pass. Sergeant Hannan led a dozen men charging toward the rustlers' camp. The augmented flying patrols from Standoff and Pincher Creek. The most welcome sight O'Reilly had seen for a long time.

Shots cracked out. Taggart's men scrambled for cover. Sergeant Hannan shouted an order and his riders fanned out into an extended skirmishing line as they charged through the pass.

"That's more than a patrol, God damn it," Slim Gude shouted angrily as he grabbed for his horse's reins. "We gotta get out of here!"

He tried to swing himself up into his saddle but his horse, startled by the shooting, whirled around and around, pulling away from him. Gude's long legs danced after it as he tried to mount.

"Shoot, damn it!" Taggart shouted at his men. "Hold them off! Most of you men are wanted down in the

States. If the yellow-legs get you now, you'll spend the rest of your lives behind bars — if you don't swing from a scaffold first."

Gude gave up trying to get up onto his horse. Instead he grabbed a rifle and ran for the cover of rocks behind the camp. Rifles blazed away at the charging Mounties.

O'Reilly threw his Winchester up to his shoulder and fired at the rustlers on the far side of the pass. Sergeant Hannan shouted another order. His men scattered, heading for the cover of trees, where they dismounted, raised their carbines and returned the rustlers' fire. A Mountie fell. The man closest to him ran to his aid, helped him to his feet and the two of them half-ran, half-staggered to the shelter of the trees.

Sergeant Hannan shouted out, his voice rising above the din of cracking rifles. The shooting stopped.

"Drop your weapons and come out with your hands raised, you men. We have you boxed in. There's more of us coming. You can't escape."

A moment later three rustlers suddenly broke out from the rocks and galloped their horses hell bent down along the valley deeper into the mountains.

"Stop!" shouted Sergeant Hannan. "Or I'll fire!"

They kept on going. Sergeant Hannan raised his Winchester, aimed and squeezed the trigger. *Crack!* The bullet sent the leading rustler's hat flying. They didn't stop. Sergeant Hannan fired again. The hatless rustler toppled from his horse. Hannan's Winchester cracked a third time. The second rustler slid from his saddle and his body hit the ground, bouncing and rolling along for several yards behind the horse. The third rustler pulled his galloping horse down to a stop and threw up his hands.

"All right," Sergeant Hannan shouted at the rest of Taggart's men. "Throw down your guns and come out from those rocks and trees with your hands up."

From where he sat his saddle at the fringe of the pines,

215

O'Reilly could see both Sergeant Hannan and the Stand-off and Pincher Creek flying patrols, and Taggart's rustlers. The Mounties were positioned among trees on the far side of the pass, where the trees swept out to form a point partway across the pass. They had a commanding view of the hiding places the rustlers had found among rocks and trees behind their camp, where the pass opened out into the valley. The rustlers' horses stood in a rocky cul-de-sac nearby. Taggart had a few more men but they were, as Sergeant Hannan had told them, "boxed in." The three who had tried to escape proved that. And more Mounties were on the way.

In anticipation of them surrendering, O'Reilly legged his horse out of the pines to ride down to take prisoner the rustler who sat his saddle two or three hundred yards along the valley with his hands up. But then a voice shouted out from the rocks.

"To hell with you, yaller-legs. Come and get us!"

Immediately a fusillade of shots exploded from the rocks. A bullet peeled bark off a tree beside O'Reilly. It startled both him and his horse and he quickly reined the animal back into the trees.

Sergeant Hannan and his men returned the fire and the mountains rang out with the crackling of rifles. O'Reilly pulled out his binoculars and glassed the far side. The bullet that had just missed him came, he suspected, from a long range Sharps. He thought he had heard the heavier bang that was characteristic of the heavy-caliber buffalo rifle. But he was too far away for his Winchester to be really effective. Besides, he was eager to join his comrades and get into the action. As he studied the far side, he tried to find a position where he could use himself to the best advantage. He wondered whether he could even get a little farther down the valley and open fire on the rustlers from a different angle, getting them with a cross-fire. But to do that he would have to gallop across several hundred yards

216

of open grass. And there was that Sharps . . . No, there was no sense in being recklessly foolhardy. He would be better advised to report to Sergeant Hannan and go wherever the sergeant sent him. However, before doing so, O'Reilly studied the rustlers' positions a little further, looking for the man with the Sharps. Most of the rustlers were in the rocks. Only three or four had taken cover in the trees. They were the only ones who had any chance of escape, and Sergeant Hannan was already ordering two of his men to mount up and ride through the trees on his right flank to prevent any escape that way.

Taggart!

O'Reilly suddenly remembered. The last time he saw Taggart, the big man was taking cover among the trees fringing the far slope. He hadn't seen him since.

Almost desperately, O'Reilly glassed the far side once more. He couldn't see the big man anywhere. That didn't mean that he wasn't still over there somewhere, but O'Reilly couldn't rid himself of the memory that he had escaped the Indian raid on the rustlers' camp in Montana. O'Reilly couldn't rid himself of the chilling fear that Taggart had somehow done the same again. He swung his glasses onto the rustlers' horses. He kneed his horse through the trees, changing position until he could see all the horses. Taggart's big black wasn't among them.

O'Reilly had just lowered the binoculars when four Indians, bent low over their ponies' backs, streaked across the grass toward the trees where Sergeant Hannan and his men were.

Porcupine Quill and three Bloods reined to when they reached the trees. Porcupine Quill had changed ponies and brought back with him three of his friends. He kneeled down beside Sergeant Hannan.

"You see *O-rile-ee?*" Porcupine Quill asked.

Sergeant Hannan shook his head. "Not yet. We've been too God damn busy, but he must be around somewhere."

Porcupine Quill looked over to the pines on the other side of the pass where he had last seen O'Reilly.

"Who are those bucks?" Sergeant Hannan asked, jerking his head at the three young Bloods kneeling among the trees behind him.

"Friends. They help."

Sergeant Hannan thought about that for a moment, then he looked at Porcupine Quill, who was proudly wearing his Mounted Police star pinned to his buckskin shirt.

"We got those rustlers holed up among those rocks," he said, pointing. "They can't make a move without us seeing them. But the sun will be down soon. I reckon they figure on holding out until night time, then they'll try to get to their horses and sneak out under cover of darkness. You see over there, where their horses are?"

Porcupine Quill nodded.

Sergeant Hannan looked into Porcupine Quill's black eyes. "You reckoned you and those Blood friends of yours could get to those horses as soon as it's dark and run 'em off?"

Porcupine Quill looked to where the rustlers' horses were. His eyes glittered. A smile came to his long, angular face. Looking at Sergeant Hannan, he nodded.

Sergeant Hannan grinned and clapped a hand on the young Blood's shoulder. "I reckon you could handle it. If any of those rustlers do manage to get out under cover of darkness, they'll have a mighty long walk. We'll be joined by more men, maybe before dark but certainly by sunup tomorrow, so we'll have lots of men to round up any that do slip out tonight."

O'Reilly had seen the four Indian braves gallop their horses to join Sergeant Hannan and his men. Through the binoculars he had recognized Porcupine Quill, but his greatest concern was Iron-Fist Taggart.

He was sure Taggart had slipped away during the confusion that had swept the rustlers' camp during the moments

218

following Sergeant Hannan's arrival. The question was—
where?

He hadn't gone deeper into the mountains, toward British Columbia. He must have gone east, out of the mountains.

I've got to get him! I can't let him slip out of this.

O'Reilly reined his horse out of the pines and legged it into a canter as he headed back along the pass. A bullet cracked over his head. He saw a puff of smoke from the trees where his comrades were. *I'm being shot at by my own side!*

"I'm O'Reilly, from the Standoff flying patrol!" he shouted at them, waving his arm wildly as his horse pounded across the grass.

He didn't know whether they heard him or not. But he rode on regardless. As soon as his horse got its stride, he legged it into a gallop. It galloped on out of the pass.

The big man was nowhere in sight. But O'Reilly was sure he was somewhere ahead. There was only one place he could logically head for—his ranch. But time was running out for him. He couldn't stay at his ranch forever. Unless he intended to somehow try to bluff his way out of the entire mess, deny any involvement at all, and make the Mounted Police prove his guilt.

The sounds of gunshots echoing around the mountains behind him, O'Reilly spurred his horse on. The mass of jumbled hills loomed ahead. Above, the sky turned crimson as the sun dropped below the soaring peaks.

O'Reilly rode all night. It was a long night, a long ride, dragged out by his unfamiliarity with that part of the foothills country, but by daybreak he was gladdened at the sight of the butte where he and Porcupine Quill had watched Taggart's ranch.

The sun rising over the rolling prairie in front of him

219

glared into his weary eyes. And his horse, too . . . tiring from constant trotting and cantering, with too few rests.

"Not much longer, boy," he said to it as he leaned forward and patted its neck. "Pretty soon you'll be able to have a good, long rest."

As he rode on he could see Taggart's ranch buildings sitting on top of the hill a few miles away.

He approached the ranch, keeping the barn and out buildings between himself and the ranch house. There was no sign of activity, and his spirits dropped at the thought that Taggart might not have come to the ranch after all, that he could be miles away. *Christ, no!* Had he made the long damned ride for nothing?

Angling around until he could see the ranch house, his spirits lifted. There was no sign of Taggart's saddle horse, but a team of horses hitched to a democrat stood waiting in front of the veranda.

O'Reilly reined his horse back behind the buildings screening him from the ranch house. If Taggart was at the ranch house, O'Reilly would have his hands full with the big man. He decided he had better check to make sure none of Taggart's men were around.

Taking his Winchester, he dismounted and moved up behind the bunkhouse. There was an eerie stillness about the place, broken only by the sound of the wind. He walked tensely, half-expecting a fusillade of lead.

He reached the bunkhouse door. Pushing it with outstretched arm, he stood with Winchester ready. The door squeaked agonizingly on dry hinges. Butterflies whizzed around in his stomach. Then he sprang in through the doorway, waving his Winchester around. But all he saw in the dim interior were empty bunks.

Stepping out of the bunkhouse, he looked over toward the ranch house, a hundred yards away. Apart from the team of horses, there was no sign of life over there. Holding his Winchester out in front of him, he padded across

220

the yard in his moccasins. As he drew closer, one of the horses turned its head to look at him. He noticed a suitcase and a small trunk in the back of the democrat. Someone planned on taking a trip.

He reached the veranda. He stepped quietly up the two front steps. He couldn't hear anything or see anything. The front door was ajar. He pushed it wide open with his rifle barrel. As tensely as a tightly-coiled spring, he stood in the doorway, listening intently. Hearing nothing, he stepped inside.

He found himself in a large living room with leather furniture, some scattered bearskin rugs and a stone fireplace. Ahead was another doorway, and beyond it he saw a table and chairs. Off to the right was another doorway, with the door partly ajar, and just beyond the edge of the door projected the corner of a desk.

Suddenly he heard a metallic clank from within the room. He jumped, startled, his heart hammering rapidly.

Sweaty hands gripping the Winchester, he padded toward the room, his moccasined feet making no noise on the floor. With each step he could see more of the room. It obviously served as an office, for behind the desk was a big leather armchair, and beyond it another stone fireplace.

Reaching the doorway, O'Reilly peered around the door. A man's back met his eyes. A big man's back, a familiar man. He was kneeling in front of an iron safe, feverishly sorting through some books or ledgers, and papers. Other books and papers were scattered on the floor beside the safe, as though they had been impatiently tossed there by someone in a hell of a hurry. The big man was so busy with what he was doing that he wasn't aware of O'Reilly's presence.

Fascinated by the man's absorption with what he was doing, O'Reilly stood watching for a moment. He seemed to be counting. O'Reilly could hear him . . . it sounded

221

like a low humming.

After a moment the humming stopped and the big man's body froze. He must have sensed something. Slowly he turned his head. The first thing he saw was the black hole of O'Reilly's rifle barrel.

Taggart's eyes widened and his mouth slackened for a moment. Then his gravelly voice rasped. "Who the hell are you? What do you want?" There was menace in his words.

The ghost of a smile flickered across O'Reilly's black-whiskered face. "Don't you recognize me, Mister Taggart? I'm Constable O'Reilly of the Mounted Police. I'm arresting you for cattle rustling for a start. There'll be other charges, like accessory to murder, and criminal conspiracy."

Taggart slowly stood up. He was holding a black metal cash box in his hands, and he was wearing a pressed gray suit, shirt and tie. His face was freshly shaved, and he wore across his matching gray vest a gold watch chain. He had cleaned up and changed after his ride from the scene of his crimes. He was dressed to play the role of the law-abiding citizen, the prominent district rancher. He was dressed for civilized travelling.

"You've got a hell of a nerve barging into my place like this," Taggart said through clenched teeth. "Where's your warrant?"

"I'm holding it," O'Reilly said, glancing briefly at the rifle in his hands. "It's called a Winchester."

Still holding the cash box, Taggart stood staring at O'Reilly. O'Reilly flicked his head sideways, motioning Taggart to step through the door. With a deep scowl, Taggart stepped forward. O'Reilly stood aside out of the way, at the same time raising his rifle barrel to allow him to pass. At that instant Taggart suddenly swung the metal box up into O'Reilly's face. The corner caught O'Reilly sharply across his forehead directly above his right eye. The pain was excruciating. O'Reilly's finger tightened around the Winchester's trigger and the weapon exploded with a deafening crash, the bullet thudding into the ceiling.

Taggart immediately followed up by lunging at O'Reilly with his shoulder. His heavy frame slammed O'Reilly toward the desk. O'Reilly hung onto the rifle, but Taggart didn't give him a chance to lever another round into the chamber. He swung a big fist that smashed into O'Reilly's face and sent him reeling sideways into the desk. He lost his footing and went sliding across the top.

Before O'Reilly could recover, another fist slammed into his face, cutting his cheek wide open. O'Reilly spun around on the desk like a top, before tumbling off to fall heavily into a heap on the floor. He was trying to pull himself to his feet when he felt a searing pain rack his ribs. With blood pouring down from his forehead and blinding him, he felt a sharp-toed boot smash into his ribs again and again. Then a sickening nausea washed over him as a boot crashed into his stomach. There was another boot to his ribs, then he passed out.

Chapter 21

O'Reilly tried to open his eyes. He could only open the left one. The right one was crusted shut. He hurt like hell everywhere. Slowly he moved his hand up to what hurt the most—his head. He touched his forehead. His hand came away wet and sticky. He held it in front of his left eye. Blood. Pain hammered somewhere above his right eye.

He tried to move. Every breath hurt like hell. Where the hell was he? What happened? His head, his face, his ribs, his stomach all hurt like hell. His head and ribs pounded mercilessly. All he could do was lie there.

He lay for a long time, gradually inch by inch moving his head, his eye crawling up the wall of the room he was in. Slowly it came back to him . . . pain-seared images . . . mountains, cattle, hard-faced men, gunshots, a fight, a night ride, a butte, a ranch house on a hill, a big man. *Iron-Fist Taggart.* Suddenly O'Reilly jerked his head up as he tried to sit upright.

Oh, Christ! He hurt like hell. Quickly he let his head fall back on the floor.

He lay on his back for several more minutes, slowly moving his head from side to side. It all came back to him in a rush. No wonder they called Taggart *Iron-Fist*.

O'Reilly rolled over onto his side. The pain was so nauseating that he wanted to throw up. But he turned over onto his stomach, drew his knees up under himself, then pushed himself up with his arms. Crouching on his knees, he drew in several deep breaths. A trick an old seaman had taught him. It took the nausea away, but he still ached all over. His head pounded ceaselessly, and his ribs . . . they felt as though a mule had kicked them. Several mules.

Gradually he struggled to his feet and leaned heavily against a wall. He ran his hands gingerly along his ribs, pressing here, pressing there.

Christ!

He must have a cracked rib or two.

Slowly he slid along the wall until he reached the doorway, then looked out into the living room. It was empty. He staggered across the floor to the front door and peered outside. The bright sunlight almost blinded him. Defensively he reeled back inside, lifting a hand to his right eye and trying to open it. He rubbed until he broke the seal of dried, crusted blood, blinked a dozen or more times, then lurched back to the door and looked outside again. The bunkhouse, barn, stables and other buildings stood silent and lifeless in the blowing wind. The yard was empty. The democrat was gone. And with it, Iron-Fist Taggart. But where?

O'Reilly lurched back across the living room to Taggart's office. He looked around at the desk, then at the safe, with its door still wide open. Books and papers lay strewn on the floor. He knelt down and looked at them . . . ledgers, cattle figures, stock prices, leasing agreements. They told him little—in fact nothing. He saw a piece of crumpled paper. Picking it up, he peeled it open and smoothed it out. A Macleod bank withdrawal slip, with figures of a large amount that had been heavily—

perhaps impatiently—crossed out, and the day's date. *The bank!* He remembered the small trunk and the suitcase on the back of the democrat.

He tossed the slip back onto the floor. He looked around for his rifle, but it was gone. His hand dropped to his waist—his gun belt was also gone. For that matter he was surprised he was still alive. Taggart could have killed him. Maybe he hadn't wanted the cold-blooded murder of a Mounted Policeman on his hands.

O'Reilly staggered out of the office, across the living room and out onto the veranda. He stood there a moment, trying to remember where his horse was. Probably Taggart had taken it. It came back to him . . . he had left it behind the bunkhouse. Stepping down from the veranda, he half-staggered, half-ran across the yard. He found his horse where he had left it. Taggart couldn't have noticed it. The animal lowered its head and nudged him when he reached it.

He tried to pull himself up into the saddle. The effort hurt. His ribs ached damnably. He renewed the effort. He grasped the saddle pommel, thrust his foot into the stirrup again and this time succeeded in pulling himself up. His head swirled, his stomach ached and pain racked his ribs, but he took the reins and moved his horse into action.

They swung around and headed along the trail to Macleod. Taggart must have gone there to the bank, where he could draw out all his money and board a train for Calgary. That must be what he intended doing, O'Reilly reckoned. That was why he had the trunk and suitcase in the back of the democrat. From Calgary he could board another train to Vancouver, then disappear. O'Reilly didn't know what sort of a head start Taggart had. He didn't know how long he had been lying on the floor in Taggart's office. He wasn't sure, but he thought a train left Macleod at midday. He looked up at the sun.

226

It was high in the sky—too high. It was nearing midday already, perhaps an hour and a half away, two at the most. Macleod was seventeen or eighteen miles away.

O'Reilly leaned forward in the saddle and kneed his horse into a canter.

The miles of rolling grassland passed by. O'Reilly forgot his aches and pains in his desperate race to reach the town of Macleod before the midday train left with Iron-Fist Taggart aboard.

As he rode, he frequently glanced up at the sky. Each time, the sun was closer to the center of the blue vastness above.

The Mounted Police barracks came into view. O'Reilly first saw the Union Jack flying from the flag pole, then the gray frame buildings and their dark gray shingle roofs. It passed through his mind that he should turn in through the gates and call for assistance, but he rejected the idea. It would take too long explaining why he was dirty and unshaven and out of uniform.

As he rode past the barracks, he could see the red-coated gun crew readying one of the field guns to fire the twelve noon signal.

"Come on, boy," he said to his horse. "Just a little bit farther."

The town lay just ahead. The horse's hoofs pounded along the trail.

They reached the outskirts of town as the nine-pounder boomed behind him. O'Reilly galloped his horse up Macleod's main street. Anyone on the street scattered out of his way, while others stood on the side and watched in startled dismay at the unexpected sight of a bloodied, black-whiskered figure in Indian buckskin galloping madly along the normally quiet main street.

O'Reilly saw the bank. Taggart's democrat wasn't anywhere in sight. O'Reilly didn't stop. The blast of a train whistle sounded ahead. He responded by pressing his moccasined heels against his horse's sides. The animal answered with a final burst of speed. Dust swirled from under its hoofs, rose, then slowly drifted back onto the street.

The horse galloped around a corner, the railway station ahead. Taggart's democrat stood beside the station. O'Reilly saw at a glance that the trunk and suitcase were gone.

The train was pulling out of the station.

O'Reilly galloped the horse after it.

The train picked up speed. For a desperate moment O'Reilly feared he would not overtake it. The last carriage began pulling away from him as he rode to overtake it.

Pounding hoofs, flying mane and tail, rider bent low over the saddle, The red carriage loomed larger. The horse thundered alongside. O'Reilly tensed, leaned over in the saddle and grasped the carriage hand rail. Gripping harder, he leaned over farther, then swung himself clear of the saddle. For an instant he swung in midair, the swaying carriage's rail in his hands, the blurring gravel of the rail track bed flashing by underneath. Then with a heave he completed the swing and landed on his feet on the steel platform.

For a moment he stood watching his horse veer away from the track and slow to a walk. He watched the shiny steel rails stretching back to the railway station that was shrinking smaller and smaller every minute.

He stood on the swaying platform a moment longer, getting his breath. The long, fast ride and his acrobatic performance had taken something out of him. His ribs still ached and his face hurt, but he was impatient to get his hands on Taggart. If by some chance the big man wasn't aboard . . .

Opening the door, O'Reilly stepped into the carriage. He quickly scanned the faces of the passengers as he

228

walked along the center aisle between the seats. The carriage was only half full and he was barely halfway through when he realized Taggart wasn't in it. But there was another carriage ahead.

Passengers stared up at him as he passed. He couldn't see his dishevelled hair, his bloodied, black-whiskered face. He didn't give any thought to his Indian buckskins and beaded leggings and moccasins, he had become used to the smell of horsesweat and woodsmoke. He couldn't see the wild look in his eyes. He only had one thing on his mind—the arrest of Iron-Fist Taggart.

He reached the end of the carriage, opened the door and stepped out onto the front platform. Without pausing, he crossed over to the rear platform of the front carriage, opened the door and passed inside.

The first thing he saw was the back of Taggart's head. The big man was sitting beside the aisle halfway down the carriage. O'Reilly started along the aisle toward him.

At that same moment Taggart, as though warned by some instinct, turned his head. Shock showed on his face as he saw the buckskin-clad figure advancing along the aisle toward him. He started to rise.

O'Reilly reached him as he was getting up. He clapped a hand on Taggart's shoulder.

"I'm placing you under arrest, Taggart, in the name of Her Majesty the Queen."

Taggart stared at O'Reilly. "What is this? You're a madman. You're stark, raving mad."

Then Taggart's tone changed. His eyes hardened. "Take your hand off my shoulder."

Every passenger in the carriage was watching the two men. The black-uniformed conductor, near the front of the carriage, was also watching.

Taggart's next move surprised the hell out of O'Reilly. He had expected the big man to do anything but what he did. With O'Reilly's hand still on his shoulder, he straightened to his full height of six feet four inches, threw back his head and laughed. But the next instant he transformed into a dazzling blur of movement, almost unbelievable for such a big man, and smashed a fist into O'Reilly's face. O'Reilly went flying back along the aisle.

Taggart looked quickly around at the other passengers and pointed at the sprawled figure in buckskin. "He's a raving lunatic. Thinks he's in the Mounted Police. Have you ever seen a Mounted Policeman looking like that?"

The blow rocked O'Reilly. Taggart should have followed it up instead of trying to gain the sympathy of his fellow passengers, for in those few seconds O'Reilly shook the momentary dizziness from his head, grasped the arms of the seats along the rocking aisle and pulled himself up.

All signs of laughter fled Taggart's face. His brows drew together as he raised his big fists and squared off to advance along the aisle on O'Reilly. The killer instinct glinted in his cold eyes.

"All right, you damned lunatic," his gravelly voice growled. "I've had enough of this shit."

Moving quickly forward, Taggart threw another punch at O'Reilly. O'Reilly ducked. The fist glanced off his shoulder, not hurting him but jarring him nonetheless. O'Reilly lashed out with a left jab that caught Taggart on the chin. It startled Taggart. But the big man simply shook his head and moved forward, swinging another punch. O'Reilly was less successful dodging this one and it caught him on his ear. Pain stabbed from his ear, radiating throughout his head.

O'Reilly stepped back a pace and let Taggart move on toward him. As Taggart advanced, O'Reilly sprang quickly forward and hit him twice on the jaw with two lightning left jabs, then followed with a driving right that would have hit Taggart high on the cheek and perhaps closed his left eye, but the big man had been in too

230

many fights to be caught like that. He blocked the punch and threw one back with terrific force, landing in O'Reilly's stomach and driving him back several feet. O'Reilly had had time to tense his stomach muscles; otherwise the blow would have doubled him up in the aisle, gasping for breath.

Fighting in the aisle of a rocking railway carriage was hard, but O'Reilly couldn't forget the beating Taggart had given him in the ranch house and he longed to pay him back. This was not the way the Mounted Police instructors at Regina had taught him and his fellow recruits to effect an arrest. Yet, despite his aches and pains, O'Reilly was getting a pleasure out of hammering back at the big man, whose reputation as a bare knuckle fighter was well known in the Fort Macleod district. Hugh O'Reilly was also something of an accomplished fighter with bare fists or boxing gloves. He had fought in bar room brawls from Halifax to Cairo, from Bombay to Shanghai, and the Mounted Police physical training instructors had given him some valuable pointers on boxing with the gloves.

Taggart moved down the aisle toward O'Reilly. Passengers scrambled out of their seats to get clear of the two fighting men, one a big cleanly shaved cattleman in a smartly cut suit, the other a dirty, black-whiskered man who looked like a half-demented squawman. O'Reilly braced his feet firmly on the rocking floor of the rail carriage and prepared to meet his opponent.

Taggart threw a massive right. O'Reilly blocked it with an upraised left arm, then drove his right fist with all the force of his shoulder. It struck Taggart just below the breast bone. Taggart's face went white.

O'Reilly moved forward and drove two more fists at Taggart, a left that caught him high on the neck and a right that smashed into his face.

Taggart staggered backward along the aisle, but he

231

grabbed at two seats, one on each side of the aisle, and stopped himself from going down.

As O'Reilly advanced, Taggart used the two seats to brace himself as he kicked out with his booted foot. The sharp-toed, high-heeled boot caught O'Reilly fully in his ribs. Stars swirled before O'Reilly's eyes as pain seared white hot through his already tortured ribs. The force of the kick knocked him halfway back along the aisle.

With a roar like a bull, Taggart rushed down the aisle, eager to close with this young upstart and finish him off. But O'Reilly wasn't in any mood to be finished off. He sprang back and met the big man's charge with a barrage of blows to the body and face. Passengers gaped as the two men fought it out. Several times the conductor shouted at them to stop fighting, but no one listened.

As the two men fought, the stamina and skill and determination of the younger man, despite his injuries, overcame the strength and ruthlessness and experience of the bigger man. Taggart was losing the fight and he knew it, just as surely as O'Reilly knew he was winning.

In wild desperation Taggart swung a roundhouse right, but O'Reilly crouched in under it and drove a hard right that smashed into Taggart's chin. The big man went to his knees.

Taggart pulled himself to his feet. He looked desperately around at the other passengers. "Stop that raving lunatic before he kills me. You all know who I am. I'm a respected member of the Fort Macleod ranching community. I'm running for Parliament. Are you going to let a raving lunatic like that kill me?"

Some of the male passengers looked around at each other. The conductor pushed forward. "Grab hold of him," the conductor shouted, pointing an excited finger at O'Reilly. "He's dangerous."

Three men closed in on O'Reilly, two grabbing him from behind. O'Reilly tried to shake himself free. "I'm

Constable O'Reilly of the Mounted Police. Let go of me. You're interfering with a peace officer in the execution of his duty."

O'Reilly fought and struggled, but the passengers restrained him. Eager to assert his authority, the conductor pushed forward.

"Hold him while I get some rope," the conductor babbled. "We'll tie him up and turn him over to the Mounted Police when we get to Calgary."

"I *am* the Mounted Police, God damn it!" O'Reilly fumed, glaring at the conductor. "Don't you remember me? I'm the constable who was on this train coming down from Calgary three months ago when those two dandies were bothering that young lady."

The conductor's eyes narrowed as he cocked his head sideways. "What's that?" He peered into O'Reilly face. "Well . . . I'll be damned! Yeah, I remember you now. But what the hell are you doing looking like that?"

"I've been doing detective work," O'Reilly said. "Let me go. Taggart is responsible for all the rustling that's been going on."

"Let him go, boys," the conductor nodded to the men holding O'Reilly. "I remember him. He's a Mounted Policeman, like he says."

The passengers released O'Reilly. O'Reilly looked quickly around for Taggart. But the big man wasn't there.

"Where did he go?" O'Reilly demanded.

A passenger pointed wordlessly to the door at the rear of the carriage. Whipping around, O'Reilly bounded down the aisle. He yanked open the door and stepped onto the rocking platform. His eyes went everywhere. Movement out on the prairie caught his attention. A man running. O'Reilly realized what had happened. Taggart had seized his case and jumped off the train. He was running across the prairie half a mile away, running

233

for his life.

O'Reilly had no intention of letting Taggart get away now. He stepped down onto the steel step. Watching the blurring ground whiz by beneath him at the rate of thirty-five miles an hour, he tensed himself to jump. Every second he waited put Taggart that much farther ahead. He let go the carriage's iron handrail and jumped from the step. He hit the grassy ground beside the railway embankment and rolled over and over. A jabbing pain shot up his left ankle.

When he finished rolling, he sat up and watched the train chuffing away rapidly northward. He got to his feet to run after Taggart, but the instant he stood up the pain in his ankle shot straight up his leg and he fell back to the ground.

"Christ! I've broken it."

Hunched on the ground beside the railway embankment, O'Reilly tenderly felt his ankle. No . . . there was no broken bone. It had to be only a sprain. But it was swelling, and swelling fast.

He got to his feet. He couldn't afford to sit there feeling sorry for himself. He *had* to catch Taggart. Right now, that was the most important thing in his life. It had become an obsession.

Gradually placing his weight on his ankle, he found he could stand on it, but only just. He set off painfully at a limping run in pursuit of Taggart, who was now smaller in the distance. Taggart had made good his head start by an additional several hundred yards. He had to be a mile away.

O'Reilly limped on. Every step hurt. He closed his mind to the pain and lurched on.

Once he fell to the ground and stayed there a moment, resting his aching ankle. Then determination and the knowledge that Taggart was getting farther and farther away drove him to his feet and he struck out once more.

234

Every bone in his body hurt. His ribs ached from the kicking Taggart had given him back at the ranch house, his face hurt from the blows Taggart had rained on it there and aboard the train. His head hurt from the cut above his right eye. Blood trickled down his forehead into his eye. But he limped and lurched on.

He could barely see Taggart now. With blood dripping down his forehead and into his eye, there were times when he couldn't see him at all. For that matter, he wasn't even sure he could see anything.

His limping run eventually gave way to a lurching walk. Gradually it sank in. He had to face it. He was beaten. Taggart had gotten away. He was about to sink down into the soft ground when he heard a call for help.

Raising his hand to his forehead, he wiped away the blood. He looked around. He heard the cry again. He placed his hand up to his eyes to shield them from the bright afternoon sun. There was a speck out ahead, in some sort of lake.

O'Reilly staggered forward once again. As he limped toward the distant sight and the sound of the calls for help, the figure became clearer.

A hundred yards ahead Taggart was up to his waist in what looked like a swamp. O'Reilly limped on.

"Get me out!" Taggart shouted, waving an arm above his head, the other arm holding up his case. *"Quicksand!"*

O'Reilly's mouth dropped open. Quicksand! Taggart was up to his waist in it. O'Reilly hopped closer, stopping when the ground beneath his feet began to quiver. Terror was written across Iron-Fist Taggart's face. He was sinking up to his chest. He was still several feet away. O'Reilly looked wildly around for something to throw out to him, but he couldn't see anything. There were no tree branches, nothing. He didn't even have a belt; Taggart had relieved him of it. He peeled off his

235

buckskin shirt, then tested the ground beneath his feet. Next he lay down on his chest as close to the quicksand as he dared go.

"Grab this," he yelled at Taggart. "I'll try to pull you out."

He threw the shirt out. Taggart reached to grab it but the sleeve fell a foot short. Struggling frantically, Taggart sank further.

"Stop struggling," O'Reilly shouted. "You'll make it worse. I'll try again.

He wriggled out a bit farther, but when he placed his left arm out for support on the mushy, silt-like sand in front of him he felt it being sucked down and he quickly pulled it back. He threw the shirt out again. It landed closer to Taggart, but it was still several inches short.

Taggart started thrashing around again. "You're making it worse," O'Reilly shouted. "Throw yourself forward this way. Try and reach the sleeve Let go of that case and use both hands."

But Taggart would not let go the case. It contained his money, his ill-gotten gains.

O'Reilly made another try with the shirt, but it still fell short.

"Let go that damn case," O'Reilly shouted. "Let it go and throw yourself forward. Use your head and shoulders and both arms. If you do that, you can reach the shirt."

But Taggart still would not let go the case. O'Reilly lay on his stomach at the edge of the swamp staring at a terrified Taggart in the face. The quicksand was up to his neck, then his chin.

Taggart sank . . . to his screaming mouth, his nose, then his terrified eyes. Then the top of his head. Finally his upstretched arm and the hand still grasping the caseful of money. After that—nothing.

All trace of Iron-Fist Taggart was gone. He had sunk

before O'Reilly's eyes, his shouts and screams and curses and pleas ringing in O'Reilly's ears. O'Reilly thought of the cowhands who had lost their lives as a result of Taggart's ruthless greed. He thought of the small ranchers who had been forced to the brink of financial ruin. None of it helped.

He lay there for the longest time, Taggart's shouts ringing in his ears.

Finally, emotionally and physically drained, O'Reilly struggled to his feet, turned around and limped slowly back toward the railway line.

POWELL'S ARMY
BY TERENCE DUNCAN

#1: UNCHAINED LIGHTNING   (1994, $2.50)
Thundering out of the past, a trio of deadly enforcers dispenses its own brand of frontier justice throughout the untamed American West! Two men and one woman, they are the U.S. Army's most lethal secret weapon — they are POWELL'S ARMY!

#2: APACHE RAIDERS   (2073, $2.50)
The disappearance of seventeen Apache maidens brings tribal unrest to the violent breaking point. To prevent an explosion of bloodshed, Powell's Army races through a nightmare world south of the border — and into the deadly clutches of a vicious band of Mexican flesh merchants!

#3: MUSTANG WARRIORS   (2171, $2.50)
Someone is selling cavalry guns and horses to the Comanche — and that spells trouble for the bluecoats' campaign against Chief Quanah Parker's bloodthirsty Kwahadi warriors. But Powell's Army are no strangers to trouble. When the showdown comes, they'll be ready — and someone is going to die!

#4: ROBBERS ROOST   (2285, $2.50)
After hijacking an army payroll wagon and killing the troopers riding guard, Three-Fingered Jack and his gang high-tail it into Virginia City to spend their ill-gotten gains. But Powell's Army plans to apprehend the murderous hardcases before the local vigilantes do — to make sure that Jack and his slimy band stretch hemp the legal way!